Rebels & Romantics

CONTENTS

For my husband,
the OG skater and surfrat who holds my heart

Chapter One

This fence will try its best to kick my ass.

It won't win.

My eyes slide up, slide down, sizing up the metal monster before me. The black painted iron roots itself into the earth and climbs skyward alongside the palm trees, ten, twelve, maybe fifteen feet high.

Matty's fingers graze the small of my back. A gentle press, not a push.

That one little touch sets my heart popping with mini-detonations.

An outright shove would be more obvious, but he would never go so far.

"You got this, Effie."

Right, obviously. As if a fence has ever held me back. With the edge of my chewed-up Vans, I kick the tail of my skateboard, clear the area. It bumps and rolls a little on the dry grass. Calculations dive in and out of my head: heights, angles, distances. Within seconds I formulate a quick and dirty plan to pull this trick off without an injury. I can psych myself into doing pretty much any- thing, and this wouldn't be my first questionable life choice where Matty Pomerantz is concerned. Let's face it, this fence is nothing more than a glorified gate to the other side, a diamond-patterned, decorative attempt at covering up its real job—keeping riff-raff like me off pretty lawns and gardens. Some kind of twisted, ornamental crap rings the top, looking suspiciously like barbed wire, like a warning. I ignore it. Scaling this fence is no different than being on my skateboard, busting out perfect tricks, one after the other, popping up, dropping down, wheels slamming the pavement.

Matty strokes my ego with endless compliments, painfully oblivious to the real reason behind my hesitation tonight. What he hopes I'll do for him isn't nearly as traumatizing as the reason why he begs me to do it. The truth is this fence is a wall better left unscaled for a number of personal reasons, not the least of which is that somewhere on the other side lives a random, nameless girl that Matty's suddenly got the hots for. It's a vicious conflict of interest I'd be smart to avoid. But no one ever said love makes you do smart things. If it did, I wouldn't be here.

Okay. Time to get my act together. My hair's out of control. I split my ponytail into two halves and tug each end to tighten it.

"I'm ready," I say. Firm as ever.

Matty grabs my face with both hands and brands my cheeks with exaggerated kisses. One, two, four, seven, twelve... I'm so cracked-out on love that I lose count. Seventy rounds of fireworks launch inside me. He licks the side of my face next and laughs like he pulled off the world's best trick. I shove him and smile, because he's so ridiculously over the top about everything, always.

My fingers claw around the diamond-shaped openings in the fence. Like every damn thing in California, the metal's still warm. The sun slipped below the horizon a few minutes ago, but it still makes my life difficult. I stuff the toe of my sneaker into one of the diamonds, look up again, focus on focusing, concentrate on concentrating. Missing a beat means breaking a limb, and that shit's for amateurs.

To my side, Matty bounces on the balls of his feet. Like always, some kind of electric energy's bottled inside him.

An alarm's been going off in my head, my mouth; it's on the tip of my tongue, and it's taking all my will not to pull the trigger and let it loose. I know the girl. Not her name, not that level of detail. But I do remember her. We crossed paths years ago, she and I. Unloading this information would score me mega points with Matty but I also have no desire to watch his eyes explode over the possibilities my knowing her opens up for him. He's already a human pogo stick. Why push it? She'll bite the dust like all his other flings. It's the only reason I'm going through with this farce. That, plus the fact that I am such a sucker for this silly boy.

A car door slams in the distance. The sound nearly blows me off the map.

Instant reminder: getting caught trespassing is one hundred percent arrest-worthy.

A security guard lords over the entrance to the complex. Matty and I spotted him sitting in the mint green pastel booth with the *Las Palmas Altas Condominiums & Gardens* sign attached to it, complete with an oversized, pink pastel hibiscus painted at each top corner. Given the chance, that guard will want to prove he's worth the money the residents on the other side of this fence pay him. No one—not even my older brother after baking himself into a lobotomy in an epic night of bong hits—enjoys sitting in those stupid holding cells down at the police station. They set the air-conditioning purposely low and parents like ours don't race to bail you out.

Matty must notice my shoulder muscles tensing up because he rockets into pep talk mode. "You can do it, Effie."

Of course I can. I will. For him, you know.

A guy like Matty Pomerantz is not the kind of guy you let down.

I start the climb.

The atmosphere is different up here at the apex. Post-sunset streaks of red, orange, and yellow tinge the sky. It matches Matty's hair. Trees seem lower from this height. The streetlights on this side of Vista Buscato—the narrow edges of town—are a little worn, a little weathered. Not the polished, decorative, ornate ones dotting the quaint sidewalks in the heart of town. In the distance, Pacific Coast Highway doesn't seem quite as wide. The luxury cars whipping around the curves heading downtown probably cost more than my life. But up here it's comforting that they all look the same. Nothing matters when you're on top of the world, and I like that.

From this height, a car's a car. They all kick up the same terra cotta dust on the road.

"You got this," Matty whispers from a thousand miles underneath me.

I twist back to glance at him. He's grinning at me.

I'm so stoked I can hardly breathe.

In the dim light, his eyes shine like in those pictures where the flash turns a person's eyeballs into matching spotlights. He's radiant, practically twitchy. This is giddy Matty, over-the-top Matty. The same Matty who bounces sky high on a skateboard, who tells me I look hot in black tank tops. He's the same Matty who'll swap this town for another in a heartbeat, even if he fits the criteria of Vista Buscato royalty way more than the rest of us skate rats do.

My fingers curl tightly around the metal. A few more moves, swing my legs to the other side, and I'm in. I dodge the pretty, faux barbed wire spokes of death, try not to straddle to the point where I render my future self infertile, and then hoist my other leg over. I drop down and stick the landing like I planned it that way.

Matty's eyes are stuck on my legs. "You okay?" His voice croaks on the last word.

Why wouldn't I be? I look down.

A thin, thin line of blood stretches from underneath my kneecap to the middle of my shin. I wouldn't have noticed but for the little pearl of red forming at the very bottom. It grows and grows until, almost like a pop, there's a release and it races down. Two more beads of blood follow on either side. It's like a game—which can reach my ankle first.

The Honorable Judge Bertram T. Pomerantz would be horrified to learn that ninety percent of my troubles stem from activities in the course of a promise to his grandson. But what else can I do? I am the one and only person Matty relies on to pull off these insane tasks he absolutely cannot risk getting caught doing. With a retired federal judge for a grandfather and a dorm room waiting for him at Northwestern, Matty Pomerantz's code of ethics looks a lot different than mine. What do I have to care about? Nothing—except him.

I run the inside of my wrist along my leg. Blood smears in all directions.

"No worries," I say.

A smile breaks open Matty's face. Whatever concerns momentarily popped into his head vanish. He leans against the fence, pressing his face at the diamonds, like he could eat the metal.

I can't stop staring at his lips. They're wet.

"Come here." His words are lush, almost too thick to leave his mouth.

Something swells in my throat. Like a throb, like a heartbeat.

I edge closer.

We stare at each other, breathing, not speaking, not moving.

Not for the first time, I think: This is it. That moment of clarity people talk about.

The look in his eyes is so open and intense I can almost see his heart beating behind the blue irises. At my brother's graduation party last year, some poser chick with nasty perfume got so close to him her boobs slid against his bicep. It was a cheap trick. I saw right through it. She told him, "Your eyes change color when it's raining, Matty. Today they're green." Except they were blue—same as always, and that day was sunny, and the day before that it had rained, and she obviously didn't know what the fuck she was talking about. His eyes are blue. Every day. Always. They are everything the color can offer.

Matty licks his lips like he's ready to say something. It's going to be monumental.

Maybe this is it. The moment. Maybe, maybe, maybe.

I push forward against the fence. I don't speak. Anything I say might come out wrong. Too desperate, too forced. I have to let this moment be. Let it roll out on its own.

He reaches for me, thrusting a hand through the diamonds. Our fingers slide together. His skin is warmer than the metal.

"Have I ever told you how awesome you are?"

I shrug. "Once or twice. But you can say it again."

He laughs. "I fucking love you, Effie Fox."

My heart triples in size. I love him too. So much.

"Okay, game time," he says. "Here." He transfers a folded piece of white paper through the fence and into my palm.

I blink. And blink again.

The spell of love or friendship or whatever you want to call it lifts. A few seconds pass before I reconcile fantasy with reality.

Right. The note. Back to the matter at hand.

This is the scripted play between us: he formulates a bullshit plan, I follow through reluctantly, he gets his way, and I promise myself I'll never do it again, even though I know I absolutely will.

A giant swirly P curls around the edges of one folded corner of the note in my hand, because people like Judge Pomerantz and his grandson actually spring for fancy, personalized stationery, while the rest of us jot numbers on torn bottle wrappers or worse—on our skin with Sharpie. All impossibilities aside, if I stare at the note long enough, I'm pretty sure the thing will spontaneously combust. Which would totally solve all my problems. Or not.

My fist closes around the paper. Better to tuck it away where I don't have to see its sharp edges. I swing my head around. "So, where do I go?"

A row of cars is lined up on my left. On my right's a clump of bushes, dried out and brown at the tips, thanks to the friendly California sun. Smoke tinges the air. Someone's barbecuing close by. Straight ahead in the distance are small homes—little identical cottages neatly clicked together, side by side. These are the ones we saw when we did our drive-by, when the security guy stood up to get a better look at us. (Matty's foot on the gas never gave him the chance.)

This is my kind of place: Vista Buscato's OG side. The cozy little pockets where people like me and my friend Joe Monroe wear flip flops and eat burnt hot dogs at block parties and sip homemade frozen drinks in red Solo cups. We're the families who've been here since the ice age, who refuse to relocate, despite the influx of newcomers downtown who ride around in luxury SUVs that are bigger than my house. I wish Matty lived anywhere other than smack in the heart of fancy-ass Vista Buscato with the rest of the phonies.

Matty's not looking at me anymore, but along the path that will lead him—*me*—to her. He's exhilarated, eyes wild. I wonder if he was ever looking at me at all. He did just declare his love for me, right? Or was that all a dream?

"She told me she lives on Rumildo Walk." His breathing's erratic, voice charged. "I looked it up. It's near the center courtyard at the front of the complex. On your right." He points past the bushes.

"What do you mean, you 'looked it up'?"

"Google street view."

Ew. "You stalked her?"

"Yeah." He smiles and nods like it's the crazy-coolest thing he's ever done. I'm pretty sure it isn't, but whatever. At least now I know what he was doing with his phone while we sat at red lights on our way up here.

I break into a jog, a note for a random girl clutched in my fist, praying to God an earthquake will crack the ground open and pull me under. Anything so I don't have to do what I know I'm going to do for him.

My knee continues to bleed. The sting is my fuel. I run faster.

Because honestly, whatever. It's just a little blood.

That's what Band-Aids are for.

CHAPTER TWO

The sun is napalm hot. Palm trees feather the sky but they don't move, they don't sway. Nothing cools you off except air conditioning. My hair's all screwy. I couldn't find a ponytail holder this morning so I'm rocking the natural, couldn't-find-a-brush, wild wildebeest look. Which doesn't help lower sweat production. But it's all good. I'm still swimming in leftover feelings of relief from last night when the mission to find Matty's mystery girl failed. If only I could get him to stop talking about her.

Before my shift at Fox Inn starts, my friend Joe and I skitch down Buscato Drive to our skate park at the end of the road.

Our skateboard wheels nearly set the street on fire.

We're cruising at warp speed, each of us holding on to opposite sides of this Brazilian guy Edgar's old-school blue Chevy with shined-up hubcaps. Our hands grab at the open window frames as the Chevy pulls us along. Behind the wheel, Edgar sucks on a cigarette that's nearly down to the filter. He flicks it out the window and it almost clips my shoulder.

Edgar owns a skate shop in Oxnard called Skate Real. Joe works there. About twenty-five people are stuffed into Edgar's car, Matty and our friend Sam included. Some of the others are members of Skate Real's pro team. Lucky bastards. Through the windows, their voices carry. Everyone's talking at once. *Where should we meet later? Anyone have beer?*

On the count of three, Joe and I fling ourselves forward sling-shot-style. We take over the road.

Joe's dark hair whips around his face. "Yeeeeaaaahh, Foxy," he says as I pass him. My heartbeat kicks up its pace as we glide down the street at warp speed.

Behind us, everyone in Edgar's car cheers. The Chevy slows and blocks traffic. Irate drivers honk.

Joe keeps gliding next to me, smiling, but then cries out, "Shit!"

He's suddenly focused on the view up ahead.

I catch my first glimpse of the Buscato Drive Skate Park. It's gone.

I mean, not literally. It's there somewhere, hidden behind the plywood construction fence locked neatly around its perimeter.

A tidal wave of disbelief swallows up all my energy.

Our momentum slows. Edgar's Chevy comes to a stop behind us. The human sardines packed inside the car grumble in a wave of bitter blues at the sight of the giant wall blocking us from our park. A muffled "Oh shit" and a "Damn!" come through the windows.

I jump the curb and land on the sidewalk in front of the park. Joe follows.

About a dozen white paper signs hang from the fence, staples hastily shot here and there. I roll up and rip one off.

SKATE PARK CLOSED
NO TRESPASSING
VIOLATORS WILL BE PROSECUTED

Everywhere we go in Vista Buscato, this shit happens. It isn't just the skate park. It's dress codes in restaurants, No Loitering signs near Town Hall, police walking the beat, pressing anyone whose wallet isn't fat enough to "Keep moving, kid!" Around here, locked gates along the road to happiness only swing open if you're a certain breed. Our kind—from the outskirts of town—don't fit the criteria. As skateboarders, we practically kickflip the criteria on its head.

Village of Vista Buscato Rule Number Four Hundred Ninety-Eight: SKATEBOARDERS ARE THE ENEMY.

Certified true fact: in virtually all of California, skateboarding is a mainstream activity. The sport started here. It's as California as surfing. Vista Buscato, however, operates under a different set of rules than the rest of the state. Here, skateboarding is seen as a gateway sport that begins innocently enough with elbow pads, wrist guards, and helmets, then quickly leaps into the most heinous federal offenses and capital crimes. Evidently, skate culture doesn't mesh with the glittering jewels of the elite who both live in and visit this town.

Joe jumps off his board and slides up next to me. He shoots out rapid-fire curses under his breath, gripping his skateboard by one truck, fingers clamped so tightly he could snap the axle cleanly in half. He rips one of the signs down and reads it out loud.

No trespassing—what utter bullshit.

Matty slides out of Edgar's car and joins us. One step behind him, our friend Sam Wills climbs out too, his domed afro skimming the top of the door along the way. He's all legs, a little on the clunky side when it comes to skating, but he's no less passionate, and no less pissed right now. He's just quieter—his military father taught him to mind his manners at all times.

Joe tosses both arms at the sky and lets out, "Gimme a fucking break!" It's loud and guttural.

He was the only one of us optimistic enough (or stupid enough, depending on who you ask) to believe the clowns at Town Hall wouldn't succeed in closing Vista Buscato's only skate park. Matty and Sam shake their heads. As for me, I'm waving a white flag in my mind.

The rest of us accepted that the park closure was going to happen, even if we're shocked to see they actually accomplished the task. It shouldn't surprise anybody that the Vista Buscato Board of Trustees chose to pull it off in the middle of the night when skaters like us couldn't pitch a public fit over it. Obviously their true goal is to purge us skate rats from the community.

"I'm sick of this shit!" Joe shouts. "They might as well put a gate around the whole fucking town."

With an elbow hanging out the window of the Chevy, Edgar strokes his goatee with his index finger. "That's bullshit, kid," he drawls in his thick Brazilian accent. "Get on that."

Easy for Edgar to say. He has power because he has money. But not at first. He was a sixteen-year-old transplant from Brazil when someone discovered him nailing rock-solid frontside heelflips, pinching a cigarette between his lips the entire time. Pretty soon The Phenom Known As Edgar Ribeiro was sponsored by a big skate company and wore their t-shirts and hats and skate shoes and probably even their underwear. Ten years later, and the dream of owning his own skate shop came true. He even built a park in the empty lot next door. Joe says Edgar's raking in money hand over fist, living the dream. People listen to him. They aren't going to listen to punks like us.

Edgar kicks the Chevy into drive and rumbles away, leaving us staring at a plywood wall.

Joe goes wild, tearing off every sign he can reach. This is the badass side of Joe that all the younger girls at school used to swoon over. Even I can't deny his hotness level increases exponentially the angrier he gets. He balls the signs up in his fists. A swath of his chin-length, dark hair sticks to his sweaty cheek. "No notice, no community vote. Unbelievable."

Sam busies himself picking up the torn pages so they don't flutter into the parking lot of the new, gleaming, glittery jewelry store down the street. He drops them into a nearby trash can.

Model citizen, my Sam. These neuroses aren't entirely his fault. Being a rule follower is in his blood. He's the son of a U.S. Marine Corps' general. Excuse me, *Brigadier General*. Evidently the title is important when your father has achieved greatness and respect. My father serves liquor from behind a bar in a wannabe trendy restaurant. I wouldn't know.

Below the threatening signs are a collection of cheery ones reminding us to clean up after our pets, with an image of a cartoon Great Dane or some other giant breed of dog, which strikes me as ridiculous considering the preferred breed in this town is anything with the word *toy* in front of it. Their little collars cost more than all the jewelry my mother owns.

Underneath the No Dog Shit signs, a piece of tape holds up one random, white paper. Its corners flap downward. Printed there is an image of a dark-haired girl with a wide smile, about my age or a year or two older, with the word MISSING in giant black lettering above contact info. I bet nothing bad happened to her. Maybe she left this place—gloriously boring Vista Buscato—of her own free will. I'd stake my life on it. Wish she'd taken me and Matty with her. I rip the sign down. I'll bet any amount of money that she doesn't want to be found.

Sam nods at the balled-up sign in my hand. "I'll throw that out," he says. I hand it over.

Matty fingers a folded piece of paper. I'm beside myself when he doesn't give it to Sam. Because it isn't one of the signs, but the note we failed to deliver last night to his mystery girl. He keeps flipping the stupid note between his fingers, still carrying the thing around like it's awaiting its destination rather than destination unknown.

I positively melt at the sight of it; I'm sweating inside and out.

My life is a twisted game of Where's Waldo, except my Waldo is blonde and boring and might as well remain nameless. Besides, let's get real. The odds of finding a person armed with only a street name and a bare bones physical description are terrible. But when Matty gets a goal like this in his head, reason doesn't drive the connections in his brain. It's all big dreams, big possibilities. It's easy for guys like him, with a trust fund and a recognizable last name. All the trappings of a perfect safety net. He has the privilege of daydreams. The rest of us peons are demoted to logic and reality.

My only option is to focus on the positives—I am the person Matty trusts the most in this world, I am the girl he texts at night before he closes his eyes. After last night's failed hunt, he and I jumped straight back into our normal grind. We sat on his front porch making playlists for his road trip to Northwestern in August. I don't want to obsess about being separated from him. Which is why I bust my ass at work to grow a cash stash so I can join him in Chicago. Hopefully, eventually. He can't live without me, and I can't live without him. And that's just how it will go, till we die, infinity, hallelujah, amen. With any luck, Matty won't find this stupid girl before he leaves. His note can sink to the bottom of the Pacific Ocean where it belongs. And I'll be the one riding shotgun beside him, where *I* belong.

Joe shakes his dark hair off his face. He eyes the top of the plywood around the skate park.

The construction fence is not nearly as high as the one I vaulted over last night. I can reach the top of it with the tips of my fingers. If the town's Board of Trustees wants to keep us out, they'll have to try a whole lot harder than this.

This uppity town might not make room for us willingly.

But one thing's for sure—that skate park is ours.

CHAPTER THREE

"I'm going in," I announce. "You guys coming?"

Joe gives me a smile that says, "Hell yeah!"

Sam slides back an inch. Matty jumps to his usual position on lookout.

We all hang back and wait for Matty's signal.

A woman carrying one of those yappy toy poodles or yorkies or some other genetic mutation waltzes out of the jewelry store.

A black convertible packed with girls rolls to the red light, doing that lazy, slow crawl along the main drive where you drink in the warm sun and scenery. These chicks aren't from around here. I can spot weekend tourists a mile away. First, they're all wearing bikinis, and if you know anything about what the California sun does to black leather interior, you'd cover your thighs to keep from burning your skin off. Second, it's a rental. An Avis symbol's on the bumper. The two in the front flip their hair and wave at Matty and Sam. The two of them wave back. Joe rolls his eyes, stiff as a cactus, and prickly too.

They finally drive off. Matty tips his chin in a tiny nod. All's clear.

Joe and I toss our skateboards to the other side. We swing ourselves up and over the wood with little effort.

Matty needs an extra leap, but he might as well be made of rubber. He makes it.

Sam has an attack of conscience.

"I'm not looking to get arrested." His voice comes through the other side of the plywood low and muffled.

"Arrested for what?" Joe says.

"They put up a fence for a reason, man. The signs say no trespassing."

I try to reason with him. "It's public property, Sam."

"Yes," Joe agrees. "We are the public. Therefore, it is our property." The sting of pissy righteousness still clings to his words. He hops on his board and busts out a jacked-up heelflip as if putting a period at the end of his declaration.

Matty shakes his head, a smile parting the swarm of freckles around his mouth and cheeks. "Not sure the Board would agree with your logic, buddy."

Joe's patronizing nod is a direct mashup of funny and frightening. "I forgot, Matthew Lawrence Pomerantz the Seventeenth. You got money. You're one of them."

"Not really."

I roll my eyes. He comes from money, so he sort of is. But that's fine. His accident of birth isn't his fault any more than it's my fault I was born to the most rotten couple of lowlife schemers who couldn't care less if I ditched school but would flip their lids if I ditched my shift at their restaurant. You can't help what you're born into, but you can help what you do about getting away from it. Just ask the supposedly-missing girl in those posters.

Joe glides away on his board like he's won the argument.

I don't have the heart to tell him the important life lesson I learned from the rich bastards who've taken over Vista Buscato, a lesson Joe evidently did not show up for. We do not belong here anymore. This town has changed. The days when Joe, Matty, and I ran down Buscato Drive chasing Mr. Henley's ice cream truck, and sat on the curb in front of Fox Inn with our arms dripping vanilla and chocolate onto the stained sidewalk—those days are long over. The sidewalks are pristine now and we haven't seen Mr. Henley or heard the musical bells of his truck in years. Cops probably got orders to give him tickets for noise violations. This town now belongs to people with a string of important names with, like, twelve words in them. It's for people who own vacation homes, weekend visitors with fat wallets. It's for imported cheese and organic tomatoes, not cheeseburgers and snow cones. We reside here, thanks to our parents and grandparents and maybe our ancestors before them, but that's it. Like so many of the old, forgotten families still clinging to pockets and cul-de-sacs on the edges of town, we get the message loud and clear. We no longer belong here.

I can still hear Sam breathing, analyzing, debating on the other side of the fence.

"Hey," I say softly. "The worst that can happen is they give us the boot." I am well aware my words are a lie.

"Your father won't care if you get arrested, Effie. Mine definitely will."

I pound the wood with my fist, hoping to jar Sam with a wake-up call. "Just do it."

Matty calls out, "Yeah, stop obsessing."

A pause lengthens.

Finally, Sam says, "Heads up!"

His skateboard soars over the fence, clattering to the ground a few feet from us. The fence shivers. The soles of Sam's sneakers slide against the wood, like he's trying to dig in, grab a foothold somehow. I look up to find his fingers gripping the top of the fence. A second later, his head peeks over, then the brown skin of his forearms and elbows. He hoists his legs up and drops down to our side, standing at full skyscraper height. He looks scarily like his father (minus the shaved head and military uniform), but with a very different sense of fashion, evident in dark blue jeans dipping several inches lower on his waist than General Wills would allow if he were here, and his hair combed and puffed into a perfect little cloud around his head.

Sam glares at Matty. "*Stop obsessing.*' Funny you should mention. How's your dream girl?"

"At ease, Sergeant," Matty says.

Joe tips his head back with a laugh.

Sam throws an air punch at him. "You guys are such assholes."

Laughter bubbles up in my chest.

We're an unlikely mix. And who knows? Maybe we are assholes. But I can't think of any people I like better. And after waitressing in my parents' restaurant, I've met a whole lot of assholes in my time serving the public. My life with these mismatched guys is a beautiful thing.

Matty pops back-to-back ollies—super air style—on his board with the new wheels, flinging his arms out like wings, like he can't hold in all the energy at once. The ollie is the most basic trick in any skateboarder's arsenal, and we've all had eons of practice. You snap the tail down hard with your back foot to create the front-end lift, and then you jump. As the nose rises, you drag the outside of your front foot toward the nose, to level out the board in midair. Bend your knees. Watch your landing. Matty's bent so deep his knees almost tap his chin. I swear he pops to airplane cruising altitude. I don't know anyone who flies higher than Matty. It's like he could grab a fistful of clouds if he wanted to.

Pop, roll. Pop, roll.

I bust out a few of my own ollies next to him.

Joe's eyes run a lap around the park, its wedges and pyramids and handrails. Our concrete paradise. His gaze floats to the plywood fence, the barrier keeping us apart from everything, and I swear he could set the thing on fire with that one look. His cheekbones are all hard angles and steely edges. He punches out a text and runs off ideas for pulling a crew together to shake things up in this town. He's forming plans. Preparing for battle. "My guess is the Town

Board finally approved a demo crew to come out and level this place," he says. "They want to build a swanky hotel here. Put a restaurant on the ground floor, too." His eyes flick to me.

Matty stops turning out tricks and asks, "How do you know all this?"

"I went to the last Town Board meeting."

"You did not." Matty's voice pitches low on the last word.

"I did." Joe nods, indignant. "I live here, same as them. I'm eighteen now. I'm a verifiable registered voter and a tax-paying citizen." He salutes Sam. Sam returns the gesture, dead serious. "They tried keeping me out. One of them told Detective Brimley to keep an eye on me, whatever that means."

Sam's eye blow wide open at the mention of Vista Buscato's head detective and perpetual thorn in our side. "Did Brimley mess with you?"

Joe waves away the worries. "Nah. He was too wrapped up in impressing the Board with his own shit to worry about me. He was there to give an update on the search for that girl Jessie Winters who went missing last month. It's like his new life mission or something."

"So, did you speak?"

"Bet your ass I did." Joe holds his board bottom up. He twists the truck that holds the wheels. "I don't let people shut me down. This is my home as much as it is theirs."

Sam smiles. The two of them are delusional.

I don't doubt Joe's ability to speak. But I know these Vista Buscato Board members, all twelve of them. Sometimes they eat at Fox Inn. From what I've learned, with the exception of Matty's grandfather—the Chairman of the Board—they are one hundred percent out for themselves. Screw how badly it hurts everyone else. They're the types of customers who do nothing but complain. The forks are dirty, the wine glasses have spots, the food's not hot enough, and where are the extra lemon wedges I asked for? I hear they harass the workers at Joselle's Sweet Shoppe next door, too. *"The dark chocolate tastes bitter today. The texture is gritty. You should discount this batch. Don't you have anything better?"* Trust me, they're not on that Board to help any of us. Like Joe always says, they're there to remind us that we serve them, not the other way around. They're there to make sure we don't ask for anything more. Because the *more* part is what they want for themselves.

"What did you say to them?" Matty asks softly. He's probably imagining the exchange between his friend and his grandfather, and knowing they share an ability to debate a point to the death, he assumes it didn't end well. The assumption grips me as well.

"I let them know I was educated on the subject. Edgar told me he went through the same process with the politicians in Oxnard when he set up the park in the empty lot next door to Skate Real. Edgar knows his shit, man. He's on a planning committee for a park in Fillmore, too. He said the town needs approval from the community board before a public space is demolished. So, I had all this knowledge and ammunition from Edgar at the meeting, right? I let them know I'm not as dumb as they think I am. The way they're going about this isn't okay with us. Closing down the skate park is a messed-up idea. Plenty of residents have young kids and this was a perfect place for them to let off steam."

"How did they react when you said all this?" I asked.

He tilts his head and squints one eye a little, like he's recalling a not-so-pleasant memory. "They didn't care for my speech. One of them started listing phony statistics about drug culture and skateboarders and how the town doesn't support people with...with..." Joe's eyes drift to the sky, trying to pick the word out among the clouds. "Unsavory—that's what she called it. *Unsavory lifestyles.*"

And yet we're standing next to Judge Pomerantz's grandson, the boy who graduated in the top three percent of our class. He can launch a backside 180 better than anyone I've ever met. Bet the Town Board doesn't know that.

"According to this Board member," Joe continues, "we're all filthy meth addicts using the skate park as a front to sell drugs and corrupt young children."

Sam clucks his tongue. "Man, I've never touched a drug in my life."

"Ridiculous," I whisper. Except for my brother Gerard. There's a little truth in the allegation there. The odds are pretty good that he is high when you catch him at the park grinding tricks on his board. But then, Gerard's high ninety-nine percent of the time. Does he even count? As for us four, none of us touch the stuff. Watching my brother light his brain cells on fire daily has certainly tainted the mystique for us. But the truth is we'd probably all fail drug tests. Even the squeaky clean people like Sam. When you run with a crowd like ours, breathing in secondhand smoke from weed is a given. Who knows what we've all been forced to inhale riding in the backseat of Edgar's car?

Joe goes on. "One of the guys on the Board—Peter LaRoche—stuck his neck out for us and suggested the Town move the park somewhere else."

"That's not a bad idea," I say.

"Yeah," Sam agrees. "Like, a place that isn't right on the commercial strip for every tourist to see. They keep the town's clean image, and we get our skate park."

"Right," Matty scoffs. "Like they're just going to hand you a brand new park."

"The Board says it's a liability issue, like injuries and lawsuits are a given. But down the road, Ventura gets away with it. Why can't we? Believe it or not, one or two of them actually listened," Joe says. "The rest of them shut me down." He grabs a lock of hair and runs it across his lips. "Turned south after that."

"Oh no," I say. "What did you do?"

Joe shrugs. "I reminded them of the Constitution. I can recite the preamble word for word, you know."

"You didn't."

"I did. I was at 'secure the blessings of liberty' when security dragged me out."

"Why would you do that? You can't just—"

"Yes, I can," he says simply.

Matty's head tips back in a laugh. "Joe the Rebel Skate Rat. Your trustworthy public defender of Boardsport Nation."

"Someone should speak up for us. If it's got to be me, so be it. We live here too. We deserve more." Joe's voice runs smooth and deadly. "I'm gathering up the troops and going all out for a new park. I'll make as much noise as I can."

None of us are dumb enough to respond. Joe's dripping with fiery heat. It all sounds great, but he's never understood the difference between *can* and *should*. It's the reason he has more arrests in his file than a crowd of people gather in a lifetime. Righteousness only gets you so far, particularly when the law stands in your way.

"Hate to break it to you, buddy. But this town is a dead end. It's shot. That's why I'm out of here in two months." Matty flips Joe the finger. "My girl's coming with me." He rings an arm around my shoulders. "Right, Eff?"

I giggle and it comes out all high-pitched and stupid. I'm horrified—how weak can I get? A torrent of waves rolls around my gut; I'm slipping, falling, diving headfirst into hopeless lovesick over this boy. Matty's arm spins me into a loose headlock. I wonder if he notices my strength fading as I fight him off. He kisses my temple before releasing me, and skates away.

Joe eyes us. "Effie's mom won't rubber stamp that."

"Please. Felicia loves me."

"Felicia loves cash, not people." A spark of wry humor runs through Joe's laugh.

Think what you want, Joe Monroe, I don't care. If I'm not careful, Matty will be fixing ugly, flannel sheets onto a bunk bed in a dorm room five million miles away while I'm stuck serving Caesar salads to weekend tourists who remind me, not so politely, to hold the funky anchovies and keep the croutons on the side so they don't get soggy. Any indication that Matty's forming plans for me to join him one day in Chicago is a win as far as I'm concerned. Matty spent summer vacations with his grandfather sending me email after email, text after text, pics, phone calls, postcards—all to show me there's a world out there beyond this teeny tiny town, and that he wished I could see it with him. He cares about me. He might be the only one who truly does. Bottom line: our dreams match. Maybe college isn't for me, but I know how to haul plates. I can waitress anywhere. I'll do whatever it takes if Matty is waiting for me when my shift ends. The reward will be a lifetime of love and limitless possibilities. I'm his forever. He just admitted as much.

Joe starts shooting out mental blueprints and ideas for a new park.

He keeps glancing at me. Gaging my interest, I guess.

I kick my board with the side of my black and white checkered Vans and avoid his gaze.

My heart aches for what I know will be a letdown. In theory, I'm one hundred percent behind Joe's plan. But what's the sense? None one of us will stay in Vista Buscato much longer. They're forcing us out. And when we're gone, what will Joe do? Skate around with the last remaining baby grommets in kneepads and helmets, then split at five o'clock when they go home to finish their homework? Some life.

"Recruiting Judge Pomerantz to our side might give us a good shot at making this work," he says, aiming a loaded look Matty's way. "You'll help, Matty. Right?"

"Sure," Matty says. His face glows, determined, but there's something in his eyes that's off. They're too hard, too focused. Like he's trying to remember where we are in the conversation. He changes the topic and starts yapping about this mystery girl he met in the pharmacy, as if she's goddamn royalty. "That love at first sight stuff is real, I swear." He goes back to busting out ollies.

Pop. Pop. Pop.

"Effie, you were there. Didn't you see her too?" Sam fiddles with the scab on his elbow. "Why aren't you in love?" He laughs like he's just hit Kevin Hart levels of comedy.

I am in love. But certainly not with her.

My brain gets stuck on a loop, wondering why the girl was at the pharmacy in the first place. What did she need? Tampons? Chapstick? Herpes ointment? Couldn't she have waited five minutes before she stepped into that checkout line and ruined my summer?

Joe takes a vert drop straight into the giant cement bowl at the center of the park and carves patterns around its sloped sides. His dark hair fans out behind him. It's crazy, but I think I can smell his shampoo from here. He shares a bathroom with his baby sister. No doubt he's sharing her shampoo too. It's one of those sweet lavender fragrances you don't forget—like when you walk into a room and a blast of familiar sensations and memories hits you just from that one whiff.

POP. Another ollie. Matty hangs in the air. That one was sick high.

"Effie's helping me find her. We're hitting Las Palmas Altas again tonight," he says.

Joe flies out of the bowl. He nearly breaks his neck swinging his head around to catch my reaction.

Sam only half listens. The scab on his elbow proves way more interesting.

I roll my eyes for their benefit, but don't dare let Matty see.

We haven't officially negotiated another bid for my services tonight. The thought of watching a replay of last night's giddy excitement over the girl makes me want to hurl, but in truth, it's progress. Matty's relying on me, his ride or die. That's one step closer to forever.

He makes a ridiculous declaration about fate next. Of course, the girl is entirely tangled in his reasoning. My stomach sinks into the soles of my chewed-up Vans at the mention of *Her*. Again, again, again.

Sam groans and fakes dying by strangulation.

I have the urge to do the same. But I don't want to seem unsupportive.

"Man, you're losing it, Matty," Sam says. "Sweating a girl you don't even know."

"I know her. We met. We talked."

"Three minutes in a checkout line doesn't count."

"Why not?"

Sam rolls his eyes. "It just doesn't, bro."

Joe tosses a handful of goldfish crackers in his mouth, no doubt plundered and stuffed in his pockets from his sister's stash. It's the closest he'll get to lunch. He casts a quick sideways glance my way as if to say, *Is he seriously still talking about that girl?*

I return the look. *Most definitely. Make it stop.*

The rationale Matty wants us to swallow is that destiny put him and the girl together. Having lived in Vista Buscato his entire life, he knows everybody who ever crossed into the town. But he didn't know her until that fateful moment.

Sam tries arguing a different logic. "Maybe she just needed antibiotics."

"Or maybe we were supposed to meet."

"Dude. You been fucking with tarot cards or something?"

Matty stands his ground. "I'm serious."

"So am I. Running into a hot girl at a store isn't magic, bro. It's coincidence."

No matter that Vista Buscato has its fair share of tourists, or that Sam himself is a transplant from another life in another city, someone we only met early in senior year when his dad's military assignment brought him to the West Coast. None of that changes Matty's thought process. He holds strong. He and the girl are two strangers on a path forcing them to collide at that exact moment, standing in line between an old man buying an eyeglass repair kit and a mom with a toddler in a stroller, hauling a value-sized box of diapers. He's always been a hopeless romantic.

The whole thing makes me want to scream. Destiny has nothing to do with it. I know that girl. She's been in this town. She's not "new" no matter how you slice it. Matty and I walked into the wrong place at the wrong time at Bella Via Pharmacy and she stepped into *my* destiny. I wish I could tell him why he's wrong about this, but I don't dare burst his bubble.

Joe breaks the silence, kicking nose grinds against a nearby bench. "Let me ask the obvious question, since no one else has." His voice is slow and measured. "Why didn't you get her number when you met? Couldn't you and Effie have avoided all the cloak and dagger shit that way?"

Matty's head shake looks less like an answer of *No* and more like a move of frustration, like a '*Haven't you been listening?*' He overestimates how much Joe cares. Friend or not, I guarantee Joe doesn't give a shit. "I tried. I asked. She doesn't have a phone."

Joe's eyes take on the same skeptical squint mine wore when Matty first told us this.

"Sounds like she doesn't want you calling her," Sam says.

Matty's freckles look like they'll slide off his face and rain on the ground. He smushes Sam on the side of the head, which is not easy to do considering Sam's height. Sam threatens to chuck a rock at Matty's head if he doesn't shut up about the girl.

I step in before he and Joe kill Matty's ever-present optimism. "She's probably telling the truth about the phone. Her dad's weird."

Matty's eyes brighten.

Shit.

Shit shit shit.

The moment the words shift from my brain to my tongue, I regret the move. It's a certified acknowledgement that I know her.

The look of confusion on Matty's face as he sorts through his thoughts is ripe. "How would you know that about her father? Do you—do you know her?"

The floodgates open. He dives straight at me.

I swallow. It doesn't help clear my panic. "I just..." I consider which words to use. Words that won't propel him even more into this crazy fantasy. "I forgot. And it's not like that. I don't really *know her* know her."

Correction: I did, a long time ago, barely, but I don't feel like dipping into the minutia.

Sam interrupts. "Is her dad, like, insane-weird or strict-weird?"

"Um. Strict, I think."

He nods. With a general for a father, strict is a language of love he knows.

Matty's eyes are open and wide as the sky. "Why didn't you tell me you know her? See what I mean? It *is* fate! It *is* meant to be!" His brain starts drawing connections and linking lifelines and all I want to do is cut through it, just hack it to death with a machete. Because she and I are not linked in any way if that avenue leads to Matty. No way.

I can't help sticking a pin in this particular bubble of his. "It isn't destiny, Matty. She's been in this town a while."

"Fess up," he says, one hand digging into my ribs in the exact spot he knows will get a squirm out of me. "What's her deal?"

I sigh. "Okay, okay."

I reveal what little I remember about his fantasy girl. No names, no firm details. My brain either doesn't recall or never grasped those facts in the first place. Years ago, she and her dad rented one of the rooms on the second floor above Fox Inn. Exactly how long they stayed or when they left—who knows? My parents' business is a revolving door of shady. In my experience, the people who hide in the rooms above a bar—even a quasi-bar and grill with good food and a killer view of the Pacific Ocean—are the sort of people who have a damn good reason to hide. And hide they did. I rarely saw the girl outdoors, and never at school. We only crossed paths when I tagged along with my father upstairs to collect the rent. Even then, I'd hardly see her. She only flashed in the background, hiding behind her father's legs. But that hair—the platinum hair I'd recognize anywhere.

"What's her name?" he says.

"I don't remember."

At the first opportunity, I find an opening in our conversation and drop into the bowl carefully behind Joe. He and I cruise for a few minutes, not stopping, just weaving lines across the cement. The sides of the bowl have the perfect curve and slope. Our wheels hum against the pavement. A symphony of pops and cracks. The most beautiful sound in the world.

Joe rips out a powerslide, twisting his torso and his board sideways, screeching like a DJ scratching at a record, finally coming to a halt right beside me. A textbook perfect trick and he hasn't even broken a sweat. He grabs a lock of my hair and gives a soft yank. I yelp and punch his arm. We've been doing this dance since kindergarten. He smiles. I smile back—first at him, then at the ground. He's unpredictable, and it makes me nervous.

He pops another goldfish in his mouth. His dark brown eyes are bright today. The sun's picking up the copper parts in them, glowing like gold bricks. He's on an uptick. "I already got your brother making flyers for my protest. You want to help me put them up around town tonight?"

"Um…" I look down at my board, at the little splinters of wood sticking out along the tail. Because how do I say it? I want to help Joe. I really, really do. But there's Matty. "I'm supposed to help Matty with his…you know…"

I can't say it; I don't want to say it.

"The girl?"

"Yeah."

He lets out a soft, breezy chuckle that's more like a sigh. "Nah. He said he'd help too. He won't bail on me."

"Don't kid yourself. Matty can't focus on anything other than her right now."

"She'll fade away. They always do." Joe shoots a glance at me.

It's a promise, the way he says it. He's trying to make me feel better, like he always does. One day Matty will let go of all the crazy flightiness. He'll stop pining after random dreams and whims, and he'll realize I've always been here. This merry-go-round ride with Matty has been spinning for as long as I can remember. He runs in circles over girl after girl, and then I get a short break when he comes back to hang with me, when the fling is over. Holding on to the good parts, those little nuggets of hope he gives me—*You're coming to Chicago soon, right?* or *What would I do without you,*

Effie?—keeps my heart from combusting at the thought of him leaving. Or falling in love with someone else.

"God, I hope you're right, Joe." I immediately regret the way it comes out—like a prayer.

I pray this whim fades like all the others. I pray and pray and pray he does not find the perfect ending, the perfect match. Because if he does, and she's not me, I don't know what comes next.

Chapter Four

Yellow pages and torn squares of silver tape pepper the street corner around Fox Inn like glitter. Bold red lettering in all caps across the tops of the pages shout out Joe's new skate park battle, urging skaters everywhere to rise up, do something about it. Joe nods like it's a mural of the greatest artwork he's ever seen. I'm one thousand percent certain these flyers are a result of the coordinated texts he sent from the skate park earlier.

My brother Gerard rips pieces of shiny duct tape off a roll with his teeth like he's ten feet from the finish line of a marathon and his opponent's breath tickles the back of his neck. He struggles to pull the sticky tape off his fingers, then slaps two yellow flyers to Fox Inn's chalk sandwich board at odd angles. Another's attached to the front of Joselle's Sweet Shoppe next door. It too hangs askew, standing out like a sore thumb against the pink and blue cupcakes and lollipops in Joselle's window display. It'll take undiluted acid to get the gluey side of that duct tape off her glass. Leave it to my brother to do something tragically unwise.

Matty and Sam spin their heads around, scanning up and down the sidewalk.

A weird tingle flushes through my hands. Hope and rage and determination all in one.

I snatch the tape from Gerard's hand and grab a flyer from the stack at his feet. I fix a flyer to the light pole on the corner. Joe, Sam, and Matty get to work too, passing around the tape.

Gerard slaps another flyer to a Fox Inn window.

"Not there, idiot!" I shout. "Mom will lose her shit!" He should know better than to dirty up the front entrance of Fox Inn with propaganda. Taping a very public statement to the restaurant's walls for all its customers to see and judge essentially amounts to Fox Family treason. I wish my brother would use his brain more often. Maybe whatever he smoked today ruined his memory retention. Circulation's compromised, his brain is starved for oxygen.

Gerard laughs. "Mom's on her third vodka tonic. I'm riding first-class today, baby." His eyes are loose and watery. I was right—he is high.

He's forgotten the most important piece of Fox Inn legislation. Fox Family Rule Number One: the restaurant's needs come first. Take a backseat and get used to it. You have no opinion unless it furthers Fox Inn's bottom line. Out of nowhere, a police car makes its way toward us.

Well. There goes our protest productivity.

Cops have escorted me home enough times that I almost consider police cars like a low-key Uber. I don't even flinch. Same goes for Joe. But Matty freaks. He tugs at my wrist, his face sweat-soaked with desperation. I already made eye contact with Sam, though, and he looks like he's about to stroke out. I can't leave him. Matty doesn't wait for an explanation. He's gone in a blink, vanishing into atoms and molecules through a black hole in the universe somewhere. It's the reason Matty's never been to a principal's office except to collect an award. He won't allow himself to get caught, even if it means he has to bail on us in the lamest of ways. Who can blame him, right? The rest of us can't get our act together fast enough. You'd think we'd be used to this shit show by now.

The car comes to a stop in front of Fox Inn. Detective Brimley steps out of the passenger side. He's in plain clothes, a prissy suit as always, but there's no mistaking who he is above all else—a cop with a badge clipped to his lapel and a gun holster beneath his jacket. A yellow flyer taped to the corner mailbox catches his eye. He laughs. Or chokes on his own saliva. I'm not sure. I don't want to ask. He heads for Fox Inn's front doors. A piece of paper sticks to the bottom of his foot. He shakes his leg like crazy because I guess bending down to pull it off his shoe wastes too much energy. It flutters away and lands face up. It isn't one of ours, but a page for the town's dark-haired, supposedly-missing girl, begging for information. Her face smiles up at the sky. She's laughing at me and my small town blues, I'm sure of it.

Brimley slips into the restaurant, but not before throwing a smirk my way.

The shit will hit the fan in approximately twenty-seven seconds. More or less. I tug Sam toward Fox Inn. We're late for our shift.

I'm three inches over the restaurant's threshold when my mother's hand slaps the back of my head. Behind me, Joe stifles a laugh. Sam flinches—the pansy.

"Shit, Mom," I say, rubbing my head.

She's in full dragon mode. Her nostrils could swallow me whole. "Get an apron on. You're late. And give me that thing." Her breath spits vodka fumes all over my face. She yanks the skateboard from under my arm. The grip tape nearly rips my skin off. She chucks it behind the host podium. It rolls next to a stack of old menus and a sticky wooden highchair. She tugs the edge of a white tablecloth over the skateboard so customers won't see it. You'd think it was a bomb. "I need you swinging those filthy wheels around clean tablecloths like I need a hole in my head." Her words rush out at just the right decibel level where she's unmistakably in rage mode but also magically unheard by anyone but the poor fool in her personal space. After years owning a restaurant, she's perfected the art of the low volume tirade.

Fox Family Rule Number Two: do not air dirty laundry in front of customers.

My family lives for rules, not many of which actually benefit Gerard and me, but whatever. It isn't like I can do anything about it other than plan my escape.

My mother hates skateboarding. Aside from her narrow-minded inability to grasp that her daughter likes the same sport as her son (and that I actually do it better than he does), she mostly hates it because her uppity customers hate skateboarding, too. It's not just about the boards, per se; it's about the nuisance everyone thinks they—*we*—are. She's been working at peeling Joe's SKATEBOARDING IS NOT A CRIME sticker off one of the outside windows for two years. I think he might secretly superglue the edges of it each time he stops by Fox Inn because she's tried everything. "Bad for business," she mutters every time she passes it, the restaurant keys singing in her hand.

Her eyes dart around the restaurant and settle on Detective Brimley at the bar, chatting it up with Peter LaRoche, that rich dude on the Vista Buscato Board of Trustees. She runs a fingernail along the bottom edge of her lipstick, tightening the line. Putting up a good front for the customers, particularly the richest ones, is the golden rule my mother will never bend on. She puts an arm around me. To anyone else it looks like we're hugging, but this woman hasn't hugged me since I was four. I'm not even kidding.

She jabs a finger at my chest. I have the customers to thank for being alive. Witnesses, you know. "Brimley said kids ripped signs off the skate park. If that was you, I'll crack that goddamn skateboard in half myself." The word skateboard is loaded with poison.

"Take it easy, Mom. I didn't rob a bank." I try to edge around her. She's a human highway barrier.

"And what about all those flyers outside?"

I shrug.

"They didn't appear there by magic! Did you put them up?"

"Not all of them."

The world's most explosive sigh climbs up my airways. Getting sucked into this glue trap does not coincide with my plans. Escaping early to help Matty won't be easy.

Fox Family Rule Number Three: when Happy Hour calls, get your ass to work.

I'll figure out my exit strategy later. First things first—play the Fox game, make a few bucks, further your escape plan. I dash behind the bar, tie an apron around my waist, grab a pen and order pad. Sam follows me, all set to organize empty beer bottles into crates behind the bar. Joe tags along and hops on a bar stool.

Good tips are worth a fake smile, so I flash my best and brightest at Detective Brimley and Peter LaRoche, even if it's with only one-third the enthusiasm my mother would like.

My father slides next to me. He pumps a cocktail shaker up and down.

Peter LaRoche flashes me a greeting with two fingers in a wave.

"Kids, kids, kids," Detective Brimley says, smiling, his arms spread out like a welcome sign. I glare at the badge dangling on a chain around his neck. I want to use its sharp, pointy edges to carve skulls and crossbones into his eyeballs.

Sam is first to stiffen. I almost expect him to salute. "Good afternoon, Detective Brimley," he says, all sunshine. I want to kick him.

Joe hides a smile behind a wipe of a hand over his mouth.

A span of silence grows.

"Samuel Wills." Detective Brimley fakes a smile. He eyes Sam's waist ine, where boxers play peek-a-boo over the top edge of a belt.

"Your father know you're hanging out with this crew again?" He gestures to Joe as if the boy is a crew unto himself. "I have it on good information that you and your friends were spotted skating near the Buscato Drive skate park. The *closed* skate park. But you weren't in it, right?"

Sam wavers. I bet he'd wrap the cuffs around his own wrists if he could.

Joe's eyes darken. I can hear the anti-establishment gears grinding inside his head. "I'm sorry, Detective. Did I hear you right? Are you suggesting we committed a crime by skateboarding?" he says carefully, quietly. That silent rage thing brews underneath the calm. I catch the edge of it as he grips the trucks of his board. His bare hands can warp the metal.

There aren't enough eye rolls to cover how I feel about this situation. Because come on. We weren't setting explosives to historic landmarks, for heaven's sake. A sigh bursts out of me before I can rein myself in. My father works the cocktail shaker as if his life depends on covering up whatever crap he knows is set to come out of my mouth. The ice inside clanks around like a drumroll.

"There's no rule that says you can't skateboard on Buscato Drive. Sidewalks are public property." The words fly out of me, annoyed, impatient, before I think it would have been smarter to keep my damn mouth shut.

Brinkley tilts his head in a way that seems about seventy-five percent fatherly and five hundred percent obnoxious. "I'm going to assume, for purposes of this conversation, that Vista Buscato Elementary School failed you all as children, seeing as how none of you are capable of reading." He reaches into his pocket and unfolds a white piece of paper. It's one of the very same signs Joe worked so hard at tearing off the fence at the skate park. Funny—Detective Brimley doesn't seem to care about the other signs posted there, like the one with the missing girl's smiling face. If that girl's parents cared enough to post signs praying for her return, why the hell is the town's lead detective so preoccupied with skaters and tackling petty street crimes? Someone's priorities are out of whack.

Brimley's eyes narrow. He casts a sideways glance at Joe, sizing us up like we're tigers loose from the zoo. Give me a break. He's the one with the gun. He flicks a finger at Joe. "I don't want to catch you riding a skateboard on Buscato Drive again, you hear me?"

"What if I'm just carrying it?" Joe's expression is deadpan. His arms splay out a little, and it reminds me of a picture my brother showed me from an underground cockfighting match he went to in L.A., with the roosters spreading their wings, intimidation set to full volume. Antagonizing the police is one of those deadly habits Joe can't seem to break.

"Keep the wheels at home, smartass, or I'll be having a chat with your mother," Brimley snaps. The detective assumes Joe's mother actually remembers that Joe exists. She's barely acknowledged him in the two years since his baby sister was born.

Joe nods. "No skateboarding or any similarly violent, criminal activity. Got it."

"We didn't do anything wrong," I mutter.

The detective's eyebrows lift. "You didn't do anything right either, Effie."

He thinks I care; I don't. Vista Buscato stopped caring about me a long time ago. Nowadays I spend my hours chatting about blond mystery girls floating around pharmacies. Priorities, priorities. Once I gather enough money from tips, I'm out of here. I'm not folding dinner napkins for the rest of my life.

Joe aims pointed looks at me and Sam in turn. "I'll catch up with you guys later."

I wonder if Sam's stomach flips as many times as mine does. Because I'm catching up with Matty, and if Matty's plans do not involve Joe, then neither do mine, unfortunately. I can't dwell on how ridiculous it sounds. It's just how it is.

Joe heads for the door. Through the floor-to-ceiling windows along the side of the bar lining Buscato Drive, Sam and I watch as Joe drops his board on the ground and jumps onto it, basically tossing Detective Brimley one big final Fuck You as he glides down the street.

CHAPTER FIVE

M y phone rings. I go stiff.

Fox Family Rule Number Four: no cell phones at work. I never follow this one. It's dumb.

My father lifts an eyebrow my way, then grabs a bottle of Jack Daniels from the top shelf. My mother would drown me with the stuff as punishment if she wouldn't have to buy a pricey replacement bottle. Luckily, she's schmoozing an old couple like her mortgage depends on it. I grab the phone from my back pocket. It's Matty. A dream sequence of him and the girl kissing floats before my eyes. I push the thought from my head. Nightmares begone. I dismiss the call even though it positively kills me to do so.

"How's the grilled chicken and veggie wrap?" Detective Brimley asks.

His words zip in and out of my ears.

"Uhh..." I can't find my place. Where are we? All I see is Matty.

Peter LaRoche glances at the wording on my t-shirt—the word WARPED is spelled out in a design of interlocking skateboards. A souvenir from this summer's roadshow music fest in Ventura. A thumbs-up advertisement for the allegedly filthy side of life, the punk side.

I chew the end of my pencil.

Detective Brimley flips a menu over in his hands. My t-shirt is nothing new to him.

My father lets out a quiet sigh and pours a shaken cocktail into Peter's highball glass. Peter kicks back the first swig of his drink. The amber haze of the liquid matches his chunky gold watch. "I have it on good authority," he begins, "that Stefanie here has a promising career as a pro skateboarder."

I nearly snap the eraser off the pencil with my teeth. This is so not a conversation I want to continue in front of my business-minded father, whose bar-wiping arm starts spinning circles at double the revolutions per minute.

"That so?" Detective Brimley continues scanning the menu. Not interested in the slightest.

"Not really." I nibble on the pencil some more. I wish Peter LaRoche would shut his face.

"Don't sell yourself short," Peter says. "My nephew skates. He says you've won a few competitions."

I struggle not to check my father's reaction. Extracurricular activities are strictly prohibited when the family business controls everyone and everything. I've learned the hard way that my parents don't need to know what I do in my free time, particularly if it's a journey down a path where Fox Inn isn't at the finish line. It's part of the reason my parents expelled huge breaths of relief when I told them I didn't apply to any colleges. Who needs higher education when a full-time job awaits you post-graduation? They never minded that I spent more time in the dean's office than anywhere else, earning myself a reputation as a burnout, even though I wasn't lighting up.

The detective pipes in again. "The chicken wrap?"

"Right. The chicken wrap," I say. "It's served with a pesto dressing. It's good."

My father knocks an elbow into my ribs. "It's our best seller!" he chimes in cheerily.

Forget Joe Monroe. The town's real enemy should be this shyster behind the bar pouring cocktails who contributed to my DNA. Aside from scamming people out of money during football season with bullshit bets bearing impossible odds, my father spends afterhours behind the bar with the soda gun squirting a carefully measured blast of water into liquor bottles. He rationalizes it, too. "Not the top shelf stuff. Those people know their alcohol. Only the mid-level shit. I'm not stupid."

Maybe he isn't. But apparently everyone else is.

"Yeah. What he said." I tick my head in my father's direction. "Want fries with that?"

"Okay. But no tomatoes."

I scribble his order down before I forget it all. *Chick wrap. No tom. Fries.*

Peter smirks at the detective. "Having a cozy lunch break on taxpayer time?"

"Nope. That's takeout. I eat on the go. I'm too busy keeping this town in order."

"Last time I checked, the crime wave missed us here in Vista Buscato."

If Peter LaRoche had a fan club, I'd be first in line for a membership. He takes another gulp of his drink.

Detective Brimley's chest pops out more broadly. "Cops in this town bust their asses. That's more than I can say for the politicians."

"You mean regular cops or the ones looking for promotions?"

"I mean law enforcement. All of us. In case you didn't read the memo in between ordering cocktails, we're working a lot of overtime on that missing person case."

"Runaways don't count as crime, Detective."

"Gentlemen, gentlemen." My father plays referee, half-laughing, half-serious, his eyes darting back and forth between the men. "Step out of the ring, please."

Their bickering is so beyond my brain waves. I'm too stuck on Matty and his call and how much it hurt to press REJECT and how my entire body itches with the urge to rip my phone out of my pocket and call him back. I have no interest in listening to these guys bitch about who has the tougher job. Plus, the more the detective's blood pressure rises, the more likely I'll be his next target.

I dart off for the kitchen.

Sam loads empty bottles into a recycle dumpster out back. He left a mess of crates and boxes in the way. Diving around them, I dig out my phone. With any luck, Matty will have a sad update that he's discovered his lovely new infatuation already has a boyfriend. Or maybe she's warned him to stop stalking her.

I call out to our chefs, Carlo and Vincent, and tack up the order slip on the line. Neither of them hears me. An argument over the temperature of the grill rages between them. Carlo turns the dial up, Vincent turns it down. They yell in Italian. I don't speak their language, but I am well-versed in swear words, and after spending a lifetime in this kitchen, I can follow the conversation.

It goes something like this:

"Moron, it's too cold! I can't cook on that!"

"No, you jackass. It's too hot. You've been burning the chicken all day!"

"You're the reason I got a head full of gray hair!"

Carlo sees my phone and waves frantically with two pudgy arms, his fear of my mother and her rules usurping rational thought. "Put that shit away, Effie. You want Felicia to fire all of us?"

"I wish. She won't do that. She needs us too much."

Carlo nudges Vincent with an elbow. "You hear that? They can't live without us."

Vincent grumbles. He's roughly my dad's age but you'd think he's ninety from his perpetually crusty attitude. He's tall and thin, with a hooked nose that makes him look like he's angry about something. "Maybe we'll get a raise." He twists the temperature dial down, then tosses Detective Brimley's chicken onto the grill.

It sizzles. Smoke wafts in a plume above his spatula. He's right, the grill is too hot. I make a mental note that Vincent is the sure bet in an argument.

Sam comes back, hauling an empty bin. His eyes grow psycho-killer huge as he catches sight of the phone in my hand.

I stop him. "Don't say a word."

He exhales heavily and mumbles something about a death wish. Whatever. Somewhere in the middle of watching his nerves shrivel and die, I've missed three texts from Matty.

Going back to Palmas tonight. It's the place to be lol. Wanna come?

I lean my elbows against the cold stainless steel counter and reply, *On my way*

Two seconds later, he comes back with, *Whoa whoa. Don't piss off Felicia on my account. We can go when your shift ends.*

Right. Like I'd ever make him wait.

No it's cool. Coming now.

I shove my phone in my pocket.

"Hey Carlo," I say. "Remember that guy who used to rent a room upstairs when I was little? He stayed for a while. He had a daughter about my age. She was all blond and cute and..." My thought breaks into a zillion adjectives and descriptions, none of which are particularly kind. Or helpful. I finish with a weak, "and whatnot."

Vincent's head turns. Carlo frowns. "Victor?" he asks.

"No, not him. Victor had no kids. And he bussed tables for us. The guy I'm talking about didn't work here. He just stayed upstairs. But it was for...I don't know...a few months, maybe?

Remember him? It was, like, ten years ago, I think. I was little at the time."

A low chuckle, loaded with judgment, bursts from Vincent. He mumbles in Italian.

"Nah. Don't remember him." Carlo smiles far too wide for someone with no knowledge.

"Come on. I can tell you're lying."

The chicken's done. Vincent arranges some veggies on top. He squirts a squiggly line of pesto dressing across it like calligraphy before rolling the whole thing up in a tortilla.

Carlo cracks a head of garlic on a cutting board with the heel of his hand. "Sometimes people don't wanna tell their story, Effie. Ain't my job to get involved."

"Give me a break, Carlo. You can't tell me his name?"

"Why you need to know? He do something to you?"

No. That's the farthest and most opposite of all things. I want to do something to *him*. Namely, remove his daughter from this earth. Crack her entire body into tiny molecules and send it into oblivion. At a bare minimum, I'd like to erase her from Matty's memory.

"I'm just looking for his kid. I need her name. That's all."

"Okay, okay," Carlo waves a hand in surrender. The odor of garlic floats around us. "His name's James Madaleo. I remember his little girl. What was her name? Let me think. It's something sweet..." His focus drifts. He calls to Vincent in Italian. Vincent shrugs. He slides two aluminum take-out trays across the countertop to me. I start bagging the detective's order.

"Got it! Got it!" Carlo thrusts a pudgy finger upward. "Charlie!"

Vincent dismisses him. "No, no, no."

"Caroline! That's it!" Carlo says. "Caroline."

Caroline. How positively adorable. I'm about to ditch work and piss off my mother to help the love of my life connect with a chick who sounds like an American Girl doll? I couldn't script this day to be more of a joke if I tried.

"Do you know where they live now?"

Vincent and Carlo's heads snap toward each other. Vincent mutters something in Italian again. He eyes me suspiciously. "You said you only need her name."

"I do. I did. But what I really want is to find her." I throw in, "for a friend."

Carlo punches air like a boxer in training. "Watch out. Effie's ready to mess a girl up tonight." Four years after the fact and he still refers—almost daily—to the black eye I gave a guy from Venice who tried to swipe Matty's brand new Carver skateboard.

Sam chuckles behind me.

"It's not that," I say. "Someone I know is interested in her." I shoot a glance at Sam. His expression falls serious. He wipes a wet plate with a hand towel.

It's only a matter of time before one of them caves.

Vincent says, "You promise this is innocent? No funny business?"

"Of course."

"Okay. Las Palmas Altas. Ten-minute ride up the mountain. 44 Rumildo Walk."

Bingo. These guys know everything about everyone in this town.

My phone buzzes. Another text from Matty.

You are the best. Iloveyouiloveyouiloveyouiloveyou.

Sam's arms cradle a basket filled with clean silverware. I position the detective's takeout bag on top. He adjusts his arms to balance it all.

"Tell my mom I had to leave."

Sam's eyes bounce around frantically. "Why? What's the excuse?" The anticipation of my mother's wrath is just as bad as the actual moment of in-person rage. In my absence, he'll receive the full frontal assault. But it's a risk I have to take, for Matty.

"Who cares? She'll be mad anyway, excuse or not."

"But we're supposed to meet Joe after our shift."

My insides momentarily churn. "I know. I know." I search for an answer that won't make me look like the world's flakiest friend. "I'll still make it." Some promises are easy to make but not so easy to keep. I hope this isn't one of them.

I toss my apron onto the counter and head for the back door.

"Be careful," Sam calls.

Why on earth would I waste my time with that?

Chapter Six

My life has boiled down to this:

A girl, a pharmacy, innumerable fences, and Matty Pomerantz.

We're at Las Palmas Altas again. Armed with Vincent and Carlo's information, I will find this stupid Caroline girl and deliver Matty's note. If he's determined to see her, so be it. I'll be his supportive sidekick through it all as the infatuation fizzles and fades without interference.

I make it over the fence but that's not the hard part. Leaving Matty standing here holding my skateboard, breathless and waiting, knowing he's not waiting for me, but for *her*—that's the part that kills me, that breaks my heart into a million pieces. I dodge the thought because it's nothing but noise. We'll be together in the end. Right now, I need to stay focused.

On the other side of the fence, Matty breathes heavily. A small, twitchy smile plays on his face. "When we're in Chicago, I'll pay you back."

My face glows red, I can feel the burn. It's embarrassing as hell. I turn my gaze to my feet.

Matty and I have a future together, despite these wild goose chases. Even he knows the reality: I'm his and he's mine. I suspected it as far back as fifth grade when he let me graffiti my initials on his very white, very new Chuck Taylors. And I knew it for sure when I caught him giving Sonny Melendez the evil eye for staring at my ass in those super tight jean shorts I wore to Gerard's graduation party.

"Whatever you want," he adds.

I want you, dumbass. But such a ballsy declaration would ruin the moment. His assumption that I'll join him one day in Chicago, that he wants me there, by his side, forever, is enough to clog my throat with a million unspoken words. "How about…" I rack my brain for an activity that doesn't sound romantic enough to scare him off. "Sunday afternoon skate sessions. We can scope out the best parks in Chicago?"

"You bet." His face cracks into the widest smile I've ever seen.

A few seconds pass before I remember why we're standing here.

I know what I have to do.

Anything for Matty.

Past the parking field and lawn, I haul ass to the heart of the condo complex. When I reach Rumildo Walk, I pace myself, hoping

I look like I belong on this side of the fence, like I've got a worthy purpose. Not being on four wheels throws me off.

All these little houses are the same. Spanish-tiled roofs atop miniature, two-story, white stucco cottages that look like you have to duck in order to stand up straight within them. You can hardly tell one from the other. The houses click neatly together in lines, with charming little walkways between them, matching tiny palm trees, small, screened-in porches along one side, and rock gardens spilling patterns across each front yard. Not one of them stands out. Not one of them screams, *She's here! She's here!* As if it would be that easy. Little black lampposts stand guard at the foot of every house, like flags in the ground. Jutting out from arms on the lamppost poles are black signs with numbers pinpointing their place on the map. Eventually, the right sign pops out: *44*.

I slow my roll and duck behind a fat palm tree in the yard next door.

It's dark out here, but the scene under the dim yellow lighting of number 44's porch is clear. Two people sit at a small table. There's a man with black and gray hair, a little too long and a little too rugged to match his stiff white button-down shirt. It's her father, I think. He's different than I remember. A little doughier, definitely more gray. He props himself on both elbows, staring at a chessboard. Across the table is a blond girl. Her—Caroline. Her gaze drifts through the screen that separates family game night from everything out here.

I gather her dad's deliberating his next move.

I gather she couldn't care less about chess.

Who can blame her? It's boring as hell. All that waiting. No wonder she was so friendly to Matty. It's Friday night and she's stuck playing chess. I thought people only do that in prison.

Getting her attention is the only way to keep this ball rolling. I need a game plan. I am so bad at this. Her dad's a complication. The thought of him making the connection between my face and Fox Inn sets my nerves into a buzz. But at some point, he's got to get up, right?

From my spot behind the tree trunk, I wait. And wait. And wait.

He takes an unreasonable amount of time to consider his next move. It's the equivalent of forty laps around the Buscato Drive Skate Park bowl. I can feel my fingernails grow in the span of millenniums that it takes for him to lift his hand, lightly touch a chess piece, then pull his hand back, like he's thought through all the possibilities and decided against the move.

I want to scream.

I tap the toe of my sneaker against the palm tree. Count the taps, pass the time. When I reach one hundred seventeen, two little kids pass by on the walkway arguing over how best to defeat a zombie in some stupid video game. Colors flash from their light-up sneakers, and I'm so mesmerized I lose place in my count. I have to start all over again.

I can't take this anymore.

No risk, no reward.

I bounce onto the walkway and stroll in front of their house. Her father doesn't lift his face from the chess pieces, but she does. As

I pass under the glowing lamppost at the foot of her yard, we lock eyes.

Recognition sparks like lightning. Shé sits up straighter.

I slip off the walkway and maneuver myself into the narrow space between her house and the next. It's dark enough here that I'm relieved to be hidden, but just light enough that I can see. I'm not at risk of bumping into the three dinged and scratched bikes leaning against the side of the next-door neighbor's cottage. I press against the scratchy white stucco wall and wait. She'll show up. Anything's got to be better than chess.

From above me, a whoosh and a scrape break the silence.

I swing my head up and around.

Here she is, shining blond hair and all, directly above me.

She pops the window's screen out and juts her body through the opening. Her braid falls forward, skimming her cheek. It's so fucking Rapunzel I could throw up. I think I even *want* to, just to clear my head.

"I know your face," she whispers to me below. It sounds like a question. "Have we met?"

Yeah, we met. That time ten years ago when she watched from a second-floor window upstairs at Fox Inn as my mom forced me—a skinny squirt of an eight-year-old grom—to climb inside a dumpster out back to look for old Mrs. Fernbaum's diamond hoop earring that the woman was sure had dropped into her bowl of lobster risotto. As my Converse sunk into what looked oddly like a combination of dog food and dog excrement, I don't believe I've ever hated my mother more, and that was a lifetime ago, so there's certainly been opportunity for hate-growth. The girl eventually disappeared from the window. (To have a good laugh, I figured.) But a few minutes later, she hopped into the dumpster beside me out of nowhere and plucked one very shiny, very sparkly diamond earring from around the neck of an empty bottle of merlot. She pushed it at my face. "Here," she said, wearing the same sunshiny smile she wears tonight.

I had to admit, I was impressed. Relief overcame me and we hugged amid the shit-stinking food scraps and coffee grinds. But as we climbed out of the dumpster, I felt stupid. I had friends; I didn't need new ones. Especially one that wasn't my speed. She still isn't. I don't do sweet.

"You don't know me," I say finally. Not really, anyway.

Her eyes float, like *what are you doing here then?*

Clarification: "Someone's looking for you."

"Who?"

"Matty."

She tilts her head. The braid dangles like rope.

"Reddish-blond hair? Freckles?"

Eyes the color of everything perfect. A smile so big you could live inside it.

Her eyes glaze over. Thinking, thinking, thinking.

Come on. What a joke. You don't forget a guy like Matty.

I don't know why he'd bother with a complete bore like her. Must be the hair.

"The guy from Bella Via Pharmacy?" I say, not even trying to hide my annoyance.

A glimmer of something bright hits her eyes.

I open my fist. The note's warm and sticks to my palm.

The weirdest sensation floods through me. Like, I suddenly don't want to hand it over. What would be the harm if I didn't? I could keep it, pretend it's meant for me, black out her name with Sharpie, insert my own right on top. Matty would never have to know. Lies could cover the whole thing up, and since Princess Blondie apparently isn't ever allowed out of her castle, she and Matty would never connect to swap stories. She doesn't know his full name yet. She'd never find him. The chances of the two of them meeting in a checkout line again are zilch. It's only happened once in the last ten years, right? My father would totally take bets on those odds. Keeping the note for myself would be loads better than handing it over to watch her marvel at the message inside. I know what he wrote. Most guys would boil it down to their name and number. This message is appropriately adorable and so wordy, so very Matty. Some romantic bullshit about how the sight of her stole his breath away. He scribbled it down in the Jeep last night, then recited it to me, like song lyrics, and waited for my reaction.

I stared at the white paper shivering in his hands.

I listened like a loyal friend should.

I pressed my fingertips to my mouth. He said, "Aw, Effie, you're all choked up. Is it that good?" I nodded and sucked back the disappointment with a mouthful of Pepsi. Of course I liked it. Except I was imagining it was directed at me.

"It's perfect, Matty." I stared down at the Pepsi can. Flames were a millimeter away from shooting out of my eyeballs to light the fucking note on fire with the red rage expanding inside my head.

I pep-talked myself then, and I repeat the same thoughts to myself now. Knowing Matty, she won't be on his radar long. The last girl chewed with her mouth open, the girl before that kept a hidden picture of her ex clipped to the underside of her car's visor, and the one before her couldn't stand the sound of skateboard trucks grinding against the curb. Too many flaws gather into a list of annoyances which then result in an eventual dump. Matty is flighty as all get-out. He'll find a solid reason to ditch this girl soon too, even if her hair is prettier than all the others. No one's perfect, but with his never-ending optimism, he hasn't figured this out yet.

I look up at her again. She's patient, waiting, probably fantasizing about her dream boy.

My dream boy. My boy with the great, big, beautiful heart and even bigger dreams. Let's face it—if I don't hand this note over, I am directly responsible for killing those dreams. I am the grim reaper destroying all hope and possibilities. And that's not who I am. If it's one thing you can count on about me, it's that I'll always do what's best for Matty.

I sigh, resolute. "He's got something to say. So. Here."

She hangs out of her window, staring at me.

I hold the folded note in the air. I don't know what to do with the damn thing. I can't reach high enough for her to grab it. An idea hits me—the windows. There's a little bit of a lip there. I shove the toe of my sneaker onto the narrow bottom ledge. Hauling myself up, I grab the top of the window—its tiny, decorative, red Spanish tiles—with the tips of the fingers. I extend my left hand. I'm elevated just enough for her to meet me halfway. My arms tremble.

The things I do for this boy.

She reaches, reaches. Plucks the note from my fingers.

There. It's done.

I drop back down to the cement. A chunk of my crazy hair catches on her window frame. If I wasn't so pissed, I'd be embarrassed. My flaws are on display in front of her perfection. When I slide the back of my hand across my mouth, it comes away sweat-slick and wet.

"Thank you," she says softly. Again, it sounds like a question.

"You're welcome," I say. It sounds like a threat.

I am literally a raging inferno.

She skims the note quickly. Her eyes spark bright as they flick down the page, full of hope and hearts and ever-after, I'm sure. I want to puke. She holds up a finger, and like a chump I obey her order to wait as she disappears, then returns with a pen. She scribbles something down on the note, refolds it, and tosses it down to me. I catch it.

My job here is done; I don't owe her anything more. Noise sparks up in the alleyway as I scrape past the neighbor's bikes. They knock together.

Her voice calls out "Wait!"

I stop. I want to shout, "Shut the fuck up!" but of course I don't. I glance back at her.

"I'm Celeste, by the way," she says in this frenzied sort of hush-yell, leaning forward until the top of her shorts skim the windowsill.

"Not Caroline?" I whisper.

Her face flashes with something unrecognizable. "No. It's Celeste."

Celeste? Come on. That's even more sweet than Caroline.

"What's your name?" she asks.

My name is a minor detail. She doesn't need to know me. Why would she care anyway?

I pop back onto Rumildo Walk like I never left. Her dad still sits before the chessboard on the porch. Deep in thought on family game night. I can't remember the last time my father wasted precious time on me. Last year he bet me twenty bucks I couldn't set all the tables in Fox Inn in under three minutes, but that doesn't count. (He won, by the way. He always does. I never start with a plan. I'm never anything but impulsive.) Celeste's dad pinches two fingers around a piece. Whether it's a king or queen, I wouldn't know. Though I suspect he'll win, regardless. Anyone who puts that much thought into things always comes out a winner.

Chapter Seven

J oe calls our first meeting to plan the protest on Vista Buscato Town Hall grounds. It's where rules are born about the
goings-on in this lame-ass town where nothing ever happens and
everything worth doing is thirty miles up or down Pacific Coast
Highway. In a city with a name you can actually identify on a
map. The meeting's venue feels horribly wrong. There's a whole
lot of officially official stuff going on in that old, brick building.
But Joe insists we have every right to be there. It's a replay of his
public property argument. He's simmering with that righteous
anger thing again—his "This Is Our Town Too" logo branded
deep into his heart. A tiny part of me, the young and naïve side
that once thought Vista Buscato was the prettiest town in all of
America, understands.

Joe's cocked with one foot on his skateboard way, way up
ahead on the walkway leading to the double doors of the Town
Hall building. He considers his move, quietly running through

all the factors in pulling off this rail slide—angles, movements, timing—not the least of which is how to manage it all without alerting anyone in the building behind him.

"He's not going to move until sixteen-hundred hours," Sam says. He licks his thumb and rubs the raw edge of the scab on his elbow. It still hasn't healed.

"Don't sweat it, Sarge," Matty says. He flips the side of his board, deck to bottom, over and over. The threat of getting caught skating on Town Hall grounds doesn't even rate a one on a scale of zero to one hundred for him. Everyone is charmed by Matty Pomerantz, even the cranky old ladies behind the Town Hall reception desk. He could get away with murder.

I don't know how much time passes, but shit—Sam's right. Entire worlds are born and die in the time it takes Joe to make a move. I'm so bored I memorize the phone number on the missing girl poster taped to the closest palm tree trunk.

On the inside I screech at Joe, *Do it do it do it!!!!!*

Up ahead, Joe adjusts his foot on the tail of his board. We've watched him land this trick before. The rest of these guys hesitate or whatever and screw up the jump. It's like they can't get the initial pop up onto the railing right. Too off center, too far backward, too far forward, pushing, leaning, never getting their shoulders square. But Joe gets the balance perfect every time. Every, every time.

No one says a word.

And then Joe goes.

He pumps forward, wheels screaming down the walkway. With a pop, he goes airborne, flying onto the hand railing into a back-slide. He glides down, arms out, legs balanced on either end of his board, teeter-totter style. His dark hair whips around his face, all thick and ropey. At the bottom of the railing, he drops down on all four wheels like it was nothing. It takes my breath away, the perfection. It's excellent.

I shout, "YES!" then cover my mouth. Too loud, but I can't help myself.

Sam's neck swivels in all directions to make sure we aren't heard.

Matty raises victory arms in the air. On top of the world, as always.

Sam's up next. He sets up the trick way quicker than Joe did. But he doesn't make the jump onto the railing. The board flies outward. He free-falls down the stairs and eats pavement bad, landing in a jumble of limbs on the concrete. His board flips and flips. It tosses out red flashes along the way, thanks to the spark plate he bought last week at Skate Real, now dangling from the tail of his board. Joe tugs it off and inspects it. "Don't worry. I'll get you another one," he says.

Sam sits up. His elbows glow pink and wet like the insides of strawberries. There's way more blood than I expected.

I wonder if we're on our way to the ER. The first time I wound up there, I was twelve. The x-ray showed a fractured ankle. The doc pointed at a thin crack in the line, but I couldn't see it. Neither could my father. It was just a bunch of white and black blurred into gray. We went to Rite-Aid and got a heat rub ointment and an Ace Bandage. Two days later I was back bussing tables at Fox Inn after school.

"Don't dwell," I tell Sam in an effort to lighten the concern painting his cheeks a deep burgundy. "Pain's all in your mind."

"Let's see you make that jump without wiping out."

"Fifty bucks, and you're on."

"Five."

"Twenty."

"Come on. Stop stalling."

I grab my board and head for the top of the walkway. "Fifteen. That's final."

Joe follows me. As we walk away, Matty rips into Sam. "That's the worst bet in the world. Effie never loses."

Over my shoulder, I throw him a smile, casual as I can despite that every cell in my body beats with fire. He smiles back. I almost explode.

Joe and I line up next to each other in front of Town Hall's doors, careful not to be heard. Joe twists his neck to the side and spits. The glob flies from his mouth, sails though the air, and lands directly in front of the double doors. His aim is perfect.

He looks at me and grins.

The expanse of pavement spreads out before us.

From the benches, Matty shouts, "Do it!"

My heartbeat pops out at least fifteen sky-high ollies.

Joe swings out an arm. It hovers against my waist, a yield sign, a warning. "Easy. Wait till you're ready."

I push his arm away. "I am ready."

"I don't want you to get hurt."

"Okay, Dad," I say, even though my own father couldn't give two shits.

I rip down the walkway and reach the perfect speed. My pop up on to the railing is super smooth. The slide down happens so quick, like always, but feels the opposite, like I'm working in slow-mo. Four wheels slap the sidewalk in a landing I couldn't have planned better.

Matty's all over me the instant I come to a stop. He wraps arms around me from behind. "Ahahaha!" he laughs, pointing at Joe, who lands behind me, coming down from an impressive 360. "She smoked your ass!"

Joe glances at us, at the way I'm covered by Matty's arms, and says, "What else is new?"

Matty lifts me off the ground till I scream. "She's a keeper."

A smile takes over my face. Because I think maybe he meant it the way I wanted him to mean it. It's the kind of reminder that keeps me going. No matter who Matty has the hots for today, tomorrow, or next week, right here, right now, I am his number one; I'm a keeper. Nothing else matters but that.

Blood's drying in starbursts around Sam's elbows. I slip out of Matty's grip, hold grabby hands out to Sam, and say, "I take cash or credit. No personal checks."

He tells me to fuck off.

Joe lands another rail slide, without the slightest wobble to his landing.

He helps Sam up and calls him a kook. Sam sweeps Joe's legs out from underneath him. They tumble to the ground. Doesn't take long before we're all laughing again.

Sam pulls cash out of his pocket. Before handing it to me, he says, "Double or nothing that Matty can't find his girl."

"Too late," Matty says. "Effie found her last night."

His smile screams insults at me. I suck in a raggedy breath.

With this huge, dopey grin, Matty skates off, banging out tic-tacs one after the other in a giant circle. He twists his body, twists the trucks. Swing right, swing left. Swing right, swing left. The repetition is gross. I wish Sam or Joe would slap the back of his head. Maybe it'd encourage his brain to skip over the glitch he's so obviously stuck on.

Three seconds ago I was a keeper. But now I'm all but forgotten in favor of a poor imitation of Rapunzel. Absurd. Somehow I spun a 180 but I'm not on wheels. My heart welds itself to the roof of my mouth. I reach for my can of Red Bull on the ground and take a giant gulp.

Joe's eyes search for mine. I look away. He's waiting for my usual wiseass comment. I don't know whether to smile and go along with it or cry because it's all so ridiculously wrong. Any reaction to Matty's excitement is weird, so I keep a deliberately blank expression. But then again, a lot of things seem weird at this moment, not the least of which is that I'm watching the guy I love daydream about the girl he loves.

Reminder: *He might love. Might. Not does, not yet.*

I am not above shaking the shit out of this Red Bull in my hand just to blow it all over the place and change the subject. I keep reminding myself that this girl is a dud, just a wooden piece on a chess board. She's as dull as ever, despite her sparkly unicorn hair. Matty will forget about her in two weeks. Last month he couldn't decide what color wheels to buy for his board. White? Red? He bought the white, agonized over it long enough to run down the clock on the return policy, and then wasted more money on the set he should have chosen in the first place. Red. I still don't think he's satisfied. He asked Joe to spray-paint the outside of them black.

Now that we're on his favorite topic, Matty plays news reporter, assaulting me with back-to-back questions. He resorts to asking what she was wearing last night because I think he wants to keep the conversation alive. I chuck the empty Red Bull can as hard as I can at his head. He yelps, but doesn't shut up, doesn't put the brakes on. The can clatters to the ground and rolls under one of the benches.

"Come on, Effie. I'd tell you."

Joe picks up the can. His gaze slides from Matty to me. My reaction is a moment worth catching, I suppose.

Blinking doesn't help clear my panic. The Red Bull buzz fuzzes things up around the edges. I give Matty the same vague answer I offered last night: "I don't remember."

Of course this is a lie. I remember every detail about last night. She was wearing a peach-colored t-shirt. For some reason I remember thinking everything about her matched in a palette of creamy peach and platinum. I wonder if her underpants fit the color scheme. The image grosses me out to no end. The last thing I want is to relive it, even if it is for Matty.

"Did you get her name yet?" Sam asks.

Matty replies, serious as ever, "Caroline."

Every cell in my body switches to red alert. I haven't corrected the "Caroline" misinformation on Matty, and I don't intend to. She must not have signed her note. If things are meant to be, he'll discover her real name. My list of mistakes grows by the minute, and I don't need to hasten the process.

Sam shakes his head at Matty. "I don't get the fascination with this girl."

That makes two of us.

Three people make their way toward us. Thank God, the conversation finally breaks. One guy rides a skateboard in oversized black jeans, and a t-shirt twelve sizes too big. The other two—a guy and a girl—have boards tucked under their arms. They're passing something back and forth. A blunt, I think. A few more steps and I can make out faces. I groan.

Of course it would be my reject brother, Gerard, the only idiot I know who'd light up on Town Hall property. On his right is this guy we hang out with. We call him Bruiser, not because he inflicts bruises on others but because he sports so many of them at any given time. He's always stoned and he always wears this God-awful wool beanie. I sweat just looking at him. One of his front teeth is permanently chipped in a cautionary tale of what happens when you're dumb enough to skitch from the back bumper of a car rather than its side. Stop signs are a real bitch when you can't see them coming. On Bruiser's other side is a skinny girl from Ventura whose name I can never remember because it's as stupid as her blond dreadlocks. I'd bet all my weekend tips they're extensions. She carries a skateboard everywhere, but I've never seen her step on it. Fucking wannabe.

"Let the protest preparations commence!" Joe says.

Fist bumps are exchanged. I offer a half-hearted wave at Bruiser and the girl. My brother gives me the finger. More or less his standard greeting.

With a proper audience, Joe says, "I hear the next Town Hall meeting is the place to be." The dreadlock chick gives a throaty laugh. "We should gather up a crowd as big as we can. Make an impact, you know."

Bruiser and my brother nod.

Sam stays quiet. He dabs at his raw elbow with the hem of his t-shirt.

Joe looks at the dreadlocked girl. "You in, Dogma?"

Dogma. That's it. I knew it was something weird. She offers a lazy, "Hell yeah," and holds out a hand for the blunt. Bruiser hands it over.

Joe glances at me and Matty. "You'll come, right?"

I wait for Matty's move.

He says, "Of course," like there's no other answer.

Next up is me. My stomach spins out a heelflip. Joe's eyes flash, a little hopeful, a little threatening. I can never tell which half of him wins out. It's not that I don't want to help. I absolutely do. This means something to Joe. And to Sam and Matty and all of our friends. But I don't intend to stick around this microscopic dot on the map much longer.

"I have to get out of my shift," I say weakly.

Gerard takes the weed from Dogma. The smell chokes me. One suck and the belligerent angles on my brother's face melt away. (Momentarily. I'm no fool. I know they'll be back.) "You're not on schedule that night."

Thanks, big brother.

"Cool." Joe's eyes haven't left my face. "So you'll be there?"

This town sucks, no question. But Joe wants this so bad. He deserves friends who stand with him. And I can't let these rich bastards take away the only thing we have left. I dip my head into a nod.

The conversation turns to the weekend's skate comp in Ventura and who's entering. Joe is, of course. Bruiser too. Gerard isn't, which surprises no one. My brother has no ambition to succeed at anything unless it involves a lighter and some ripe bud. Loser. Joe pushes me to enter, and even though it doesn't mean any-thing—it's not like my parents will allow me to pursue a future in Vista Buscato that doesn't involve bar towels and silverware—I'll do it. Because kicking ass on wheels is always a good time.

Gerard offers the blunt to Sam. Sam raises a hand, declining.

"Oh. You're one of them now, huh? Military man." Gerard blows out a stream of smoke. He laughs but the sound's not genuine. It's the laugh my mother lets out right before she pours herself another glass. Bruiser joins him. Before long, they're pelting

Sam with Skittles from an open package Gerard pulls from his pocket.

Sam's father has him on a leash. It's tight and short and stifling. But at least General Wills cares. He's shooting for a life for Sam where his son's self-sufficient, successful, happy. Our parents are nothing more than our bosses. They're not shooting for anything other than a fully-functioning business and a steady stream of income. I thought my brother understood this.

"Lay off him, Gerard," I say.

"Fuck you, *Mrs. Pomerantz.*"

Sam's head spins in my direction.

Gerard's dig hangs in the air. I feel so utterly stupid.

My entire face—no, my entire *head*—goes hot.

Joe pretends he doesn't notice, but his eyes meet mine. His jaw locks down tight. Every angle in his face is intensified, edging on distaste for what Mrs. Pomerantz suggests.

Matty shouts, "Watch your mouth. That's my wife you're messing with."

Laughter breaks out, and I finally join in, because it's not like I can do what I really want to do, which is kick my brother in his throat.

"Go home, Gerard," I say.

He throws out his arms. "I am home."

Which is exactly why I hate this place. He, my parents, and everything about Fox Inn and its phony menu with overpriced food, keeps me here. It's a list of the things I can't get away from. It's prison. *They* are my prison. I wonder, despite the crazy circumstances, if that girl in the missing person poster is happy she's gone, if she feels free. I certainly would.

A half hour later, when the three of them head back the way they came, their heads floating from the weed fog, I make my disgust known. "Look at them! You really trust my brother and those guys to help?" *And not fuck everything up?* I want to add but don't.

"Strength in numbers," Joe says. "We need everyone at Town Hall."

Matty nods.

Sam picks along the edge of his thumbnail. He's played with army figures his whole life. Even he knows the biggest army is useless if its members can't—don't even know how to—battle. And those guys, they don't know anything. They can hardly stand in a straight line.

"They'll stay outside," Joe assures us. "I'll have them chant, make a picket line or something. You three can come in and be voices with me."

Sam and Matty throw unwavering support into the mix. I don't see why either of them cares. Sam's leaving Vista Buscato in a few weeks, off to San Diego for Marine Corps boot camp. Why would he fight for a skate park he'll never get the chance to ride in? And Matty—he's already halfway gone. Tuition's paid, dorm room assignments are set. All that's left is to leave. I'm torn between wanting to remember the countdown of days we all have left and not wanting to acknowledge the finality of it all. Like Joe, I'm *supposed* to care about this town. But I don't know if I do.

Joe waits for my response. This could be the dumbest thing we've ever attempted. We're rolling out a plan to challenge the Board, and it's basically the same as igniting a fire that could potentially burn everything to the ground. I'm pretty sure we won't come out winners. And yet, something familiar glows around Joe as I look at him. I know what it's like, feeling as though no one's on your side. Like your dreams aren't worth a damn. So I slap his hand in solidarity. His palm is hot and dry.

"I'm with you," I say. And I totally mean it.

CHAPTER EIGHT

My back pocket's on fire with a buzzing phone.

I need to get my shit together.

It's Saturday night, prime tip-making time. The more tables I wait, the more my bank roll doubles, and the closer I get to leaving this town. But the texts from Matty won't stop rolling in, and staying focused is impossible.

The most recent text: SHE LEFT A LETTER FOR ME AT THE FENCE

She, he says. Like I'm supposed to equate every feminine pronoun with this girl.

Who's she? I type. A tickle of satisfaction runs through me when I make it clear that *She* is not my everything. I don't know this *She* he's talking about.

He doesn't even notice.

NOT JUST A NOTE—A LONG, LONG LETTER.

I follow up with a vague reply of *Cool. Talk later.* Because I don't give a damn about this girl and her apparent ignorance of modern technology in favor of letter swapping. Not my fault she doesn't own a phone. If my relentlessly hardass mother catches me texting, I'm dead.

Ditching my shift last week to help Matty turned out to be a bad idea for more reasons than the obvious. It was a flagrant violation of Fox Family Rule Number One. My mother softened an inch when I told her I did it for Matty, because it stoked her dream of seeing me tied together with the trust fund-owning grandson of the town's one and only wealthy judge. She still hasn't let go of the mantra she was raised with: look pretty and marry rich. I think she regrets falling in love with my father and his empty pockets and swindler heart all those years ago. But still, rich Matty or not, I knew I'd face punishment. She gave me a double table load tonight as retribution and she's been riding my ass all shift. The fact I asked to have off tomorrow—on a Sunday, of all days—adds another layer of disgust to her crappy attitude. If she catches me texting, I'm dead.

I try to push thoughts of Matty and the girl out of my mind. It doesn't work. Because my phone buzzes again. And again. What if he says something important—other than about the girl? Like he needs me or whatever. The temptation is too much.

In the kitchen, I hide in a corner and read his next text:

SHE WANTS TO HANG OUT

I'm hot and nauseated. Sweat pools at the small of my back. This thing cannot move forward. It's not supposed happen. He's supposed to fantasize about his mystery girl, obsess a little, make an idiot of himself, maybe hurt her feelings, but he's not supposed to take it further. I thought this would be over in a flash. Like in sophomore year when he decided he no longer wanted to hook up with Lori Malcomb after discovering she chews cinnamon gum. "That shit's gross," he told me and Joe. "What other weird stuff is she into?" A similarly ridiculous cinnamon gum reason is supposed to break his trance over this new girl.

A letter. Wow. That's great, I write, even though it's so not great. I can't think of anything worse.

And then, because I'd be an asshole if I didn't at least ask the obvious question, I write *What did she say?*

A notification pops at the top of my screen. It's not Matty this time, but Joe.

Meet tomorrow at 11. Edgar's driving.

Tomorrow's skate comp is less than twenty-four hours away. Edgar told Joe that he pretty much knows every girl who plans to enter, and, hands-down, I have the skills to win. An unexplainable, almost embarrassing degree of excitement has grown inside me over the prospect of steamrolling over the other entrants in this contest. Just to show everyone that I'm good at something, that I'm not a complete fuck-up, I have a path—one I can carve for myself. Joe's excited enough for the two of us, which is awesome.

Another text rolls in.

HER NAME ISN'T CAROLINE.

And just like that—all my good feelings fade to black.

Okay, I respond.

IT'S CELESTE VAUGHN

Turn off caps lock pls.

HER NAME IS CELESTE VAUGHN.

I heard you

IM EXCITED

I can see that.

CELESTE CELESTE CELESTE CELESTE

My insides suffer like the porterhouse steaks meeting their demise on the grill. As Matty cycles through deepening degrees of love-induced lunacy, I'm stuck here where I can't do a thing about it except send replies and play the loyal buddy and serve another plate of panko-crusted salmon. Because this is the hole I dug myself into. It's entirely my fault. No one forced me to climb that fence for him; no one asked me to squeeze her address out of Carlo and Vincent. What was I thinking? Shit. I let this go too far.

A new text bubble fills the phone's screen. I cover my mouth to keep from throwing up when her name materializes there.

CELESTE VAUGHN. IT'S A BEAUTIFUL NAME. RIGHT?

Oh, dear God. He's flushed and heated over a girl who hangs from balconies and probably still wears princess pajamas. I want to cry. I don't respond.

SHE SAID WE CAN MEET TONIGHT

AT 8

BUT

My heartbeat kicks into a sprint.

I know it's coming. The dots in the text bubble shimmer before the axe drops on me.

I NEED YOUR HELP

And there it is. Story of my life.

Vincent flips the steaks. The kitchen spikes to four hundred degrees. I loosen the apron around my waist. I can't...I'm so hot.

Carlo plops dollops of garlic mashed potatoes onto two plates, then slides them across the counter toward Vincent. His eyes squeeze tight with concern. "You okay, kid?"

"I'm good, yeah."

"You look like shit."

"Thanks."

Vincent drops the steaks onto plates but forgets his usual artsy garnish. The gray-haired food master is suddenly too engrossed watching me. Carlo, too. They know something's up. How could they not? They watched me use scissors to hack off the bottoms of my feetie pajamas in this very kitchen many, many years ago when my parents stuck me and Gerard here with sleeping bags on busy weekend nights. I'd say they know me better than most, for good or for bad. Like family, like uncles.

I run the plates out to table three before they ask more questions.

Behind the bar, my mother's on her seventeenth or thirtieth vodka tonic. I lost count. But she's smiling, which is a good thing. My phone vibrates against my ass. I am undeniably weary.

The chatter in Fox Inn grows louder by the minute as the sun takes its final plunge below the horizon. The sky's hazy, dull, and gray. Orange splotches up the edges. I wish I had the luxury of sitting there at a glossy mahogany table, sipping a drink, gazing at the beach in the distance, watching the sun drop, letting minutes ooze into one another. These people have no idea how lucky they are.

My phone buzzes again. Damn it.

Table four orders another round of drinks. I squeeze past the crowd waiting to be seated at the host's podium.

Through the front door, Matty steps inside.

He's clean and sharp and gleaming. Those adorable freckles dance across his eager face. It doesn't take a genius to figure out he has plans for the night and they don't include bumming around with Joe. He beelines to me. A light cologne scent wraps around my head. I make the most absurd and illogical wish that he's wearing it to impress me. My father would say a wish like that is just a bet with bad odds.

He pulls me close. "I have a problem." The whisper, the words, all of it comes out hot and hurried against my ear.

I want to say in return: *I have a problem, too. I'm in love with you.*

But I decide on: "And you need me because...?"

"*Because*? That's the dumbest question I've ever heard." He shakes me by the shoulders. "Because you're my fucking rock, that's why."

The traitorous cells in my heart let a tiny smile bleed through. I'd be lying if I said his needing me is a drag. It isn't. It's a thrill. A more worthy cause would be nice.

"You stopped answering my texts."

"I'm working. See?" I wag the order pad in his face. He swats it away.

"I'm meeting her tonight."

Back on the girl again. She never goes away for long.

"What does that have to do with me? And if you say I have to climb another fence, I'll slap the shit out of you."

"No, not that. I have no way to pick her up."

"You have a car," I say dismissively.

"That's not what I mean. Her father would never let her leave with me."

"She under house arrest or something?"

"She says he won't let her date."

My efforts to hold back an eye roll fail. He sees it.

"Effie, please."

He bends down a smidge so we're at eye level. His face hovers an inch from mine. Our noses almost tap. I try to focus my gaze anywhere but on his eyes. They are so, so blue. When I look at them, I fall apart.

I sigh. "What do you want me to do?"

"You can pick her up. Go get her for me. It's the perfect icebreaker. You two know each other."

"That's overstating things."

"Don't make me beg. You know I will."

He opens his mouth. Something ridiculous, like a song or whatever, is sure to come screaming through his lips, so I smother his face with my hand. "What makes you think her father will let her leave with me? I'm a stranger."

He bites my hand, then laughs when I yank it away. "You're not threatening. You're a girl." Finally, he notices.

"I'm working." To be fair, at this moment I'm not. And my tips will certainly reflect that. Table two is clearly ready to leave—jackets on, glasses emptied, wallets at the ready. Their faces have that unmistakable searching quality. *Where is that damn waitress?* "And anyway, I'm taking off tomorrow. My parents don't know, but I'm going to that skate comp in Ventura with Joe. They'll never let me have off if I bail on tonight's shift, too."

He takes a step backward, drops my hand. "Shit," he says, all thrill and excitement deflating.

"I—I'm sorry...I mean...it's just that Joe and Edgar think I can win," I say like an idiot, and immediately wish I could take back the pitiful whine in my tone. He's slipping away.

"Of course. Go. You'll win."

"I don't know. It's stupid, I guess. It's just a comp, right? I can skip it."

"Would you do that for me?"

What kind of Mrs. Pomerantz would I be if I didn't? He needs me.

"Ride or die, right?" I say with a smile. I hope it doesn't come out as fake as it feels.

"Oh my God, you're the literal best. I owe you my life."

You owe me everything.

"I have no idea how I'll get past my mother, though."

He starts bouncing on the balls of his feet. His whole body's set to pop. Like right before he busts out a perfect ollie. "If she sees you're with me, she'll let you go to Antarctica. We'll tell her you won't be gone too long."

The more he talks, the more I regret my decision.

But love is sacrifice and I'm willing to do whatever it takes.

I grab his hand and we race to the bar. The liquor bottles lined up behind my mother's head sparkle and gleam, each illuminated with little points of light suspended above them. She stands in my father's place, dragging her hand across a chalkboard mounted to the wall where we post the evening's specials. Tonight, we're testing out some fancy new pan-seared mahi mahi recipe Vincent came up with. Because apparently hamburgers aren't classy enough for this town.

"Hey, Felicia!" Matty says with an easy smile.

"Matty! Look at you!" She presses her upper torso over the bar's edge for a full-length view of him. Her chest busts forward. Three guys at a table against the wall go silent as death as they ogle her boobs. I want to die—but first, I want to cover her with a tablecloth or something. All the body parts I worry about her over-showing are on display, spilling across the polished wood. You'll make more tips this way, she once said as she forced a denim miniskirt on me under threat of death. Later, when she'd consumed enough vodka tonics to render herself legally blind, I pulled a pair of bike shorts out of my P.E. bag in my dad's office and wore them underneath the skirt. Just to get back at her in my own way.

She thrusts a finger at his brand new, straight-out-of-the-box docksiders. "Bet you wouldn't skate in those beauties, huh?" She nods like it's the greatest observation ever. Matty smiles. I hold back a gag. "Where are you heading tonight?" As her words come out, she glances down at our hands—still joined, warm palms pressed together. I want to let go for her sake, because she'll quiz me about this later, but I also want to keep holding on. Forever.

"I'm going out," he says in a mouthful of excitement.

"Take me with you."

Not your garden variety joke. Matty pauses two beats.

My mother is a lush. Chances are excellent she will unintentionally embarrass you. Chances are rock solid she will embarrass herself.

I roll my eyes. "Mom. Stop."

"I was kidding." She reaches across the bar and slaps Matty's arm.

He laughs again, though it's not a smooth sound. He clears his throat and says, "I'm taking someone out to La Jolie Dame."

Errrrrr...HALT EVERYTHING.

Matty's text series of breaking news bulletins did not mention this nuance. I clutch my heart because I'm afraid it will dive out of my chest onto the sticky wood floors. When did this happen? How did he leap from exchanging notes on torn slices of white paper to spoon-feeding the girl at a table for two, bathed in moonlight and oysters? The closest Matty's ever come to taking me out to dinner was covering my In-N-Out Burger order when I forgot cash. And I'm damn sure he didn't stress about it the way he's stressing right now. La Jolie Dame is the classiest restaurant in town, and my mother is wildly jealous of their impeccable reputation. It's one of those white linen places with old, snooty waiters and a menu you can't read without a French-to-English dictionary. It's up in the mountains near Buscato Point where the view of the Pacific is so wide and so high you feel like you can tap the mountaintops with your fingertips.

I do my best to keep my face even, my emotions in check. He pumps a few squeezes through my hand, as if to say *We're winning! She's caving!* Of course she is. I'm not the only Fox charmed by Matty Pomerantz.

"La Jolie Dame, huh?" My mother's eyes fly to me. Her jaw cracks almost into a full drop. She's set to say more. It'll be stupid and ridiculous and it will blow my whole day and night. I shoot her a silent *Shut up*.

Like the certifiable asshole that she is, she coos, "What a lucky girl!"

And what kills me, what positively rips me open from heart to guts, is that she knows the girl involved in Matty's evening is not me.

"It's nice to see you boys clean up for someone," she says. "She must be very special." She looks straight at me. I'm sure a tirade of lectures awaits me later about how I'll never find a boy if I insist on acting like one, and maybe if I let my hair out of the ponytail every now and then I'd have a boyfriend, and I should try wearing something other than those dirt-caked old Vans. Comments like that are what make me wish this restaurant and all the people in it would just slide into the Pacific Ocean, like the next Lost City of Atlantis.

My hand is hot and gluey. Matty untangles his fingers from mine. He's lost in a fog of Cupids and hearts. "She is special. She really is," he gushes. "Hey—you might know her. She's—"

I jump in front of him. Stop the information train.

I get to the point because obviously Matty cannot. "Mom, I have to leave. Matty needs me to pick up the girl for him. But I'll come back. Give me 30 minutes?"

Matty and I glance at each other, and I can tell by the way he scratches his ear that he's nervous as hell.

"Phil!" she shouts. "Phil!"

Matty and I jump. A few heads in the restaurant turn.

My father pulls up to the bar in a trot, eyes wild, hair the same. A pencil's tucked above his left ear, which means he's playing magician, running numbers in his back office. Making cash disappear with a flick of his wrist, straight up his sleeve.

"Effie's taking a break."

"Again?" he says. He talks around the cigarette hanging from the left corner of his mouth. It's not lit. He's been trying to quit for months. His strategy—the I-feel-better-knowing-a-cigarette-is-near method—doesn't work. At least once a day, and sometimes ten times, he lights it off a burner. Anyone with half a brain knows he's teasing himself. And yet he insists he's quitting, actively embarking on a smoke-free adventure. Setbacks are part of the process, I guess. Either that or he's a phony, just like the rest of them.

"I'm taking her tables," my mother says. "You're bartending."

Matty shoots me a hurried glance. This was absurdly easy. Same as when I convinced my mother, years ago, that Matty requires a free bowl of Lucky Charms every day after school because after losing his parents in the car accident and moving in with his grandfather, the only things in his pantry are oatmeal and fiber supplements. Felicia would do anything for Matty. It's probably genetic.

My father trades places with my mother. "What's the occasion?"

"Hot date," she teases.

Matt's smile genuinely overflows.

My heart implodes. I'm shriveling inside.

"She a skater?" my father asks.

I'd be blind if I didn't notice the quick flash of his eyes in my direction.

Matty shakes his head. "Nah." A stupid question.

I'm splayed open, bleeding on the floor at everyone's feet, spilling out until I'm empty.

No one even cares.

"This mystery girl got a name?" my father asks, grinning.

Please. I cannot hear her name again. I yank on Matty's arm. "We're going to be late."

Matty calls out thanks. My parents wave and wish him luck. He pauses at Fox Inn's front doors, where small panes of glass set into the wood shine silvery with reflections. He stoops a bit for a clear shot of himself in the glass, then runs his free hand through his hair and primps. This view of him—this backwards reflection—is all wrong. The Matty I see is not the Matty I know. His eyebrows cock too far to the right, his nose seems off-center slightly, and I'm not sure but is the right side of his top lip thicker than the other side? He stops making love to his mirror image and looks at me. He grins, face back to normal.

His smile fills the hollow spots inside me.

This is why I do it. *This* is why I can't say no to him, no matter the cost.

But the flipped version of Matty in the mirror stays rooted in my head. I think maybe that's the guy Celeste sees. Or maybe that's the guy he wants her to see.

We step outside into thick, warm air. Everything feels off, and the heat doesn't help.

"You wouldn't let me tell them who she is," he asks. "Why?"

"Long story." *Like, really long.* "You nervous?"

"Nope. I'm fantastic." He tosses the keys to his Jeep skyward and catches them on the drop.

Regret rises inside me.

The Jeep loops through mountain roads same as on our other trek to Las Palmas Altas. The top is down, but the passing wind on the drive doesn't help cool me. I'm boiling from the inside out. Making matters worse, Matty won't shut up about the reservations at La Jolie Dame. It'll be a surprise, and won't she love it? I think a girl like that has probably already been there. Restaurant management likely named a dessert for her. Matty paraphrases her letter to me word for word as if I'm dying for the details. I am dying, but not in the way he thinks. I sink into the seat, I drown under the dashboard, I roll underneath the floor of the car and die on the side of the road. He runs me over with two tons of steel packed into every word.

"She feels the same way, Effie." His head whips from the road to me and back. "It's crazy. In her letter she said she couldn't keep her mind off me since we met. Can you believe that?"

Of course I can. It's exactly how *I* feel. I offer him a tiny smile.

"She said she can't imagine not seeing me again." He waves a hand as if to erase his last few words. "No, no. She said: 'We have to see each other. I don't care about the rules.'"

"What does that mean?"

He raises his shoulders. "No clue. Probably something about her dad. But it's awesome, right?"

"I guess, yeah."

"And to think she's been here all these years. We wasted so much time. What day am I leaving for school again?"

The day the apocalypse will come for me? "August twelfth," I reply.

"Right." He taps the steering wheel. "So that gives us…"

"About two months."

Six weeks, three days, twenty hours, and approximately thirteen minutes.

But who's counting?

Weeks ago it was only a matter of me and him and a whirlwind of energy between us. He's everything—every happy moment, every beautiful thing I've ever wanted to have, every dream for getting away from this boring life, of having a future of my own. He's all of it. I only needed one simple moment to change the course of our futures. Six weeks seemed like more than enough time for that to happen. But now it's a timeline riddled with far too many complications. I blinked, and he's already halfway gone.

The road opens at a clearing in the palm trees. It's dark as hell. Streetlights are few and far between up here in the mountains on the edge of town. But little pink and green spotlights in some bushes along the side of the road guide us. They shine directly on the Las Palmas Altas welcome sign, with its muted pastels and swirly font. Matty slows the Jeep. Not so friendly and not so welcoming is the tiny, mint green building up ahead with simple, block letters labeled SECURITY. Matty stops before we get too close.

"Okay." He unclips his seatbelt. *Snap.*

And he's gone. Out the door, into the dark road.

He gestures for me to take the driver's seat.

I climb over. "What do you want me to do?"

Everything's a whisper now. "She laid out the plan in her letter. Tell the guard your name and that you're here to pick up Celeste Vaughn. He'll ring her, she'll give the okay, and then he'll let you pass. It's easy."

"What about you?"

"I'll wait out here."

Out where? In the road? He could fall off the side of the mountain and no one would even know. "But it's so dark. What if—"

He laughs. "I'm fine, Effie. Just go." He leans into the car, grabs my face with both hands, and plants a kiss on my forehead. "You're the best."

He dips away toward the Las Palmas Altas welcome sign, disappearing behind a cluster of cactus plants with pads the size of tennis rackets.

I squeeze the steering wheel. Ready myself.

I am the best. I absolutely am. I'm going to deliver Celeste to him tonight. And he will see—*oh my God, please let him see*—that no one can replace or imitate or substitute someone as vital as me. She is a whim. I am forever. She's complex. I'm unwavering, unquestioning. No one would ever choose complications and roadblocks over ease and trust. And Matty won't either. He just needs a little more time to see that. It's part of the process.

With any luck the process won't take six weeks.

CHAPTER NINE

Something tells me I'm not supposed to honk.

Which, of course, makes me want to throw the entire weight of my body against the horn.

But there's Matty to consider.

I'm his rock; I'm a keeper.

So I check my attitude and act appropriately. It kills me.

The security guard, who is unfriendly to the point of open hostility, directs me to the parking field nearest Rumildo Walk. The screened-in side porch of number 44 is dark this time. The chessboard rests on a small table there, prepped and ready for a game that won't happen, at least not tonight. She's breaking free. We're the same in that way—trying to get away from our parents. Hoping to cut the cord. Only, her father gives a shit about her leaving because he legit loves her. Mine only cares because he'd have to hire another waitress.

I stand before the front door.

What next? Ring the bell, knock, shout an obscenity?

This feels awkward and proper and not even one-tenth easier than the last time I was here. I'm much better at climbing fences.

The front door swings open wide, killing my decision about ringing the bell.

Out pops Celeste, and all the lights from inside their cottage spill out with her. It's so bright I throw an arm up to my head instinctively. She smiles in surround sound. This could be the very same smile she used to zap Matty with her lightning bolt at the pharmacy. It doesn't work on me. I know I should be nice for Matty's sake, so I try to return the greeting. I really, really do. But I think I growl instead.

Justifiably, the situation calls for removal of her teeth one by one.

This is so hard.

Her smile falters a bit when she realizes I'm not going to reciprocate. I wonder what does it—the sound of my heart crackling into stone or the repeated thwack of the tip of my Vans against the terra cotta pot of flowers to the side of the door? I'm kicking it, rhythmically. She looks down with something like concern flashing over her face. My toes don't hurt; I don't feel anything.

She calls to her father. He strides quickly to the door.

He's tall, stooped, with wide shoulders. Dark eyes that dart around so fast you'd think he's dizzy. He and the tiny blond fairy girl standing between us look approximately nothing alike and it occurs to me that DNA is a strange and wondrous thing.

"Daddy, this is my friend." She passes me a pointed look.

I'm busy thinking: *We are not friends. We never were.* I almost miss the handshake her father offers, but Celeste clears her throat and looks at me meaningfully, like the tempo's off. I better get back with the rhythm. I take his hand. It's warm and soft and huge.

"Effie, this is my father, Kevin Vaughn."

"Kevin Vaughn?" I say because it sounds weird to me. That's twice Carlo and Vincent gave me the wrong information. Or maybe it's just my memory screwing with me. I'm still stuck on Caroline. So.

"You can call me John Doe if you like. I'm flexible." Some kind of nervous laugh—too forced—bursts from his mouth. A smile leaks through the awkwardness.

I nod because whatever. I don't care what his name is anyway.

"We'll be back in a few hours, Daddy. It's only a movie." Celeste hugs him with a chokehold around the gut, tight enough for me to consider reporting it to the police as an assault.

He looks down; she looks up. His eyes are dark, but they're warm, with the kind of wrinkles around them that can only form on someone who's done a lot of smiling over the years. My father has those. But only when he's counting money.

"Thank you. I love you, Daddy."

"And I love you."

Birds tweet. Rainbows materialize. Roses bloom through the cracked cement at our feet. It's Disney Princess on steroids. What the fuck am I doing here?

She lets go and edges closer to me, to her great escape.

He slides hands in pockets like he doesn't know what to do with his arms if they aren't wrapped around her. "Be careful," he warns, eyebrows raised in significance.

I don't ever recall, in my entire life, either of my parents telling me to be careful. I remember threats, ultimatums. I remember weekly schedule sheets with my name appearing more times than any labor laws would allow. I remember miles and miles of frustration and impatience on both sides. But I do not remember affection.

I kick the pot of flowers a little harder.

Celeste lays more yeses and thank yous on him as she backs away. Just enough to set the stream of overflow to overkill. He watches as we walk to the parking field. When we reach the Jeep, he closes the door finally, sucking all the light back into their house.

Celeste squeals and claps at the sight of the closed door. "Oh my goodness, it worked! Matthew told me you could make it happen and you totally did!"

Her excitement is everywhere. It's blinding.

I grab one of her arms roughly and shush her. She stops moving but doesn't stop smiling.

I am absolutely disgusted from the inside out that she and Matty swapped notes about escape plans involving my help before he bothered to ask for it. He knew without any hesitation that I'd follow through for him. Faith is a tricky thing. He has enough in me that I should be flattered. I should be; I want to be; normally I am. But as I climb into the Jeep to deliver Celeste to him, I'm not sure I feel anything other than a hallucinogenic degree of rage.

The word chatterbox comes to mind as we drive back to the complex's entrance.

He's here, right?

Where?

I can't believe I'm doing this.

You don't understand—this is huge. My father never lets me leave his side.

I toss out one-word responses, because really, I don't want to engage.

The security guard waves and calls out "Have fun!" as we drive out of the complex. She's human sunshine. He's positively cheery now that she's with me.

Past the exit, I pull the Jeep around the corner. Matty pokes out from behind the cactus where I left him. The radiance in his smile could swallow the universe. He trots over to the Jeep. His hand closes around the driver's side door handle.

I am suddenly distinctly aware that Celeste sits shotgun.

Once I remove myself from the driver's side, there is nowhere for me to go but in the back. This is not okay. I refuse to be demoted to the backseat for my efforts. If it were any other person sitting shotgun, I would rip them from the spot and leave claw marks as a deterrent to the next would-be trespasser. But Matty's already pulling the door open. He looks straight past me, right at her. And she's smiling that big, stupid grin again.

Between the two of them, I'm a phantom, I'm invisible, I'm not even here.

My fingers lock around the steering wheel. I won't get out. I won't do it.

"Effie, I owe you my life." Matty reaches out for a hand slap.

The pull is magnetic. I remove one hand from the steering wheel to clasp his. A force rises within me. I don't want to let go of him. It's this crazy, overwhelming feeling of having to hold on because if I don't, none of my dreams will come true. She will slide into my place, and Matty and I and all our plans for getting out of this town will be done with.

The big grin he aims at Celeste matches the doofy way he keeps swinging his head around me to look at her, like a puppy behind a gate.

He lets go of my hand. His smile cracks a bit when I don't move.

What choice do I have? Give Celeste what's mine or go the asshole route and kick her out of the front seat. I'm not here to make friends with her but I sure as shit cannot make a move that would alienate Matty. Wrestling his fairy princess for a few inches of leather beneath my ass won't go over well.

So, I'll take the back. For now. For Matty.

But I don't get out. I throw myself over the seat and land in the back. It's less of the cool and casual hop I intended, and more of the faceplant-along-the-leather variety. I search for grip, grab at anything. A glorious skin-sucking squelch rises from under my sweaty, sliding hands.

To which Celeste yelps, "Oh!" and strains her neck to check my landing.

Matty laughs. Like I'm ridiculous.

I think I am. This whole thing is.

I clamber onto the seat, roll my legs up, tuck into a ball. Something stings my right shin. I must've ripped my skin on the edge of the center console. But it's not bad. I don't even look.

"Are you okay?" Celeste asks.

Her eyelashes match her hair—blond, almost like they're dusted with gold. Am I seeing things or does this girl actually glitter? I'm revolted and awed all at once.

Matty slides behind the wheel. "Effie's made of steel. She doesn't crack."

Whether his answer pleases me or guts me is debatable. He's, like, one thousand percent certain I'm okay. Effie Fox is the strongest person he knows. She scales fences, she delivers notes, she lies to her parents. She's his right-hand man. Nothing stands in her way. Not even girls with glittery hair and cheeks the color of crème brulee.

A series of clicks pop from up front. They're buckling up.

Screw the seat belt. Who needs it? He's right—I don't get hurt. I refuse to let this scene bother me. Celeste, better known as Girl #457, will fade like all the others. I'm a keeper. I'll be the one left standing at the end.

Before shifting into drive, his head turns to Celeste. "Hi," he says softly.

She tilts her head in a shy smile. "Hi."

Something changes between them; something withers inside of me.

The skin on my neck tingles. I should not be watching this.

The ride back to Fox Inn is positively nauseating. For the record, claustrophobia is alive and well in this backseat. I do not belong here. I cross my legs and shake my top foot till it's drumroll fast. I'm sweating, despite the wind. Thick chunks of damp frizz frame my face, and not in the cute, halo way. Up front, Celeste's blond, sparkly, fairy hair blows out around her. It's all a mirage and Matty sinks into it, headfirst.

The air around them heats up from excitement. Inquiries and answers race out, one on top of the other. They laugh as they stumble. Every question out of her mouth is one I am not only able to answer, but want to answer, just to show her that some of us know Matty better than he knows himself. I lip sync his responses and get them all right—every single one. The alternating medley of lyrics to their love song runs like this:

"Why's your dad so strict?"

"What college are you going to?"

"You were home-schooled?"

"My mother died when I was a baby."

She calls him Matthew. I want to hurl a stream of vomit and obscenities onto the road. *Matthew.* Stop that. The only person with permission to call him Matthew is his grandfather, and he would have a fit if he saw Matty driving around town with a skate rat and a princess without a pedigree.

Matty surprises her with his dinner plan. He's so excited for her reaction to La Jolie Dame that I almost tell him to keep his eyes on the road or he won't make it there.

Celeste's face is blank. She's never heard of the place.

To which I reply, "Are you fucking kidding me?"

"I've never been to a restaurant without my dad before. Can you believe that?" she says.

Actually, yes I can, all things considered. Her father is a prison warden. I can't imagine she's ridden in anything other than an armored vehicle with tinted windows and a five-point harness instead of a simple seatbelt.

They start talking about colleges and majors. I lose focus on the conversation and look at the sky. After a few minutes, Celeste turns in her seat and smiles at me.

"Effie?" she asks. "What school will you be going to in the Fall?"

"She's coming with me to Chicago," Matty says before I can respond. Then he laughs.

I wonder what the hell is so funny. The punchline of the joke is me, apparently.

Celeste's eyes swing between the two of us like the essence of third wheel has just shifted and she's not sure which wheel she qualifies as. "Oh nice. You're going to Northwestern, too?" Her voice is soft, tentative.

"Nope." I shrug and say, "School of hard knocks."

Her eyebrows twitch.

Matty's eyes flick to me in the rearview mirror, sharp with a warning: *Be nice.*

I am nice. Under the right circumstances. "I'm not going to Northwestern. I've been enrolled at University of Fox Inn since birth," I explain. "It's a lifelong curriculum. I major in customer ripoffs."

Matty chuckles.

Celeste's eyes bubble with recognition. "That's it! That's how I know you!"

A story begins—one of her father and his search for a job after they relocated to California from the East Coast over a decade ago. Her statements have this annoying, singsong lift at the end, like questions. It's charming and adorable and disgusting. As far as she says, their plan wasn't to settle here permanently, but to head north—Portland, Seattle, she can't recall? Her chess aficionado Daddy was a counselor at a homeless shelter back in New York City, so he looked into jobs where he could help the less fortunate? Flexible hours to accommodate homeschooling? They hopped around for as long as Celeste could remember and she was tired, you know? She wanted a place to tape posters of unicorns to the walls and permanently set up her Barbie Dream House? (Or something like that. I don't care enough about her story to focus on it.) After he found a job at a shelter in Ojai, she lobbied for them to stay in Vista Buscato because it was so quiet and pretty?

Evidently she's good at twisting Daddy's arm.

"Do you remember me, Effie? We rented at Fox Inn once. I remember you. Always on your skateboard." Again, it all sounds like a question. "One time when my father was talking to your dad, I drew a picture of a castle with chalk on the sidewalk in front of Fox Inn's door. Your mother was so angry. She brought out a bucket of water and a sponge and made me wash it off. I don't think she cared for me very much."

"She doesn't care for anybody," I say.

"Except me." Matty laughs.

"Or maybe she doesn't care for hot pink chalk castles?" Celeste asks with a little giggle.

This girl is exactly who I thought she was: frivolous, silly. A waste of time. I try not to laugh, but a little snort leaks out.

"You don't like castles either, I guess? What would you choose to draw?" she asks.

I'd choose to die? How about that?

"At University of Fox Inn, kids don't have time for doodling on the sidewalk. We work," I say. "Long, boring shifts. We have to keep the business afloat and food on our table." That's my story, in a nutshell.

"What will you be doing in Chicago, then?"

The obvious response—*I will be loving Matty*—seems inappropriate given that she's the one accompanying him to a romantic dinner, not me.

"I love this song," I say, and order Matty to turn up the radio. My foot bounces and shakes so hard I think it might fly off my leg. I force myself to bring it to a stop, but the stillness only lasts seven seconds before the cut along my shin starts to sting. There must be blood. I don't want to feel it. I shake my leg again.

Matty turns the Jeep onto Buscato Drive. He stops at a traffic light one block away from Fox Inn's corner. A man and woman stroll the sidewalk alongside the Jeep. They're holding hands. She's in heels—the super fancy, shiny kind. And he's in brown leather shoes with those stupid little tassels over the toes. I bet they've been to La Jolie Dame. I bet they know which silverware to use and when. I bet any amount of money they'd be horrified if they saw the things I write in marker on the sides of my Vans when I'm bored. People like me don't mesh with people like them. Only perfect people like Celeste do. Look at her riding shotgun. She's a star.

I can't do this anymore. My hands are all over the door handle.

"Let me out."

"I'll drop you in front," Matty says.

"Let me out here. It's fine."

"Don't be ridiculous."

I'm about to jump over the side—the top is down, after all—when his eyes flick upward to the rearview mirror. I force a smile. "This is kidnapping, you know. Pops will not be happy when I press charges."

He grins at the reminder of his grandfather. Or maybe it's at the absurd suggestion that he would ever wind up in jail.

Celeste's eyes dart back and forth from me to Matty. She laughs, but it's packed with nervous energy, like she doesn't understand the dynamic between me and him.

The light switches to green. He guns the engine until we're right in front of Fox Inn. When we stop at the curb, the locks click open. The sound should feel like freedom but it's more like a death knell.

No need for goodbyes. I jump out.

Matty's right behind me. "Effie, wait."

I hop onto the sidewalk. He follows.

"Slow down." Confusion dulls his eyes, his mouth. He reaches for my hand, but I step back. He grabs at nothing. His face goes serious. There's no bounce in him. "I just wanted to thank you."

"No worries. I got your back. You know that."

Don't you? Don't you know that? Can't you see?

"Maybe I'll bring Celeste by after dinner. We could have dessert at Fox Inn and wait for your shift to end."

My entire body burns. Lava fills my veins. "Felicia's got me on kitchen cleanup after," I say, shaking my head.

His gaze drops to his feet. "Okay, well…um…maybe I'll swing by the comp with you tomorrow? We can celebrate after you wipe out the competition."

The goofy grin is back. I feel my edges soften.

Celeste watches us through the frame of the Jeep's open window. She glows. Her smile aims at me. It's big. It's real. She wiggles a hand in a cheery goodbye wave. I think how funny it is that her head is so perfectly positioned in the center of the frame. She's lucky. She's someone who nails it, who gets things right every time. We couldn't be more opposite.

This is the kind of girl Matty hyperventilates over. Not girls like me.

I lift my chin at Fox Inn. "Gotta get back inside. Felicia will freak if I'm gone too long."

"Sure." He nods.

What do I do now? Pat him on the back? Slap him five? Offer him a condom? This is horrifically awkward. I'm trying so hard not to look at Celeste as she watches Matty, but it's impossible to avoid her face. A thought slides into my train of thought: is that the same way *I* look at him? With something like hope and awe?

"Have fun at dinner," I say weakly.

"Thank you so much. For everything." He pulls me into a tight hug. Cologne slides up my nostrils. I want to throw up. It's a struggle not to squeeze my arms around him so he can't leave. He kisses me on the cheek, whispers, "Wish me luck."

I open my mouth, but nothing comes out.

A wish like that wouldn't make sense. Because I hope his luck runs out tonight. And when it happens, when all the happy circumstances and chalk castles and pretty hair comes to an end and he sees she doesn't offer anything more than the countless other girls he's lost interest in, he'll come back to me. It's the pivot point I've waited for all these years. The light bulb moment. But it can't happen until his luck runs out.

"You won't need luck," I say. "Just be yourself."

"I hope you're right."

Of course I am.

She's going to love him; he's easy to adore. That's not the issue. I'm praying for the moment he realizes he doesn't love her.

Matty jogs back to the driver's side of the car. "I'll text you later."

I don't wait to watch them drive away. I bust through the doors of Fox Inn. The restaurant swallows me up. Gerard mans the host station. He pushes an apron at me. My mother comes through the swinging kitchen doors, three plates stacked along one arm. Her gaze runs the length of my body and pauses at my right leg, which I'm certain bleeds. She rolls her eyes. No one around here gives a rat's ass if the blood leaking out of me is from a simple scrape, a gunshot wound, or a byproduct of an ever-breaking heart. My life is absurd.

A nagging, stabbing thought pierces me over and over. Wishes and dreams don't come true for girls like me. They come true for gorgeous, lucky girls with names like Caroline Madaleo or Celeste Vaughn. Girls with an unlimited supply of future.

Chapter Ten

The first text I received this morning didn't mention Celeste, and I'm beyond grateful. It was from Joe.

Time to win that comp. U ready?

He and I wait in the Buscato Drive parking lot with some other people for rides to Ventura. I squint against the sun sparking off the windshields of the cars parked around me. Palm trees are cool and all, but when they're ninety miles high, they don't offer much shade.

Edgar rolls up in the Chevy. Crazy loud punk music blasts from the open windows. I'm fairly certain my mother can hear it all the way at Fox Inn and will come running with a baseball bat momentarily. Edgar waves everyone in. I stall and scan Buscato Drive for Matty's Jeep. He said he'd be here. When my choice is Edgar or Matty, the winner is obvious.

Joe pulls the car door open for me. I hesitate.

The question mark on his face vanishes when Matty's Jeep rounds the corner. His jaw locks into a hard right angle. I open my mouth to say something. I don't know what. Maybe try to explain so that he doesn't feel ditched or second-best or whatever. But he jumps into the Chevy and slams the door shut behind him without a word.

Matty comes to a stop at the curb behind the Chevy. His hair is wind-warped and orangey yellow, flickering like flames. The July sun teases new freckles out on his nose. He waves at me, and it's like my heart free-falls off a cliff. He's here. For me. Only about six weeks remain until he ships off to college to join a fraternity and go to keg parties and sit hungover the next day at a university library table. But who cares? Today, I'm the one riding shotgun.

We follow Edgar and make the turn off Buscato Drive. At the next intersection, a signpost greets us. White lettering and arrows on a green background show us all the possibilities for a ticket out of Vista Buscato: Pacific Coast Highway—California 1. North or South. Either way is beautiful. Mountains to one side, lined up in neat cones looking like anthills in the distance. Shoreline on the other side, with the dusty beige of boiling hot sand and aquamarine blues of the ocean rippling beyond. Matty turns south toward Ventura. I tug my hair out of its ponytail. It streams behind me as we pick up speed. Matty glances at the storm of hair whipping a tornado around my face. He laughs.

Thankfully, his dream girl's off the radar as both our phones ring like crazy with calls and texts from Joe.

dont stop anywhere

gotta be on time

the entry window closes at noon

We trade gripes about Joe being a pain in the ass. Keeping the conversation to topics that don't include Celeste or college is a good thing. I don't want to deal with stuff that threatens to take him away.

We hit the high part of Pacific Coast Highway near Ventura, the spot where the entire city unfolds before you like a board game. I feel like I'm everywhere at once—in the clouds overhead, in the water down at the beach, walking the length of Ventura Pier. I don't know if it's being with Matty or the sight of the city or what, but I'm so happy my heart could burst. Not for the first time, I let the fantasy of being his girlfriend take over. We're a couple; we have a future together; we'll make something of ourselves; we'll never be apart.

When we hit the skate park, I pay the entry fee, fill out the forms, sign the waivers, and I'm all set. Matty and I thread through the crowd to find our friends at the back of the park. Edgar sits on the top bar of the low, chain link fence, decked head-to-toe in Skate Real gear. Joe's there, too, wearing his lucky Bones Brigade cap, the white one Tony Hawk autographed a couple years ago when we saw him doing a demo on the set of some skate documentary in Santa Barbara. Joe's wearing a Skate Real t-shirt too.

As we wait, Joe goes off about the Vista Buscato Board of Trustees again, listing a dozen reasons why they should transition our skate park to the abandoned Wiley estate on Halberd Court. "We can't always be the residents getting the short end of the stick, you know?" he says, like we should all agree. The Wiley estate is near where Matty lives, where Buscato Drive's shops and restaurants morph into fancy-pants landscaping. They say a vineyard owner once owned the land, but that doesn't matter now. To us, an abandoned property is just another place to skate. And seeing how we don't have a park anymore, any and all paved surfaces are fair game.

The comp starts. We shift forward to watch the guys compete, one by one.

Joe's turn comes. His tricks are pretty good but he's not on his A game. There's no way he'll beat the skinny kid from Santa Monica unless he kicks it up a notch. It's when he transitions toward the bowl and the crowd starts to murmur that I think he's got this win locked up. He drops in, pumps hard around the sides, and makes a few simple turns around the bowl. The speed is out of control. I wonder if his wheels will lose grip. He's all over the place—swinging along the slopes, catching air, upside down, right-side up, and back again. Finally, he shoots up toward the lip. It looks like he'll fakie backwards into the pool, but he kicks his board into the air in a spiral like he planned it that way. His board flips, suspended, disregarding all laws of gravity, as Joe jumps up and out of the pool. The board finally makes its descent. He catches it. Bruiser and a ton of other people belt out a chorus of *Yeah, Sick, Damn.*

The judges give him a great score. He places second. Not bad at all. He and Edgar slap the dozens of hands stretched out to them.

The announcer calls for the girls' round to start.

Before I walk away, I shoot Joe a fist bump, but he grabs my hand and pulls me close to him.

We wind up pressed together as the crowd around us shifts to watch the next event.

"Go out there and kill it, Foxy," he whispers in my ear.

Heat clings to my hair, my chest, everything. I can't tell if it's from the sun beating down on this park, warming the concrete, or his breath against my ear or the way his body feels against mine. A flush of warmth floods through my face. I have a feeling I'm blushing, which horrifies me to no end, because this is Joe. *Joe.* I don't crack around him, and I certainly don't get amped-up feelings like the ones kicking my heartbeat into overdrive right now. He pulls off his lucky hat and plops it on my head. Lavender shampoo left traces in the fabric. I'm dizzy. He's never getting this hat back.

Instinctively, I glance at Matty. He throws me a thumbs up.

I blink a few times. I'm stunned, totally out of it. I head closer to the park entrance to clear the dazed feeling in my brain.

The first girl up is some super short, beachy type from Santa Barbara I've seen hanging at Skate Real. She does a killer job at first but stumbles on her rail slide landing and doesn't go near the bowl at all. The second girl is decent, but pretty much does the same heelflip with every trick. She's good, but not versatile enough to win. Three more girls go, and I'm not impressed. I can win this. But I have to get my shit together, play it smart.

As far as my skills go, I'm a street skater. I can turn a trick anywhere. But I'd be a fool to think I can win this comp if I don't at least nail a few runs around that bowl. The best street skaters usually know a thing or two about vert drops. I've carved a bowl enough to acknowledge that it feels pretty good once you've decided to make the drop in.

For vert skaters, pushing past your initial fear is huge. It's a lot like falling in love. You can work on your form, practice how to glide, carve, dig deep on the turns, swerve into a tailslide. But that initial drop is the hardest part. You know it's going to be great, but do you really want to take the risk? Are you prepared to let go and fall? You might land all tangled, broken. Joe always says, "But you still felt the rush, and that alone is worth it." Maybe he's right.

I look back at my friends by the fence. Joe's staring at me like I cast a spell on him or something. It's crazy. *He's* crazy. My stomach backflips.

When the time clock starts, I gain enough momentum to rock out three perfect heelflip variations before I set up each rail slide. The transitions in this park are the best. I nail every trick. My moves are tight. As the clock nears the end of my time, I know this win is a lock-up if I can blow out something special. I hold my breath, say a prayer to Tony Hawk and Stacy Peralta and all the other skate gods, pick my board up by the nose, and take a run to the edge of the bowl. I bomb drop in—no ollie pop, just a full-body freefall drop down with my board locked in my hand in a death grip so tight my fingers ache. My heart is in my throat. I fly, all legs and arms. At the perfect point, I shove my board under my feet. Faith must be on my side today because I land on the deck in a perfect stance, knees loose and light. I immediately dig deep into a carve, then powerslide to a stop just as time runs out. My hair whips me in the face. Throngs of people around the park's edges go full blast with cheers.

I climb out of the bowl. Everywhere, my name's popping from people's mouths. The judges don't take long. With a 9.3224, I snag first place.

Joe lifts me into the air. Every cell in my body soars as he spins me around.

Matty jumps all over the two of us. My eardrums nearly burst from their tandem shouts, "You won! You won! You won!"

"It was totally my fucking hat," Joe says.

"Hat's mine now." I twist it backwards.

Joe doesn't protest, just laughs.

Edgar elbows his way into our trio. "Yo, Effie. I got a spot for you on my team if you're up for it." He pushes a weird handshake on me. Trying to keep up makes me feel ridiculous. "Stop by Skate Real this week and we'll talk sponsorships." A view of my own reflection stares back at me from the dark lenses of Edgar's sunglasses. I'm flushed and sweaty. Hair's sticking up all over under Joe's hat. Matty and Joe are directly behind me. I've never been happier.

Hands reach out to grab at me like I'm some kind of celebrity. Eventually, when congratulations ebb away and people disband, chasing down parties and skate parks in other towns, Edgar declares a celebration at Skate Real. Everyone's stoked. They practically bow at his feet.

Matty digs the keys to the Jeep out of his pocket. "You ready?"

I flip my board with the toe of my sneaker, deck to bottom, bottom to deck.

Take a chance. The clock is ticking.

This could be my lucky day, finally. The perfect day for celebrating, for winning, for moving things forward with Matty. "Yep. But let's not go to Skate Real."

"Where to, then?"

"Ice cream at Ventura Pier?"

"Whatever you want."

I tug Joe's lucky hat tighter on my head and link my arm through Matty's.

Chapter Eleven

Ventura Pier shoots out into the Pacific like a road to everywhere. Endless possibilities on crusty, old wood. It's my favorite place on earth.

Foot traffic runs on the right side of the pier as if people can't shake off the road rules and habits. The whole thing feels claustrophobic. I edge into the middle to break out from the herd and go at my own pace. Matty follows.

He eases his speed and slides next to me, "You trying to ditch me or something?"

"Never."

"I can take a hint."

I hit him hard in the shoulder.

He laughs and bounces away. "You're such a bully."

"You love it."

A poster with the smiling face of the dark-haired girl missing from Vista Buscato made its way to Ventura too, taped to one of the light posts along the pier. I smile back at her. I bet she's happier now, wherever she is.

Matty and I reach the end of the pier.

He wraps a hand around a wooden post holding a sign—Ventura Pier, Since 1872.

I wonder if it will be here when he returns from school. If he ever does.

Two seagulls loop in a circle over our heads, screeching.

He tilts his face to the sky. Heat flushes his cheeks pink. "Did you register at VC yet?" he asks out of nowhere.

I slide my gaze away. No, I did not register for classes at Ventura College, despite his constant nudges. Nothing makes me want to fall asleep faster than thoughts of boring professors and notebooks and pages upon pages of assigned reading. Besides, it seems silly to even entertain the thought when I plan to meet him in Chicago. One day.

"I told you—just go for one semester. Then transfer out."

I roll my eyes. Getting away from this town may be my dream, but I'm not convinced college is the way to do it. I just haven't found any alternatives yet. "Wherever I'm going, college isn't in the cards."

"What do you mean, *'wherever I'm going'*? You're coming to Chicago. It's the place to be in winter." He wags his eyebrows up and down. "The sooner you get some credits under your belt, the faster you can transfer."

I wish he'd shut up with the constant reminders that he's leaving soon. Life will be measured in college semesters for him, but long, painful weeks for me, and I don't want that part to come. I have to get used to him being gone, even if it's only temporary, even if I'm meeting him in Chicago soon after.

"I'll lend you money," he offers, "if that's what you need."

"Can we stop talking about this?"

"You know I won't survive at Northwestern without you there to push me around and remind me to study."

Please. Studying has nothing to do with Matty's smarts. He walks into a testing room and aces whatever they put in front of him naturally. That kind of luck is priceless. Everything comes up roses for him.

"Come on," he presses. "Take a few classes. Get some credits. I'll help you look into schools near Northwestern. It's not even negotiable."

His smile ignites a round of rockets inside me. I can hardly catch my breath.

"College is the only way out of here," he says like it's fact, like it's law.

"Not necessarily. I could start my own skate business. Or ride for a team."

He shakes his head. "Please. Don't start that Joe shit with me."

Joe, who gave me the lucky Bones Brigade hat I'm wearing right now without a second thought. Joe, who celebrated my win like it was his own, who convinced me to enter today's comp in the first place. Joe's more motivated than all of us combined, just in different ways.

I shove Matty. "That was low. He's your best friend."

He throws hands up in protest. "Listen, I love the kid. I'd cut off my right arm for him. But I mean, what's gonna happen when he's thirty? You can't ride a skateboard for a living forever. He's choosing a tough road."

A road is a road, though. It gets you from where you are to where you want to be. The ones with potholes or gravel and dirt have just as much character as the ones paved smooth. Right? Or maybe not. Matty makes it sound like something else.

Hopelessness squeezes me. This contest win—what does it change, really? As long as I stay in Vista Buscato, my dead-end job at Fox Inn is all I can bet on. The aching reality of my non-future here smothers me.

Before we came to the pier, Matty and I took a walk through Ventura and passed by the famous blue historic sign that says, "Shop, Surf, Stay." And it occurred to me then: people come from all over the world to see sunny, beautiful California and its rolling hills and endless mountains and wineries and palm trees and hot, hot sand. And we coerce visitors to stay—*STAY*—when so many of us can't wait to get the hell out of here. If I don't make it to Chicago, if I'm stuck decaying year after year at Fox Inn, will Matty lump me into the same category he's lumped Joe? The Going Nowhere Pile?

Fear takes over. Words fall out before I can stop them. "What if I can't get out of here, Matty? My parents, the restaurant..." I struggle not to crack in front of him. *What if our roads don't run parallel?*

"There are a thousand ways you can break out. You will, don't worry."

"How do you know that?"

"Because you've pulled off some pretty monumental shit already."

"Like what? Skate tricks? So what."

"No. Like *life*." He throws a free arm out toward the water rolling beneath and beyond the pier. "You literally leap over every obstacle. If you want something, you go for it. You're strong. You're a survivor." He pulls me into a hug.

The skin on my neck tingles. I'm pretty sure I'm blushing. I turn my eyes to the water.

Endless blue ocean stares back at me. Ripples roll outward on a path to somewhere bigger, somewhere great.

I press my face against his shoulder.

Something wet hits my hand. I break away from Matty and look down.

Bird shit. Right on the back of my hand.

"Are you fucking kidding me?" I mutter.

I look down at the weathered, broken wood of the pier beneath my feet. What didn't occur to me before is suddenly so evident now that I'm not drowning in Matty's embrace. Bird shit is everywhere on this pier. Splattered along the railings, the wooden boards underneath our feet. It's even dripping in spots from the top of the Ventura Pier sign.

California is the most beautiful place in the world, and still it's not perfect.

I don't know why I ever thought Matty and I could spend the day together without something messing with it. Fate always fucks with my happy ending. Always.

Matty drags me out of my hole of self-pity. Screaming insults about rare avian diseases and bird plague, he runs in a circle around me. Naturally, everyone stares. He's ridiculous and immature, but he always manages to pull me out of a funk. Now I'm laughing too. I love this kid so much. I chase him, holding my stained hand out in front of me. People walking along the pier back away from us. Laughter puts a kink in my breathing.

Finally, Matty stops running and says, "You know that's good luck, right?"

"Is it?"

"That's what my grandfather always says. When he was a kid in Chicago he broke up a fight between two of his friends who were arguing over a ball. He shoved between them, and a bird shit on his shoulder. It sort of ricocheted and got all in his hair, on his ear, everywhere."

I cringe. Matty's laugh is raucous and loud.

"They were all howling so hard they couldn't remember what they were fighting about in the first place. To this day, Pops says it was some kind of divine intervention. That mediating the fight and having the bird shit on him was what paved the way later in life for him to become a judge, resolving disputes for a living."

I can't hide my skepticism. "Do you believe that?"

He shrugs. "I don't know. They called him Shithead for a while afterwards, so there's definitely a downside."

"What does bird shit on my hand mean then? How can that be good luck?"

"Maybe you'll own a nail salon and do manicures one day?"

I screw my face into a tight knot. "No way."

"You could become a hand model. I bet lots of jewelry companies need them."

"Doubtful."

"Well, it's got to mean something," he says with finality.

Really? I'm waiting for the clouds to part, the heavens to burst forth, and for him to finally see our fates twisted together in this glob of bird shit splattered across my knuckles, but this is the prediction he gives me? That I'll become a hand model? He doesn't even consider that this good fortune might have something to do with me being here with him. His interpretation wouldn't ever, ever bend down that avenue. The thought doesn't occur to him. He's so blind. Or dumb. I don't know which kills me more.

Suddenly, standing with my hand outstretched like Frankenstein doesn't feel funny and immature and spontaneous like it did when I tucked my hair beneath Joe's lucky hat earlier today. It feels stupid. I swipe my hand across the wooden railing once, twice. Bird poop smears onto the pier and off of me. There's still a little left, though. I go for one last swipe when a sharp twinge shoots through the side of my hand.

I jerk away from the railing. A dagger-sized splinter has driven itself six feet deep into my flesh. I think it's pierced straight through my hand and into my heart. It certainly feels that way.

"Oooooh," Matty says, examining my hand. He sucks in a breath. "That's got to hurt."

"Not really." I dig at it and pull it out.

"Your hand is taking a beating today."

Wrong. It's not my hand, it's ME. *I'm* taking a beating. Every day. Can't he see that?

We head down to the beach to wash my hand off. I kick my Converse off and wade into the ankle-deep water. I dip my wrist under. The final dregs of bird shit melt away. I let the saltwater do its job, set this day back to a clean start. I shake off the woe-is-me mood hovering over me. I'm fun. I'm unique. I'm the girl he can't live without. I'm everything he's ever wanted but he just doesn't realize it yet.

Water rushes past our ankles in two rounds of tiny waves before I finally come up with something to say. Holding up my clean hand, I say, "Am I lucky yet?" I aim for a light and spontaneous tone. I hope it works.

He stares at my hand like he's truly considering the meaning of all this good luck business. "Actually, I think I'm the lucky one." His expression goes all foggy, dreamy.

My stomach flutters.

This is it: the moment where he acknowledges his feelings for me. That he's lucky to have me. That I'm lucky to have him. That we're together.

"Everything in my life feels like it's clicking into place. It's like luck times one thousand. Things are perfect. I graduated, I'm going to Northwestern, I'm hanging with my friends every day. I have you."

A smile spreads over my face.

"And I found Celeste."

I take one step back. *Fuck. Not now. Not her.*

He says in all sincerity, "I owe you so much, Effie. Without you I wouldn't—"

I cut him off with, "No problem."

"Celeste changed my whole outlook on life. I didn't know I could feel this way after a handful of hours together, but it's real. We talk about everything. We finish each other's sentences. People always say stuff like that and it sounds so dumb, but it really happens to us. We like all the same things. And we have all the same pet peeves, too. She gets irate over those idiots who tap on the glass at aquariums, just like me. Sick, right?" He goes on. And on. And on. He's talking so fast I can barely keep up. I just nod, nod, nod. With pink, freckled cheeks, he smiles at the sky. "I am officially the luckiest guy in the world."

His words are the cruelest sort of torture imaginable. I recoil, fighting for composure. Silly me. I thought luck was on *my* side today. I should have known. Sometimes shit is just shit and that's all there is to it.

"I'm happy for you," I say.

I mean it. Kind of. I also don't. But whatever. What else am I going to say?

"I never knew how great it feels to be on the exact same wavelength as someone else."

I know. It happens every time I'm with him. I bend to pick up a shell, then flick it into the water. "Too bad you're leaving soon."

"Oh my God, Effie!" He pulls my arm so hard I almost fall over. "I forgot to tell you!" It's insane how high he jumps in place right now. Like, literally sky high.

"What? What?"

"She's going up north for college, too!"

"Where?"

"Michigan!"

The look of recognition that book-smart kids wear when reciting college names obviously does not appear on my face. He explains, "It's only about a five-hour drive to Northwestern." He's still bouncing.

"Oh." I fake a smile but I think it comes out looking like I have gas pains instead.

The flight between LAX and Chicago O'Hare Airport is only four and a half hours. I know. I googled it. And yet he's already riding in a car speeding along some Godforsaken Midwest highway to spend time with a girl he barely knows, when he could easily get on a plane and come back to see me in less time. The whole scenario is so fucking fairytale-inspired, I could spit venom.

"Wasn't she homeschooled, though?"

"You can still get into college if you're homeschooled," he says, like I'm ignorant to the ways of the world.

Maybe I am.

His bouncing has turned into full-blown jumping jacks.

I want to tell him to stop. Jumping for joy is overrated.

Seagulls swing in a giant figure eight overhead. I plop down on the sand. Matty gives up jumping finally and joins me. We lay back together. He breathes heavily, winded.

"This thing with me and Celeste. It's like fate."

Or something. Maybe it's just bad luck and awful timing for me.

"So, she's smart?"

"She's brilliant."

Of course she is.

"You really like her, huh?"

His eyes close for a pause and he smiles. Like he's dreaming. About her, obviously. A final whoosh of breath leaves his mouth, and with it comes the words, "I think I'm in love."

Every molecule of air in the atmosphere vanishes with this revelation.

This time it's not a joke.

I can't breathe. I can't breathe.

My lungs shut down. I'm overheated and sweating. All this talk of love and dreams and I'm not a part of it. He has chased and he has obsessed and he has even gone a little cuckoo over a pretty girl or three over the years. But nothing like this—like *love*. Hearing him say anything even remotely like those words in my presence, about anyone other than me, is essentially the commencement of the end stage of my life. My hopes, dreams, possibilities are all snuffed out. And what's worse—at least eighty percent of this situation is my fault. I led him to her. All that good luck he speaks of, it all clicked into place because of me.

He says it again. "I'm in love." Softer this time. Sweet, like candy.

He is in love with her—Caroline, Celeste, whoever.

A seagull squawks from somewhere on the sand behind us.

I don't speak. My mouth is open and I struggle to take a breath but I can't.

He is in love.

After one fancy dinner date with her. After one sweaty joyride up Pacific Coast Highway in the Jeep. After one three-minute conversation in line at a fucking pharmacy that he ordinarily would never venture into except for that day when he offered to pick up his grandfather's blood pressure meds.

He is in love.

I will never breathe again.

He flips onto his side, runs fingers along my arm. "You okay? Does your hand hurt?"

His touch shocks me back to life. I stiffen. The sun is hot and intense like I'm on a roasting rack in one of Fox Inn's giant ovens. I need a breeze or air conditioning or something. Anything but Matty whispering about heaven and angels named Celeste. I can't do this.

"I'm fine." My voice comes out ragged. I clear my throat. "Just a little...antsy. Can we keep moving?"

"Sure."

We spend the rest of the afternoon near the water. As promised, he buys me ice cream to celebrate the skate comp win. As I choose my flavor, he tells me Celeste's favorite—salted caramel—as if I should tuck the detail away for future reference. The information sticks to my brain tissue like a scab. We sit on the sand as we lick our cones. But it doesn't taste the same as always.

As I'm biting at the first of many beautiful chunks of marshmallow in my rocky road, willfully ignoring Matty's declarations of love just an hour ago, he asks some guy walking by about ferry rides at Ventura Harbor. Then he turns to me. "We should totally do that one day." I'm all for it. I suggest the special midnight ride on the Fourth of July after my shift at Fox Inn. Matty's eyes burst like a sunrise. "Celeste would love that," he says, and it all makes sense. A ferry ride. Romance and evening moonlight. Shooting stars and midnight kisses. Here's adorable, romantic Matty again, with thoughts and ideas aimed to please a girl who isn't me.

I nod like a good friend should because it makes him happy. But it feels so strange now. Like, for the first time in my life, I'm not sure his happiness ever included me. I don't know what to do with that thought.

Chapter Twelve

Ventura Harbor's Fireworks Show is apparently where the cool kids are tonight. Matty is positively overflowing with anticipation over his Fourth of July date with Celeste. Earlier, he casually tossed out a question about my plans, like I am an afterthought. I faked excitement over hanging with Sam and Joe later at Buscato Point. But I'm going to be on that ferry. Somehow.

Sam plucks at his palms in Fox Inn's kitchen. "Tough night?" I ask.

"You have no idea." He rolls his eyes. "I got so many splinters, man. Last night Joe insisted on building a homemade ramp. We were banging nails until three in the morning. Then my dad had me up at five-thirty for drills. Try doing a hundred push-ups with these hands." He raises his palms. Fresh hell—they're a battlefield of scratches and pockmarks and what looks like little bloody dots. "It's all part of Joe's plan for the Wiley property. Like, for real. He drew up plans and everything. He and Edgar designed a whole skate park. Have to hand it to him—he's got vision." He pinches the end of a splinter.

A flash of guilt shoots needles at me. My hands should carry those marks too. I'm Joe's friend. He ought to be able to count on me.

Sam inspects his palms. "You think I need ointment for this? I don't want an infection."

My groan doubles as an answer. Big Baby. He'll never survive boot camp.

He ticks his chin up at me. "Where'd you and Matty go last night? Meet up with anyone?"

"We didn't hang with his dream girl if that's what you're asking." Thank God for that. "We just went to a movie."

"He still jocking Caroline?"

"Her name is Celeste."

"Does it matter?"

"To him it does. He can't stop saying it."

"Shit, man. That's bad."

That's what I'm saying.

I prepare a coffee for Detective Brimley, who recited his order to me—coffee, with a splash of cream, *just* a splash, no sugar, *none at all, not even a half teaspoon*—like I couldn't be trusted to get it right. It took all my strength not to ask him why he and his team haven't found the missing girl yet, but I'm not dumb enough to suggest the guy can't do his job when he'll probably be on the lookout for kids like me tonight.

"You okay?" Sam asks. He's working the coffee machine. He pours a cup for himself, but doesn't add anything to it, just sips it black. Like he can harden himself by not softening the coffee with cream or sugar. His lips pucker. I don't even think he likes coffee.

"Why wouldn't I be?"

"I don't know. Joe and I were talking about it. We just figured..." He stalls, averts his eyes.

The level of discomfort between us skyrockets.

The kitchen is too hot. I need air.

"She must be cool if he's so into her, right?" Sam continues. "I mean, this time seems different, doesn't it?"

It does. My heart shrivels.

I'm so hot. I can't think. I rush to the walk-in freezer and step inside.

Sam follows me and watches as I lift my arms. The frosted air reaches my armpits.

"Can we stop talking about her?" I ask quietly.

"You're the one who brought her up."

I did? Maybe I wanted to hear Sam remind me how run-of-the-mill Celeste is, how Matty won't remember her name in a week. But Sam went the other route and reminded me how very much I stand to lose if this living, breathing porcelain doll and her perfect fairytopia universe don't go back from where they came.

"This is Matty we're talking about," I say. "He'll be over her soon. Give it two weeks." I say it with a hell of a lot more conviction than I feel on the inside.

"Yeah. You're probably right."

Something in the way Sam studies me makes me want to move to the other side of the kitchen. Preferably somewhere dark and solitary. A hole in a cemetery comes to mind.

I pass him a large take-out cup of coffee—splash of cream, no sugar. "Run this out to Brimley for me. He probably has a warrant for my arrest by now."

"Wait." He winces as he takes the cup with a shredded palm. "You coming to the Point with me and Joe later? He keeps asking if you'll be there."

I let phony indecision play around my face. "Uhhh...yeah. Probably."

But I have no plans to head to Buscato Point. I can't sit on my ass while Matty falls headfirst for Celeste. His *I am in love* pronouncement plays over and over in my head no matter how hard I try to eject it. This turbo-charged, fast-forward relationship—it can't be. It just can't be. Things moved too fast. With one whiplash movement, he's in love. I drown in this intense, all-consuming need to understand why a simple fling progressed into love so quickly. I know she's adorable, I know she's sweet, I know he's charmed to pieces over her. But what drives this fantasy forward? I need to know these things. Nuances, details. They tell a story, and the story tells me what my next move should be. I absolutely cannot lose him. That ferry cannot depart without me.

Molding a believable story as to why I need to be in the vicinity of Matty and his fairy princess has me wrapped in knots.

Later in the night, when we leave Fox Inn, Sam and I climb into his dad's SUV with the blacked-out windows. We promised to pick Joe up at Skate Real after our double shifts, then head to Buscato Point to watch the fireworks display, which is small and beat and not exciting at all. I'm not sorry to miss it, I'm just sorry I have to come up with a believable reason to bail.

Sam's appropriately confused by my sudden interest in Ventura. "I can't drop you off there. It's the opposite direction," he says.

"Come on. I need a new set of bearings. Mine are all gunked up with sand and shit."

"It's after eleven o'clock. All the shops are closed."

"The one down by the pier's having a midnight madness sale for the holiday."

"Are you kidding, Effie? We're heading to Skate Real to get Joe. They sell parts, too."

Clarification: *he* is heading to Skate Real. I am not.

"Skate Real doesn't sell the brand I want."

He runs fingers lightly over the puffy dome of hair on top of his head. His dark eyes glaze over, thinking, thinking, thinking. He's not dumb. Matty's only mentioned his Ventura ferry plans about six hundred times. It doesn't take a genius to put two and two together.

Finally, he says, "You're stalking him, aren't you?"

The question buys Sam a punch on the bicep. "If you won't drive me, I'll skate there," I say, and tug on the door handle.

"Sit down, tough guy. I'll get you to Ventura." He doesn't sound happy about it.

A million questions pour from his mouth along the long way. My ears bleed as we crawl through Harbor Boulevard's traffic. I do my best to shrug and stick to my story. The one and only set of bearings I want is sold in a store in Ventura, where Matty just happens to be taking his one and only love on a date tonight. It's all a crazy coincidence, I tell him. Stick to the story, stay focused. As we pass Ventura Pier, memories of bird shit and other disasters dirty my thoughts.

At a traffic light, a group of four or five baby grom skateboarders crack the noses of their boards against the sidewalk in an amateur attempt at nosesliding.

"Wouldn't you rather be doing that tonight?" Sam asks, pointing.

I offer him a twenty just to shut the hell up, which he grabs, and promptly stuffs down the front of my tank top.

When we're close to where I need to be, I grab my board. I tell Sam to let me out at the red light up ahead.

"Hold up. How will you get back?"

I jump out, drop my board, and take a second to get my bearings. *You Are Here*.

The light switches to green. Sam hesitates. Cars honk behind him.

"Don't worry about me," I tell him. "I'll figure it out."

I always do.

Chapter Thirteen

The ferry doesn't depart for another few minutes. Leave it to Sam, military man-to-be, to keep me on schedule, even in traffic. I cut into a parking lot on the right and ollie over some concrete parking stops to get my energy out.

Ventura Harbor is even more beautiful with the setting sun as a backdrop. Boats reflect upside down in the water, all yellow and white. It's a mirage, flipped and mirrored. It's funny how Ventura was once a place filled with promise and possibilities. A simple competition win made everything rosy. The city is completely different now that Matty is in it with Celeste, not me. He's here with her. No skateboard under his arm, no ripped cargos, no Chuck Taylors with scuffs around the toes. I bet he's wearing cologne again. All cleaned up.

I skate past the cute village with all the shops in a row. Couples sit daydreaming at outdoor café tables in front of the butter-colored walls of the ice cream shop where Matty bought me ice cream and confessed his love for a girl whose bedroom walls are probably covered in posters of puppies and kittens. Did Matty and Celeste stroll down this path tonight too? Did they sit at one of the tables and share a salted caramel cone? The image squeezes my insides.

I jump down a set of low steps. The pavement sends up a bright crack when my wheels hit ground again. I wish Joe were here to see me nail it.

The ferry office sits at the boatyard. A small wooden sign nailed to the door lists the ticket prices. Somewhere in my head I can hear my father saying, "What a racket! They have nerve charging that much when they're cruising to nowhere." The old man at the counter robs me in exchange for a ticket. I remind myself the ends will justify the means. He points at the marina and says, "Go ahead and board. They depart in less than five."

The time's come to unwrap my brother's hoodie from around my waist and tug it over my head. The sweatshirt smells like weed, and it puffs out a bit around the middle. Smelly and oversized or not, this disguise is essential. I face immense embarrassment, on an unreal level, if I'm caught by Matty and Celeste playing James Bond on a ferry packed with tourists. The odds of them putting two and two together—the girl underneath the hooded, oversized Independent Trucks sweatshirt—is low. I tug the edge of the hood so it skims my eyebrows. A whiff of my brother's unwashed hair shocks my nostrils. The lengths I will go to.

The ferry bobs in the water over at the dock. People mill around both the upper and lower decks. I bet Matty and Celeste are already on board. I bet he's showing her everything *out there* that she can't see from land. My stomach crystallizes into glass. On the inside, I'm breaking. I tell myself: Maybe tonight he'll notice that her teeth click when she speaks or her eyes are too shifty or she talks in questions or she's clingy or whatever nonsense he comes up with to strike a black line through the name of a girl he's lost interest in. I wait for it. I hope. I pray.

The boat pulls away from the dock and heads to Channel Islands Harbor. We bounce atop the water. Wind tugs at Gerard's sweatshirt as we pick up speed. I adjust my disguise a few times. Lay low. I weave through the crowd on the lower deck, gripping the trucks of my board hard. It dangles at my side. I blend and stalk at the same time, which is an incredibly challenging thing to do, as it turns out.

Finding them isn't tough. After all, Celeste glows in the dark.

I spot them on the upper deck, crammed between two tourists wearing Disneyland sweatshirts and an oldish-looking guy with a Santa-white beard and a cigar clenched between his teeth. His arm hangs around a girl who looks my age. I can't tell if she's his kid or his date and just thinking about the latter scenario makes me a little queasy. I decide to loiter behind the Disneyland couple with my body set sideways. They laugh annoyingly loud, but they're much less threatening and a lot more magical.

The boat's engine thrums. Beneath the edge of my sweatshirt hood, I peek at Matty and Celeste. At first, they lean with elbows on the railing, their backs to me. But then the boat anchors. The firework show kicks off, and he turns to face her. I lean closer for a snippet of what they're saying. I'm practically eating Mr. Disney's armpit.

The light show reflects on Celeste's skin. Matty looks only at her, because he's seen fireworks thousands of times, and I guess the view of her face is better than any of that. He brings both hands to her face, cups them around her cheeks. She stares up at the sky, open-mouthed and wondrous, like she's never seen fireworks before.

Explosions detonate inside me. Loud, blasting, disastrous.

I creep closer, catch the words they set into the air.

"I feel like my life only just got started when I met you," Matty says.

Oh God. And mine has ended.

He runs the backs of his fingers along her cheek. "It's like I took my finger off the pause button and pressed play." He looks down and does that sweet, goofy head shake of embarrassment that makes his hair go all shaggy. He's worried she'll think his words are silly. They're not. They're everything.

She grabs one of his hands and kisses it.

He's so elated, he's flying.

The higher he soars, the lower I sink.

I don't want to feel this way; I don't want to feel anything.

"Celeste. I just...I—I..." His words are a jumble of half-started words and gasps. He huffs a few times, like he's readying himself to say something epic, like when he tells me, *"Effie, I love you, you're fucking awesome."*

I wrap my arms around my skateboard.

No, no, no. Don't say it to her. Don't go there.

"I—I want you to know—I—I—think I love you."

The words are bullets shot straight into my chest.

It takes everything within me—all of my strength, head to foot—not to hurl myself into the water and let it fill my lungs. She's only known him a few weeks. That's all.

I clutch my stomach. This can't be.

Something went wrong. It wasn't supposed to turn out this way. She was supposed to be another of his random hookups, not his perfect match.

I thought I pressed his play button. I thought we were going to hit fast-forward together.

The fireworks ramp up now, intense. The gasps from the crowd pick up, too, pushing out at a faster tempo. Red explosions come first. Then white, then blue. Giant balls of popcorn. Chaotic and uniform all at the same time. They grow into dazzling starbursts, bigger and bigger. As they fade away, a series of rockets, one after another, shoots up into the sky. They reach full height, then pop like a cannon blast. I tremble from the inside out. I grab the railing.

Mr. Disney notices me and says, "Y'all okay, Miss?"

I nod. What I really want is to beg him and Mrs. Disney to get me out of here, take me with you, back to Texas or Louisiana or wherever you come from. I can't do this anymore. I can't live a life without Matty, without a future.

He kisses her now. Under the fireworks, under a million lucky shooting stars.

Celeste is making out with Matty—*my Matty.*

I can barely stand.

A trail of silver and white sparks drizzles downward like rain. A little rogue wave moves us. The boat rocks to the side, then back again. People around me adjust their footing. Matty's hand lands near mine on the railing. Too close for comfort. I have to leave.

I race to the deck below and find the restroom. It's a tiny little box, no bigger than an airplane bathroom with a dingy metal toilet. Navy blue sanitized water stains the inside of the bowl. I lock the door, press my forehead against it and breathe. In, out. In, out. I count to ten, then twenty, thirty. Still, the nausea stays within me—the tight stomach, the burn at the back of my throat, the absolute hopelessness of it all. The feelings don't fade.

The cruise ends. I don't leave the restroom until I hear the clunks and clicks of the ferry hooking back up to the dock. Throngs of people swarm off the boat. I spot Matty and Celeste a little ahead of me, their arms around each other. She's so tiny, he swallows her up.

Look at this picture of love. Just look.

I can't deny it. They are in love.

It's enough to make me head back to the restroom and throw up.

He has the perfect girl tucked under his arm.

Under mine is a skateboard.

How fucking stupid.

How epically, tragically stupid I am.

All my life I waited to hear him say those things to me.

All my life I stood by him, supported him. I was the perfect friend. I hoped, prayed, waited. When two people care about each other as much as he and I do, the next step is obvious. I was in it for the long haul. Ready to take the leap and run off to Chicago. To hell with my parents, to hell with Fox Inn, to hell with Vista Buscato.

It was only ever a matter of when.

But suddenly my *when* seems more like an *if.*

Or maybe, if I'm being honest, it's a *never.*

What happened to "I can't live without you, Effie"?

What happened to "You're coming with me to Chicago"?

What about our playlists and road trips and our great escape together?

What happened to "I fucking love you, Effie Fox?"

I thought I was his rock, his girl. I'm a keeper.

From my spot in the parking lot tucked in a grove of palm trees, I hide only a few paces from Matty's car. I beat them here. Riding on wheels covers a lot more ground than a romantic stroll. They load themselves into the Jeep. The top is down. Her hair flows free, wind-whipped from the ferry ride. She looks wilder than I've ever seen her. Urgency pops in her eyes. She leans over and kisses him. He seems surprised, even pulls back for a second. My pulse jumps. Maybe this—*this*—will be the move he'll dislike? She's too forward, not as demure as he thought. But then he gives her that wonderful, beautiful smile, and they lock themselves together in another kiss.

I'm going to be sick.

My hope, my denials, the back pats I gave myself—it was all for nothing.

Somewhere in their frenzied heartbeats pressed together is the truth I needed. Seconds turned into minutes, into hours, into days, and through it all, Celeste hasn't gone away. She is a living, breathing, burning reminder of everything Matty wants and everything I will never be.

His fingers run through her hair. Her mouth moves in sync with his.

Numbness takes over. I can't watch; I don't want to watch; I have to watch.

Pretending and denying won't work any longer. This is real.

They say the truth hurts. I wouldn't know. I can't feel anything.

Chapter Fourteen

People mill around the Town Hall grounds. Some on foot, some on skateboards, a few on BMX bikes. A crew pulls off perfect 360 grinds on the building's steps as Matty slides the Jeep into a parking spot. Bruiser, my brother, and the dreadlocked girl, Dogma, are here too. They don't chant or raise signs or do anything to indicate they're here to protest. They hold skateboards. I suppose that in itself is protest enough.

I have to hand it to Joe. When the rebel side of him rouses up an army, he does it right.

"Wow. Some crowd. Everyone's here," I say.

Matty nods. I wonder if he's thinking the only person missing is Celeste. My heart shrinks. I don't want to think about her anymore. Matty thinks about her enough for the both of us. This past week since the ferry ride has been slow, cruel torture.

Our phones beep in unison.

Group message to me, Matty, and Sam:

next up on the agenda

Joe's inside at the Board meeting and he's not backing down.

General Wills insisted on coming with Sam to the meeting, as if he couldn't trust the rest of us to keep Sam out of trouble. With any luck, he and Sam scored seats close enough to Joe to put out any fires that might arise.

We make our way down the wide hallway to the large meeting room in the back of the building. The lights are bright enough to shine holes through skin, show the worry under my façade. It's not worry for me—I have nothing to lose. But Sam and Matty—they have futures they can't screw up. And Joe. How many times can you get arrested before they throw the book at you? He's definitely reached some kind of limit.

People rent this spot as a sort of community center, for ceremonies and other special occasions. On party days, balloons skim the ceiling, cakes and cookies from Joselle's Sweet Shoppe spread over the tables, streamers and banners cover the walls. My Pre-K graduation party was here. It was the last time my parents ever showed up for something. We sang *This Little Light of Mine*, and when the song ended, I waited for my mom and dad to beam and go all teary-eyed like the other parents. Please. I should've known better. They didn't even bring a camera. Who needs Pre-K ceremonies when there's silverware to set and napkins to fold?

The meeting room is hot and stuffy. A rectangular table sits off to the side. A silver urn of coffee and a stack of white takeout cups sit atop it. Powdered sugar spills across the ugly, hunter green, plastic tablecloth from a now-empty box of donuts.

Joe's in the audience, in a row toward the middle with Edgar seated next to him. I barely recognize Joe when he's cleaned up, without a t-shirt with a skate slogan. Tonight, he's in a button-down shirt and belted slacks. His hair's tame. The wild and winded look pressed down into sleek waves. He looks more like he belongs on the dais, not in the crowd. We slide into seats next to him as the Board's conversation continues. Several people stare, like they're curious about us skate rats. Or disgusted. Maybe a little of both.

The Board members face the audience, seated behind a long table. They're propped high up on the dais, staring us down. It's us against them. We're so deeply, deeply far apart, the division between our two sides stretches out like we're on separate planets. And why? All because we like playing on wheels. It's ridiculous.

Joe passes me a paper detailing the meeting's order of business. He points at the third line. A parking ban on Buscato Drive after 7:00pm. Snatches of conversation in the room ring in my ears. Arguments rattle back and forth.

That's why we have the municipal lot. Let them park there.
It's a sanitation issue, really. We need the streets clear for cleaning.
You're killing Buscato's after-hours businesses.
It's only drunks at that hour.

Joe raises his eyebrows at me, tips his head in the direction of the chattering voices in the front of the room. I think he wants me to raise my hand. Like, join the discussion or something. I don't care enough about Fox Inn to give a shit where its customers park. That's my parents' problem, not mine.

Eventually, the business over parking regulations ends. Someone on the dais makes a pronouncement—I can't hear what he says, but it can't be good. People around us grumble. Two rows up, Joselle's shaking her head. Her white hair looks like cotton candy. The woman is always, always happy, and it shocks me to see her without a smile.

A thin, hoarse voice I know—Judge Pomerantz—calls out, "Next order of business. Discussion over the Town's acquisition of the vacant property on Halberd Court formerly owned by the Wiley family." The impossibility of reconciling Matty's gentle grandfather, the man I've always known as Pops, with this stiff and uptight Chairman on the dais blows my mind.

Matty sinks down a few inches.

A Board member at the end of the dais grabs a stack of handouts. He passes them to the first row occupants with the smuggest of smiles on his face. The rest of the stack makes its way down each aisle. I know this Board member well. He's a heavy hitter at the bar with one of those black American Express cards. Pressed collar popped up around his neck. Shoes always shiny and perfect. I wonder if he has a different pair for every day of the week just so neither gets too dirty.

Edgar gives Joe a nod of encouragement. Joe stands. He addresses Judge Pomerantz. "Sir, if I may speak?" His tone shocks the shit out of me, all courteous and proper, like he might curtsy next. It's a new angle for him. He's playing the game. I can't believe it.

Judge Pomerantz nods. "Certainly."

Detective Brimley stands to the side of the seated Board members. He coughs into a closed fist. A uniformed officer suddenly shifts to the end of our aisle, his eyes on Joe. Directly across the room, I cast a look at Sam and his father. General Wills doesn't move. But his eyes dart around, sizing up the scene. Sam fidgets, presses a thumb to his mouth, nibbles at his nail.

Joe launches into his argument.

"We respectfully request that the Wiley property be used as a skate park."

It's hard not to notice the tsunami wave of eyes rolling up on the dais. As far as I can count, at least five of the Board members openly chuckle. It's so obnoxious I want to chuck my dirty Vans at their heads.

Someone calls out, "Who's this '*we*?'" Another person shushes loudly.

The room quiets again. Outside, noise kicks up. The bite of wheels against pavement, the scratch of metal biting the curb. White painted hand railings don't stand a chance tonight.

Joe's face hardens for a moment, but he isn't deterred. "I've invited some friends to show their support outside. I'm not the only person in Vista Buscato who's interested in creating safe conditions for skateboarders." Like robots with an auto-on function, each Board member's face snaps to the ruckus beyond the windows. "Residents in this town would like to benefit as much as the tourists do. Other cities—Ventura, Fillmore, Carpinteria, Oxnard, Ojai—they all have successful skate parks." Edgar's nodding. Matty's mouth hangs open. I know, I agree. Joe is more articulate than

I ever thought he could be. Pride overwhelms me. Goosebumps pop on my arms. "It's a fun outdoor activity for kids. Parents can get involved at sponsored events and contests, and it's a great way to utilize property like the Wiley estate that's in foreclosure and would otherwise be—"

"How often are police called to those parks, huh?" a voice calls out from the other side of the room. "What kind of fun are we talking about?"

A man in front of us with a jaw like a bulldog spins in his seat and says, "The kind of fun they had on July 4th when they stole fireworks from the town's stash. They wrecked Buscato Point with beer bottles and that marijuana crap!" He pronounces it *mary-wanna*. Ridiculous. Such a stupid stereotype.

The energy in the room buzzes with muffled chuckles.

I struggle not to kick the back of the man's seat. Matty looks down at his lap.

He was doing something different on the Fourth of July. So was I.

Joe doesn't falter. "In those cities, infractions at skate parks—*if any*—are minor." No one takes particular issue with this, so he turns back to the Board. "The property is already in prime condition. It wouldn't take much construction to get it up and running. I work at a skate shop in Oxnard, so I've made a lot of contacts in the industry who can help." He shifts an arm toward Edgar. "My boss here knows an engineer who—"

One of the Board members—a woman—leans forward. "Mister...?"

"Monroe," Joe answers. "Joseph L. Monroe."

Matty, Sam, and I exchange glances. We don't know Joseph L. Monroe. We know Joe. Skater, risk taker, high school hater with an arrest record as tall as he is. We know that guy, the mutineer, the dark horse. We are not familiar with Joseph L. Monroe.

"Mr. Monroe. Thank you for your suggestion. However, the Board conducted an economic study of Halberd Court prior to its acquisition of the Wiley property. We determined, based on surrounding property values, that the most financially prudent way forward would be to demolish it with a view toward commercial development."

Matty sucks in a long breath between his teeth.

The woman's words enter my ears, run a circle in my head, and flow right back out. Property values, financial prudence, commercial development? I know what these things mean but I can't focus on her nonsense reasoning. I'm too busy staring at Joe. His jaw tightens like someone's cranking screws. They were never going to approve his suggestion anyway. This is just a dog and pony show to keep us quiet. Edgar's already shaking his head. I wonder when he'll give up the act and put his Skate Real cap back on.

"Surrounding property values?" Joe shakes his head. "There are no other properties on Halberd Court. The Wiley estate is the only property there. It *is* Halberd Court."

"Precisely. We can develop the entire street. It's a wise solution for our community."

Joe's energy puddles onto the floor. He looks down, like he's lost his train of thought.

The lady on the Board rattles off more numbers. Finances, retail sales forecasts, and projected development start dates and shit like that. Matty leans forward. He's perked up, listening intently to the details. I try, but the noise from the skaters outside pulls me away. I focus on Matty's face and try again. *Pay attention.* On the other side of me, Joe's still standing. I'd like to kick his legs out from underneath him. *Just give in, Joe. People like us don't win. It's a losing battle.* But he wants this so bad. He's listening and, I'm sure, forming counter arguments in his head.

The room drops into silence for a few moments as people leaf through the brochure handed out a few minutes ago. Matty snags one sitting on an empty chair. We lean together for a look. On the cover, in tacky, curly font—*Westin Development. Creating Brighter Places, Cultivating Communities.*

Please. We already are a community.

We just suck at it.

Matty's fingers flick through the pages. These are not visions of friendly, warm, tree-lined streets filled with tiny mom-and-pop shops. These are high-priced boutiques, all mirrored and silver and gold, with names you see in Beverly Hills. Carbon copies of the ones that already infiltrated Buscato Drive. The community cultivated by Westin Development does not include people like us. Matty, maybe. When he's Matthew Pomerantz, the Honorable Bertram T. Pomerantz's grandson. But certainly not me. And definitely not Joe. The rest of us, the old, leftover families here since the dawn of time, they just keep on pushing us out.

"Wait a minute," a guy in the front row shouts, and I'm snapped back into the moment. I lift myself up a little for a better look. It's Steve Conroy, the guy who owns the bike shop down at the other end of Buscato Drive. I got my first two-wheeler from him. His shop's been around even longer than Fox Inn. Steve smacks a hand against the brochure. "This is a Westin Development brochure. They're a high-end developer. How the hell will that help the community? What's going on here?"

Peter LaRoche—the only Board member who actually dares to converse with us skaters, lifts a hand to gather people's attention. "In the interest of full disclosure, I should tell you that I am also on the Board of Westin Development."

A thrum of chatter rises in the room. Brochure pages flip and flap. It's hard to hear the rest of what Peter says but I think it's a bullshit assurance about how he's not corrupt. Like it even matters. *Look around, Effie*, I remind myself. You don't fit in. You don't belong here, and neither does your family, no matter how hard they try. Our Foxhole will never do as well as La Jolie Dame. We're as disposable as our drinking straws.

Matty snaps the brochure shut. He shakes his head in disgust. I do too.

His phone buzzes, vibrating against my leg, the one pressed to his. He slides it out of his pocket. Celeste's name lights up the screen, bright and angel white. I could cry. *NO.* I want to take the phone and chuck it out the window. Light it on fire. Drown the damn thing in the Pacific Ocean. Anything but watch her name materialize like magic in Matty's hands every time I'm about to forget. She's gotten hip lately, calling from those burner phones you pick up at roadside quickmarts and gas stations. Her father would shit a brick if he knew.

One of the Board members, a man who looks older than the universe itself, leans toward Judge Pomerantz. "Let's put it to a vote."

The vote takes less than thirty seconds. It's unanimous. No skate park.

The old man on the dais says, "Can we move along now, Bert?"

Matty's grandfather turns to the Board member who addressed Joe. "Betsy?"

She nods. "This issue is closed."

Steve Conroy throws his hands up in defeat.

Joe stares at the dais. "Wait. I'm not finished. Can we get a community vote on this? I understand you thought it was a good idea to close the park on Buscato Drive, but replacing it with a newer, more improved one in another location would—"

The woman named Betsy shuffles papers, clearly irritated. "You don't have a constitutional right to engage in your sport anywhere you please."

"I'm not saying I do."

Her eyes flick to Detective Brimley way down at the end of the dais. He moves forward and raises one hand at Joe. *Silence.* "Son, please. That's enough."

"Don't call me son."

Matty's head snaps up. Edgar shifts in his plastic folding chair.

The whole place falls quiet as death.

Ladies and Gentlemen, Joseph L. Monroe has left the building. The effort required for me not to explode into applause is like moving a mountain. I wish I had Joe's courage.

"I don't appreciate you silencing me." He keeps going, directing a stoic, assertive voice at the Board. "This decision is a farce, same as the skate park closing. You never intended to get the residents' approval. You already made up your minds. How many business owners are in favor of this? Let me see a show of hands."

The faces around the room are wary. Some don't bother looking up from the brochure at all. I don't know what to do with the Jekyll and Hyde people here. When I hand them a menu, they smile; when I hold a skateboard, they rip me apart.

Matty is so lucky he's getting out of this town.

"Mr. Monroe." Judge Pomerantz's voice is light, but loud enough to carry over the hushed conversations popping up around the room. "The Board is permitted to take action on this matter without explicit approval from residents."

"How? Don't we live in a democracy?"

Behind us, a woman remarks snidely, "Let's hope he doesn't filibuster this time."

Judge Pomerantz remains focused. "We are chosen each year by the community and have authority to act on behalf of the town."

"With all due respect, I've read the Town's By-laws. I don't see—"

"Please permit us to move on."

"I can't do that."

My stomach bounces up, down, sideways. Matty reaches for my hand.

"Joseph, please sit down," the judge says, softer than ever, and a flash of Matty's grandfather—the Pops I know—leaks out behind the glasses. His eyes are warm. This is the man who used to let us all stay up late on the weekends watching Netflix, the one who gave me a corsage on graduation day after he'd heard my parents weren't attending the ceremony. The flowers were white, delicate. I still have it in a drawer in my room, all dried out and browned at the edges.

Joe does not move. And he most certainly does not bend a knee to sit down. Joe is always serious and always thinking, but this guy—the one they're challenging—his eyes rage like he could light the room on fire. Maybe this *is* the real Joseph L. Monroe.

The judge's tone drops to a down-and-out last chance warning. He straightens himself in his chair. "Joseph, you will be removed if you cannot control yourself."

At the end of our aisle, Brimley nods at the officer, who pivots toward us. His eyes are clear and focused and one hand's hovering over a set of handcuffs clipped to his left hip. He reaches for Joe, who's shaking his head violently, erratically. Out of nowhere, General Wills takes up a post at the opposite end of our aisle, next to Matty's seat. He's wearing normal clothes but he's stiff, like his uniform's still buttoned up around him.

"Let's split," Matty whispers. He squeezes my hand.

I glance at Sam's spot across the room. His seat is empty. Edgar's disappeared too.

Joe shouts. "No! You're not tossing me out! I have every right to be here!" His eyes blaze.

Matty tugs my hand. We dash down the aisle. I look back once. General Wills stands beside Joe now, pressing hands all over him, trying, it seems, to coax Joe into submission. On Joe's other side, the officer grips his right elbow.

We're supposed to stay and fight. Be his voices. I feel like a fraud. I'm not supposed to leave Joe to fight this battle alone. I'm not supposed to hold the hand of a boy who's in love with someone else. And he's not supposed to love Celeste in the first place. I squeeze Celeste out from the corners of my mind and grip Matty's hand tighter. Being connected to him is the only thing that pulls my thoughts away from her, from my shitty life, this waste of time, dead-end town.

We race together through the open doors.

Chapter Fifteen

Outside, the Town Hall grounds are chaos.

The crowd got wind of Joe's situation and they're not happy about it. Some guys throw trash cans at the sky like rockets. Contents spray everywhere. Water bottles, tissues, crumpled newspaper. People peer in the windows of the meeting room and shout support for Joe. I spot Edgar with arms outstretched, like he can hold back the crowds with his bare hands. If he thinks he can talk sense into people, he's nuts. It's as useless an endeavor as Joe's wasted time in that Town Hall meeting.

Matty and I step into the center of the commotion. Arguments break out, and no one remembers the rules—the ones saying you can't assault each other, and you most certainly cannot assault a cop. I spot one scuffle, then two, then three, and my head is spinning before I can count them all. People are going to jail tonight. I so don't need this shit. I think of Edgar and how he sprang into action. Matty and I need to do something. We need to step up and help Edgar take control of this. It's what Joe wants, and if he were out here, he'd be doing exactly that.

Sam sits alone on a park bench in front of a statue of a bald eagle with wings stretched to full spread like an angel. We push toward him. He's bent forward, hands spread over his face. His chest rises and falls. Hyperventilation mode. I almost want to find him a paper bag to breathe into or something, but when we edge closer and I see his features more clearly, I realize it's more about relief than anxiety.

"Guys, I'm sorry," he says, breathless. "My father—he made me leave. I wanted to help."

"It's okay. We know," Matty says. He understands. He has the same priorities.

What's my excuse? My parents are behind Fox Inn's bar right now, stirring drinks and throwing back a celebratory shot for each cha-ching of the cash register. They're not here to order me to bail on my friend. That decision came on my own. We left Joe at the apex of a crisis. You can pretend you're brave and loyal all you want but when your actions pretty much spell out the opposite, you're nothing but a fraud. I'm absolutely disgusted with myself.

Matty runs both hands through his hair.

Sam covers his face again. Blood coats his left thumb. I force him to let me look.

"Someone threw a bottle. I tried to pick up the pieces but…" He doesn't finish, just inspects the sliced skin. "It's bad, isn't it?"

"No, I don't think so." But it totally is.

Spending my whole life in a restaurant, I know the rule—brooms only, no hands. At a minimum, you scoop it up with a dishrag. I throw a nasty glare at the crowd, because I feel like I should do something on Sam's behalf.

There's a lot of blood. His face goes gray.

I don't know what to do. I grab the hem of my tank top and press it against Sam's finger.

He swallows loud enough that I hear the soft squelch of it.

I tell Matty to come look, but he's too busy checking his phone. I don't want to think about the name above the text bubble.

After a slow count of ten, I peek at the cut. The fleshy pad of Sam's thumb's ripped down the middle cleanly. But it's not as deep as I thought. "It's just a heavy bleeder. Once it stops, you'll be fine."

He winces as I press my top against it harder.

On the lawn, Dogma argues with a police officer who's trying to tug the skateboard from her grip. She's just a poser; she's probably never even stepped on the damn thing. But then, I'm supposed to be speaking up like she is, like a hero, and mouthing off to further the cause. Who's the poser now?

"Matty, we have to do something," I say hurriedly. "People are losing their shit out here. We need to scale it back before we make ourselves look worse."

His eyes go wild. "Are you serious? We can't control this." He throws an arm toward the crowd. "They're animals."

The comment—and the flippant way he says it—rocks me. "These are our friends."

"You know all these people? I don't."

"Not all of them. But they're here for the same reason. We're all skaters." I stop myself from saying what I really want: *If they're animals, so am I.* Because I don't want to hear his response to that, where he separates himself from this world we live in and leaves me in it.

An uncontrollable buzz of adrenaline rips through me—the same one that makes me mouth off to Detective Brimley when I know damn well to keep my trap shut and play the game like a good girl. But Joe played the game tonight and look where it got him.

The fucking game is rigged.

My sneakers slip a few times, but I manage to climb onto the back of the bald eagle statue spreading her wings behind Sam, whose mouth falls open in a mile-long gape.

"Effie, what are you doing? Get down!" Matty hisses.

The statue wobbles once, and I almost lose my nerve, but I've had worse falls, so I keep it together. For Joe's sake. For all our sakes.

Starting a chant seems like the only way to draw this crowd's attention. But what do I shout? Perched on top of the eagle's head, I know I'll be heard, so the message I spread is important.

Some guy with black and blue hair I recognize from school points at me. "That's the girl who won at Ventura!" A couple more voices behind him rise in unison—"That bomb drop was sick, yo!" "Woohoo!" "She's here!"

And then the message comes to me: WE ARE HERE.

I shout it. And I continue shouting, and shouting, until my throat stings and I can't hear myself anymore. But the words are still there, this time carried by the crowd. Matty and Sam join in too. No more bottles and paper wads fly through the air. The only things raised up high now are clenched fists and cries of victory. This must be why Joe does this, because it makes you feel like a hero. I wish he were here to see the solidarity.

Suddenly, shouting rings out from inside the building.

The crowd outside quiets.

Even from all the way out here, through the open doors of Town Hall, you can still catch glimmers of movement inside the main hallway. Joe's flailing, limbs everywhere. Here's a friendly factoid to keep in mind if you're ever arrested: spitting at a cop might earn you a few elbow shots to the ribs when no one's looking. It'll take forever before Joe can twist his upper torso on a ramp turn without wincing.

They pull him down the hallway; they drag him across the floor. Eventually they reach the front doors of the building with Joe in handcuffs.

The atmosphere blasts open like a cannon shot. Whatever success I had in pulling everyone together crumbles in an instant when people see their leader overpowered. People go wild. Joe stops struggling for a moment to take in the view. Sam gets to his feet and salutes. Joe spots us and nods.

General Wills steps out from behind them and catches Sam mid-salute. He glares. Sam's arms fall. As his father approaches us, Sam snaps to attention, standing upright like the obedient soldier he is. General Wills threatened Sam with some crazy program—like a pre-boot camp boot camp—if he gets into any trouble. I pray Sam doesn't have to explain his part in this. The posters taped to the front of the building are all his doing. I climb down from the eagle statue. General Wills eyes me with disgust.

We watch as they guide Joe into a squad car at the curb.

I think General Wills wants us to watch. It's proof that civil disobedience is nothing but anarchy. It kills me that we can't do anything to help. Sam and his father slip away, but not before a firm order to go home. "Things could get worse," the general says. But Joe's on his way to jail—again—and I can't imagine things will dive any lower. For all the times he's spouted shit about the Constitution and freedom of speech and power to the people, it's never gotten him anywhere. Unless you measure progress with handcuffs. That's just not how things work in a town like Vista Buscato.

Matty keeps swinging his head around at the doors to Town Hall. Probably wondering when his grandfather and the rest of the Board will step out of the building. Personally, I doubt they will. With the commotion outside, I'll bet they're hiding, discussing how best to erect a structure higher than the Great Wall of China to keep themselves safely tucked inside. Or, more likely, to keep us out.

Matty tugs on my arm suddenly. "Celeste's here."

"What?"

No, no, no. Please, God, no.

"She's here. I can't believe it. Celeste!" He bounces on the balls of his feet, waving in her direction. That's all it takes. One sighting of her and he's a jack-in-the-box. "Celeste!"

Stop saying her name. He is forever saying her fucking name.

He whistles. The shrill signal splits my eardrums, and I'm re-minded of the same sound at the end of recess in elementary school—how we'd all sigh, defeated. I feel the same way now.

I see the white-hot spark of her hair in the crowd before I see her face. She weaves through the crowd, looking as though she's been yanked all over. Like a doll rescued from the bottom of a toy pile. Her shirt's hanging too far to one shoulder, hair is tugged out of the braid in spots, and her face—the one that smiled far too much that night in the car—is wide-eyed, packed with fear.

Matty throws himself at her. The motion knocks me off center, and I have to spread my arms out to steady myself.

Instantaneously, a black cloud shifts over my head.

Rain will fall in five, four, three, two…

They kiss.

I'm sick.

My whole body wavers. I'm stuck in a tailslide. I grab the side of the statue for support. The eagle stares down at me. I went from hero to pathetic in the span of one minute.

They sway together in a hug. When they finally disentangle, he runs hands over her sides and her hair—smoothing, soothing, checking for injuries. "Are you okay? Are you hurt?" Like his porcelain doll would crack under the pressure of all those skate-board wheels. Squaring the vision of Matty's delicate, breakable angel with my memory of the friendless girl who squished around next to me in a filthy dumpster ten years ago makes my head throb. She relaxes and smiles. He smiles too. Happiness and sunshine all around. I stifle a reflex gag because how the hell did I wind up in this position? I pretty much handed her to him on a silver platter.

It takes superior strength not to press my fingers around her neck and squeeze. I am no longer surprised he hasn't found an absurd reason to get rid of her. I am furious.

They talk over each other. It's a duet, a harmony, a swan song of *How did you get here? I lied! Your father will kill you! He doesn't know! Holy shit!* If he tells her she's brave, I will take off my shoe and beat him with it.

"Hi Effie," Celeste says. Her voice pitches upward. Unsure. A question.

"Hey."

Visuals flash through my head, streaming by on a fast-forward picture slideshow, of their love story from pharmacy checkout line till now. I can't make it stop. I am painfully aware that he still holds her hand, even though she's no longer in danger of being mauled by the crowd of protesters. My heartbeat quickens. I want to run all the way across town to Fox Inn, grab the biggest knife I can find, and slice the two of them apart, forever.

"Nice to see you again," she says.

"Yeah, same here." I try to sound casual, but it comes out rushed instead.

Celeste's eyes dart back and forth between me and Matty. "Do you think we could go somewhere? If my father finds out I'm here, I'm dead, you know?"

No way will Matty leave. He and Joe are too tight. Matty cares what happens to people in this town. Or he did until Celeste came into the picture.

He pulls Celeste close to him, cradling her under one arm. "Sure," he says.

The entire universe shifts under my feet. That tailslide feeling again.

"You coming, Eff?"

"No," I say, like *Of course I am not coming*. Is he for real?

He runs his gaze over the crowd. "We shouldn't stick around here."

"I'm not leaving. We came to help Joe."

Matty's face shifts for a second with that reminder. Another bottle sails through the air, cracks against a tree trunk. Glass explodes in every direction. Celeste jumps. Matty squeezes her tighter. He reaches for me with his free arm.

"Come, on, Effie. Let's go."

He tugs on the bloody hem of my tank top. All the desperation in my heart wants to grab his hand, never let go, despite the beautiful girl tucked under his arm, the one burrowing into his side. But that puts me in the backseat again. And who wants that?

"Go, Matty. I'm fine."

"Effie!"

"I'm not leaving!"

I want to say, *AND YOU SHOULDN'T EITHER*. Judging by the way he clings to Celeste's arm as she begins a slow backpedal, he wouldn't listen to me anyway.

Somewhere close by—I can't see where, exactly, too many people crowd my vision—more glass shatters. Someone falls. Three or four people go down like dominoes.

Celeste spins and breaks into a run.

Matty's still holding his arm in the air where she used to be.

"Go!" I tell him.

"Shit," he snaps and turns to race after her.

He disappears.

I didn't think he'd do that. Of all the possible outcomes, this one didn't occur to me. And yes, I told him he could leave, I even ordered him to do it, but I didn't actually believe he would.

What was I thinking? The depths of my stupidity are absurd.

A wave of anger reaches my core—a place so deep I didn't even know it existed. I want to scream, I want to throw something, I want to run and run and run and not come back until Matty returns with me. A guy bumps into me on the right and I shove him hard enough that he stumbles. He looks at me like I'm nuts. Maybe I am. I'm stupid and impulsive and I never, ever think things through. I'm dangerous.

Three police cars stop in front of Town Hall. Cops get out and press hand-held radios to their mouths. They push people back. The crowd shrinks, tightens. Which makes things worse. Bodies slam into each other. That's when the pushing starts. I'm shoved forward, backward. Bounced to the left, slammed from the right. And here it is: the commotion every Board member sitting up on the dais inside that meeting room expected. We fall right into it.

It's so predictable. All the chanting and unity I conjured up earlier is gone.

The crowd thickens.

I don't understand if people are dispersing or charging.

It's madness; it's a stampede.

I can't get locked up tonight. I can't.

My phone beeps with a series of texts from Joe. Group messages to me, Matty, and Sam.

where r u guys?

they're booking me for disorderly conduct again

someone has to bail me out

they're gonna take my phone any sec

don't fuck me over

Then, one for me alone: p*lease effie*

My insides fold in on themselves.

I search for a glimpse of Matty and Celeste somewhere, anywhere, but can't find them.

Hoping by a miracle to find Sam and his dad, I push through the crowd. There's no sign of them on the sidewalk. Sam's probably home already, disinfecting his thumb. Or sucking it.

Several people line up next to each other, sardine-style, on the ground at the curb. Plastic zip ties join their wrists together. One of them is way older than the rest—gray-haired and a little thick in the middle, the way men become after they've ordered one too many steak and eggs at Fox Inn week after week, year after year. Thin, weathered skin sags around his eyes, like crepe paper. I think I recognize him. Maybe? It's dark and he's stooped over. I'm not sure. He might be a Fox Inn customer, but it's hard to get a clear shot from the side of his face. A cop bends to say something to him. His chin lifts, mouth open with an answer. A full frontal view faces me, illuminated by streetlights overhead. I know it can't be, but he looks like Celeste's father.

He shifts. Swings his hair out of his face with a flick of his head.

A memory hits me then, a chess piece pinched between two fingers.

It is him. He's one of a dozen people they're loading into a police van.

Holy shit. How?

James Madaleo or Kevin Vaughn or whoever the hell he is has zero interest in protesting skateboarders' rights. He's here to find her. And now he's going to the slammer.

I bolt back into the crowd, to where Matty and Celeste disappeared. But my legs falter, the soles of my sneakers scuff on the sidewalk in a start and stop motion. Which way did they go? The Jeep isn't in the parking lot anymore. I encouraged Matty to leave, and he took the bait. The truth is so majorly fucking crushing that I don't want to think about it.

People shove past me. Shouts hit my ears. A skateboard shoots upward, hits a light post, and cracks into a vee from the force. Something sails through the air my way—a rock or a bottle or can or something. I try to dodge to the left but wind up slamming myself into three girls leaving on their skateboards. Boards go flying, and we hit the ground together in a pile. The thing I avoided —some kind of canister—cracks the pavement not more than two feet from us. It hisses, leaks, positively rages with smoke and fog. The haze covers everything, everywhere.

I know this. I've seen it on television.

This is tear gas.

I run as fast as I can. I have no choice.

My eyes drip, burn, melt. I have no idea where I'm going. All I feel is fire where my eyeballs should be. This is five thousand times worse than when my mother forced me to chop onions all afternoon for cutting school in ninth grade. Carlo and Vincent helped me flush my eyes with warm water afterwards, and I wish they were here now to help. Tear gas is no joke.

I blast into a body, shove the person aside. I think they fall. I don't know. I can't see a damn thing. Whoever it was throws an arm around my neck and pulls me to the curb. I'm shoved down. I feel others beside me. I blink and blink, but the burn rages on.

"Well, hello, Stefanie Fox."

The voice hits me in the gut. Coffee—splash of cream, no sugar.

Detective Brimley pins my wrists together from behind. He binds them.

I'm cuffed.

Chapter Sixteen

"You know what Brimley calls a perp who's been locked up as often as I have?"

I don't answer Joe. I just roll my eyes.

"A career criminal." He chuckles. "I should be flattered. Right? At least he thinks I'll have a career."

"You did it to yourself."

"I did it for us."

Anyone who proudly proclaims that their multiple arrests are sacrifices for the greater good is either stupid or misguided. It's simple. People are arrested because they get caught. I do not sit on this metal bench in a holding cell with sweat soaking through my bra as a gift for anybody. That's absurd. I'm here because I accidentally assaulted a cop in my temporary state of tear-gassed blindness. I'm here because I should have left with Matty. I should have listened to him, Celeste or not. This is all her fault.

"How'd you get in here, anyway?" Joe asks. "Brimley said you jumped a cop."

"It wasn't intentional. I couldn't see what I was doing." I point at my eyes because he missed the obvious. If they look as bad as they feel, he must be an idiot not to realize. "Tear gas kind of messes with your vision."

"Are you okay?"

"Don't act like you care," I tell him.

"Are you crazy? Of course I care. Obviously."

"You only care that they took away your place to do ollies. That's all."

"No. I care about everything that affects us."

"Yeah, well, I care about people, not *things*."

"Person, not people." His stare is intense. "You only care about one person."

Bubbles pop and fizz and spill over in my belly.

"That's not true," I say. If only the words came out as strongly as I thought they would.

"Your actions speak for themselves."

"Is that really what you think of me?"

He pauses, tugs on a piece of hair, then flicks it away. "I think a lot of things about you."

Something hot and weird ignites deep inside my chest. I don't know what we're talking about anymore.

My gaze flicks to the tiny girl sharing our holding cell. She sits quietly on the bench across from ours, legs bent, knees tucked beneath her chin, flip-flops strewn on the floor as she picks at her toenails. A faint peanut butter odor clings to the air around her. She watches me and Joe with bloodshot, tear-gassed eyes. Joe asked her name earlier but she didn't answer, just tugged her skullcap tighter over her head. Which totally made me sweat as I watched because there's no air conditioning in these cells and why the hell would you wear anything like that in July anyway? I hope she doesn't have the brain power to realize I'm weak and driven only by my love for a boy. Because Joe is right—I care more about Matty than anything or anybody else. I'm aware how ridiculous that is.

Joe starts grumbling about unlawful arrests and peaceful protests, breathing life back into his argument over the unfairness of the town's by-laws and junk. I wish he'd shut up.

I press the side of my head against the gray cement wall. *Stop talking, just stop talking.*

"What's wrong?" he asks.

"We're in jail."

"So?"

"I don't enjoy being here."

"And I do? I wasted a call on my mom, and she can't even come get me. My sister's already in her crib. We can't find a sitter on short notice."

"What about your stepdad?'

"Tim's on an overnight flight." He aims an exhale at the ceiling. "I'm stuck here until tomorrow. So please, save your complaints for Matty. I'm sure he'll blame it on me too."

"I don't blame you. I'm just...whatever."

Telling Joe that my foul mood has nothing to do with him and everything to do with Matty would just prove his point. Tonight will be difficult enough. We're sitting in a jail cell. It's already a mess.

"I saw you chanting. That was awesome. Thank you." The quiet, calm Joe is back. He's soft and thoughtful again.

The overwhelming feeling of control I had in that moment at Town Hall, when I soothed the crowd and pulled them all together, breaks through my irritation. I was heard, for once. What I said was important. Blinking hard, I wish myself away from here. I glance at the girl again but she's too busy digging at her toes to care what we're talking about. I bang my foot against her bench. *Whack, whack, whack, whack.*

A police officer stops to open our holding cell. With him comes a wave of cool air from the front end of the precinct, like a glorious jet stream of air conditioning. It fades within two seconds. He waves the girl out. "Your parents are here."

Joe holds out his knuckles for a fist bump. She leaves him hanging.

The door closes and we're locked in our hot box again.

Barely five seconds before Joe asks, "Where was Matty?"

"I don't know."

I love Matty too much to spill all the details of his transgressions and misplaced loyalty. I don't want to admit his failures. It's embarrassing.

"He swore he'd stay the whole time. Gave me the big speech about how no one would touch me if I were with Judge Pomerantz's grandson. Why would he leave?"

"Maybe he got spooked when the crowd went wild." It's not exactly a lie. But that's not why he left. He might have stayed, I think, had Celeste not run off. Had I not ultimately encouraged him to go. I leave out the Celeste detail. I don't want to hear myself say it. And Joe doesn't need to know that part.

Joe's head falls back against the concrete wall behind us.

I bang my foot on the bench leg some more. My big toe goes numb.

"If I had a dime for every time that kid put himself first, I could buy the Wiley estate myself," Joe murmurs.

"That's ungrateful. How many times have he and the judge bailed you out of this place?"

"They didn't have to. My mom or Tim would have come for me."

I mean, maybe. But he would've waited a lot longer and endured a lot more grief.

My father's voice bounces off the walls down the hall. My nerves crackle, electrified. This conversation is going to suck. The last time I got busted—a total misunderstanding involving Bruiser's BB gun, Sam's snail-paced run, and my reluctance to leave him behind—my parents put me on kitchen cleanup duty for a month. Spider webs of cuts marked my hands for weeks afterwards, thanks to steel wool scrubbing action.

A set of keys clinks down the hall. The sound grows closer. An officer walks in front of our cell. I stand, assuming he'll break me out, but he passes us. His footsteps stop at a cell on our left. Keys jingle again. There's a creak and a slam as he lets someone out. I grab the bars and wait for my turn. In two seconds, the cop walks past with Celeste's father in tow.

I press my face between the bars for a glimpse of the person bailing him out down the hall. If it's Matty and he chooses to spring Celeste's dad over me and Joe, I will lose my fucking mind, I swear. The walls will not be able to hold in my rage.

They turn a corner. I can't see. The unknowing shreds me up inside.

I kick the bars.

Joe asks what I'm so aggro about. I don't answer. He's already pissed at Matty. The next phase frightens me.

Brimley himself comes down the hall with my father. A filthy bar towel is tucked into his belt and an unlit cigarette juts from the corner of his mouth. Brimley unlocks our cell door and waves me out. He quickly slams the door closed again. He and my father pump arms in a handshake that lasts an unnaturally long time. My father thanks the detective profusely. Meanwhile, behind closed doors he's developed a list of slurs to describe the detective. His favorite is The Blue Bully. Gerard's is Big Fat Dick.

The detective and my father walk down the hall toward the main office.

Now that I'm free, I don't know what to do with myself. I just stay there like an idiot.

Joe stands inside the cell and comes closer. He raises his arms to grab the bars over his head and leans forward, one hip cocked to the side. Sexy as ever, even if he's still in his fake prep boy Board meeting uniform. He flashes me a tiny smile.

"What are you waiting for? Go," he says in a hoarse whisper.

My chest burns. I don't want to leave him here. He's alone in an overheated, uncomfortable jail cell waiting for friends who'll never show. This is wrong.

"Go," Joe says again.

My father and the detective are halfway down the hall.

"Will you be okay?"

"Yes!" He laughs in that exhaling way he always does. A glimmering line of sweat runs along the edge of his hairline.

I can't stop looking at him looking at me.

"I'll be fine. It's okay."

I don't know. I don't know.

Joe's fingers wrap around the bars. I lean forward and grab the bars too. He slides his hands over mine. They're hot. Somewhere in my core, a fluttering feeling kickflips a full revolution. He smiles again, bigger this time. It's totally genuine. I don't think anyone has ever smiled at me like that, not when their own world is imploding.

We're in this together, I want to say. But I don't have the nerve.

"Really, it's okay."

"Effie!" my father barks out.

I pull out from underneath Joe's hands and backslide away.

The bars partially block my view of him.

This feels cold and criminal. The farthest thing from brave. I don't look back as I jog down the hallway.

When I'm in the main office signing release papers, I wonder if Joe still stands there gripping the bars or if he's given up and dropped to the bench again. My head hurts.

Outside, my father pauses to whip a lighter out of his pocket. A flick, a flame, and his cigarette glows red. He blows the smoke upward. The sky's on fire.

"Your skater friends aren't doing you any favors," he says, displaying the cigarette in the air like it's my fault.

"They're not responsible for me getting locked up, Dad."

"That's right." He's got that patronizing parental nod thing going on. "I forgot. You assaulted a police officer."

"I did not assault him. I had teargas in my eyes and—"

"Save it, Effie. Get your act together. Your mother and I work our asses off for you and Gerard. We expect more."

What a joke. The hardest work they do is drinking all the liquor and generally loitering in a business that can easily operate without them. I see right through his bullshit.

"You're getting more shifts," he warns. "A few doubles should straighten your ass out."

"How is that even legal? I already work six days a week."

"Your mother is furious with you."

The force with which I roll my eyes almost causes nerve damage.

"You're a lucky girl, Effie." He takes another drag. "The future's already laid out for you. A family business, a job to rely on. Put a little effort in, and you'll be set for life."

He must think I'm stupid. We both know it's not a little effort, it's a lot. Let's face it—Fox Inn does okay, but it isn't rolling in cash like La Jolie Dame where even the bathroom attendant doling out warm hand towels scores big tips. Or so I've heard.

His promise needs an adjustment: I'm not set for life. I am shackled for life.

Spin it any way you want, I know what it really is. And I'm definitely not lucky.

Lucky was when I wore Joe's Bones Brigade hat and won that skate comp. Lucky was the exhilaration running through my body when I stood up for something important and shouted, "We are here!" Lucky was my time with Matty on Ventura Pier before he went all lovesick and started pounding Celeste into my head again.

I want to punch my father but that only ever works for Gerard. "You're acting like I robbed a bank at gunpoint. All I did was go to a protest, which is a perfectly legal thing to do."

"Who told you that? One of your punk friends? Did they also tell you that people get arrested at protests?" His head dips toward mine. Cigarette breath puffs near my ear. He jerks a thumb toward the station. "You got any idea what I do to keep that asshole off my back? You know how much it takes to get him to look the other way?"

By *that* asshole, I assume he means Brimley. But why should I worry about my father's sketchy business operations? Phil Fox's problems are his own making. He risks his dream business with bad judgment on the daily. No one forces him to take bets from old-time locals in the weeks leading to Super Bowl. No one coaxes him to snake cash out of the register and hide it in a bulk canister of coffee grounds in the giant freezer in the kitchen. I know all his tricks. I'm not blind. And what do I care about his consequences? One of my best friends—possibly the bravest person I know—is sweating out his water weight in a jail cell behind us. The consequences of Joe's sacrifice are far more important.

Thoughts of him sitting alone fog up my head.

My father must realize he lost me because his tone softens. "There's more to life than skate parks."

He stubs his cigarette out on the precinct steps.

There's more to life besides a whole lot of things. Ferry rides, fireworks, fairy tales.

It depends who you ask.

Chapter Seventeen

On the ride to Fox Inn, my father launches into a rousing speech involving how a few weeks of hard work and extra shifts will shape me up. I'm on kitchen cleanup duty, effective immediately. Whatever. This punishment has nothing to do with my behavior and everything to do with me remaining Fox Inn's indentured servant. I'm only half-pissed, because I can deal with a few extra shifts. I don't like it, but it's more money in my pocket and more money means I'm out of here. Joke's on him, really.

Fox Inn is mostly dark except for the small overhead pin lights illuminating the liquor bottles behind the bar. Carlo and Vincent are already red-faced and sweating over prep for tomorrow's brunch crowd when I step through the kitchen doors. One of their phones is cranking out songs in Italian. They sing along, Carlo scrubbing the grill and Vincent pouring melted chocolate into a piping bag.

The second I walk through the doors, a barrage of questions hits me.

What happened?

Why'd you get locked up again?

Can't you stay out of trouble, Effie?

I blow them off with a question of my own. "That man we talked about, the one with the daughter. Can I ask you—"

"Don't remember him." Carlo shrugs.

I slap the counter. "Yes, you do. We've already been through this."

"Oh no! She's mad!" Carlo says. "Hurry! Grab a mouthguard. She aims for the teeth." He drags a damp cloth along the stainless steel countertop where I left fingerprints.

"Why does he say his name is Kevin Vaughn?"

Vincent's deep voice chimes in. "You still on him?"

Carlo mutters, "She is."

They exchange a look and fall quiet.

"Come on, guys. Don't hold out on me."

Vincent drizzles chocolate sauce onto parchment paper. It's a perfect alternating pattern of curlicues and dashes. I aim to kill him with kindness, stroke his ego a little.

"You should have been an artist, Vincent."

"I *am* an artist," he says flatly.

My father bursts through the kitchen doors then, clapping his hands. "Let's get this place cleaned up, guys. Chop, chop." He hovers over a small vat of hollandaise sauce sitting on a warming plate, and sniffs. "Stretch this another day."

Vincent mutters something inaudible.

My father slips back into the restaurant.

Carlo sighs. "This guy, this guy," he mumbles. "*Stretch the hollandaise.* How we gonna stretch that for the morning? The flavor's all wrong. Felicia will have a fit." He pulls a gallon-sized container of sour cream out of the refrigerator and whisks it into the sauce. The stretched rendition is more than a little on the white side. Vincent peeks over Carlo's shoulder and dips a spoon into it. They taste it and start yapping in Italian. Carlo lifts a shoulder when he catches me watching them. "Don't take it personal, but your father's a cheap bastard."

I have not taken a single negative comment about my father personally since the day I watched him rig a bet to trick some poor, unsuspecting tourist out of a hundred bucks. We locked eyes, and instead of offering an explanation—something, anything—he shrugged and said, "Never seen him before. Wouldn't do it to a regular customer." So if Carlo and Vincent want to call him a cheap bastard, I don't mind. I might even tuck the phrase away for future reference.

Carlo eyes me still standing there. "Look, kid. I don't ask for birth certificates when I meet people." He pops one shoulder. "Madaleo's a nice guy. He didn't have a lot of money when he rented upstairs. I don't know what he's doing these days but years ago he worked at a shelter in Ojai. He went to church and prayed to the Madonna more than anyone I know, except my Nonna, may she rest in peace." He makes the sign of the cross over his chubby body and kisses his fingertips before releasing the kiss up to the heavens. Vincent does likewise. "Your mother pressured your father to cut him loose. I think he owed back rent or something."

"They kicked him out?"

"That's what I hear."

"But that's so extreme. Couldn't they have worked something out?"

Carlo shrugs again. He wipes his forearm across his brow. His hairnet shifts. "You know your father."

All too well. "Right. Cheap bastard."

"Effie!" My father's jumps back into the kitchen, holding the ugliest, filthiest mop with stringy gray ropes dangling at the bottom. The thing's falling apart because he's obviously too cheap to buy a new one. He pushes the mop at me. "Bucket of soap and water's by the bar. I want to see my reflection in those floors."

Carlo follows me out of the kitchen. He squirts a Windex bottle in every direction.

I pretend I give a shit about dragging this stupid mop over the hardwood floors.

The music inside the kitchen changes to what sounds like a sappy love song in Italian. My father stayed behind to speak with Vincent. Their voices mumble out a low, steady, almost inaudible thrum below the music.

Another thought strikes me. "What's his real last name? Madaleo or Vaughn?"

"Vallone," Carlo whispers.

Time slows down like wheels losing momentum uphill.

Vallone? I don't understand.

A sharp click cuts through the music.

Carlo holds his Windex bottle up like a gun, pointed in the direction of the sound—the side door emergency exit. The door clicks once again. Shut.

That exit has a horizontal push bar for a handle. It locks from the inside. On the other side is a dumpster in a dark alleyway between our store and Joselle's Sweet Shoppe. There's no door handle. You can't get in from out there. From the kitchen, the next song revs up. It grows louder. My father and Vincent's hushed voices slip below the volume.

"Effie?" a soft voice calls out. "Effie?"

I move closer.

Celeste stands under the glow of the red exit sign above the door, half hidden beneath the hood of Matty's favorite North-western sweatshirt. She pushes back the hood. Her hair's mussed up, scooped into a hurried ponytail. A few glossy strands stick up in odd spots where the hood tugged them out of place. Even in the restaurant's dim lighting, she still glows, angel-bright and gorgeous. But something's off. Her eyes flick to the windows—left, right, up and down Buscato Drive. I get a hard and rash feeling from her. This isn't the Celeste I know. This girl looks more like me.

No, no, no. I blink hard. Then again. It's another mirror reflection screwing up what I thought I knew.

Reminder: she's a fairy, she's a glittery unicorn, she's a useless princess. She can't be crafty enough to get past locked doors. I push her aside and jiggle the door's push bar.

"How did you get in?" I ask.

"I know a lot about not getting caught." A flash of fright rips her eyes open wide.

I know a lot of things too. Of one I am certain: a girl like me snakes her way past locked doors. A girl like Celeste Vaughn does not. Particularly when the girl appears to suffer from a catastrophic degree of fear. She's super twitchy.

"What are you doing here? Where's Matty?" I ask.

"He went home. I came to talk to you alone."

For the first time, her words aren't laced with question marks. They are direct. I'm not sure who this girl is and what she did with Celeste. She whips her head around, spots Carlo. He lowers the Windex bottle.

"You can't just walk in here when we're closed." It's a stupid comment. But I can't think of anything else. And I don't want her here.

"I need to talk to you about Matthew."

Matty, Matty. I don't know this Matthew guy.

"Can you give him this?"

She passes me a folded notecard. On the outside is a generic pattern of a cross, exactly like the ones Carlo sends our family at Christmas. I'm not sure if I should flip it open—there's no envelope—so I glance at Celeste. She nods. I unfold it. Inside, the name Claudette Vega runs handwritten across the card. The mark crossing the double T in the first name is barely more than a stiff, hurried sideways slash hovering above the letters. A Santa Barbara street address takes up two lines below the name.

"What is this?"

"Tell Matty I left. He can find me there."

I'm so confused. "You were just with him. Why didn't you tell him then?"

"Things happened too fast."

"What things?"

"Just do it. *Please*." I don't like her tone. Her lips are hard and white.

"Can't you text him? Call him?"

"They might look at his phone. I can't risk it."

I thrust the thing back at her. "Look, I don't know what game you're playing. Give it to him yourself."

"I can't." Her eyes dart to the exit. "I don't have time to explain."

She lifts a finger to my face. Despite myself, I inch back. I know a threat when I see one. "I'm not coming back to Vista Buscato. Ever. You cannot tell a soul." Her voice hardens. She swings her finger to Carlo, another person she needs to warn. He pretends not to listen.

She backpedals to the door.

"Wait." I grab her arm. "You're leaving? What's with the name?"

What's with *all* the names?

She hitches the door open a crack and peers into the dark alleyway outside. Her head twists left, then right. She raises the hood of her sweatshirt. Tucks her hair underneath it.

"Tell him I'm sorry," she whispers.

It's almost impossible to hear her above the kitchen music. A man's voice croons, *"Ti adoro, ti adoro, adorrrrrrrooooo."*

She turns back once to say, "I wish I had more time, Effie. We could have been friends."

I highly doubt that.

The door snaps closed. I immediately crack it open to watch her leave. She's a lightning flash, running, already at the end of the alley. She pivots onto Buscato Drive. She's gone.

I don't understand. What the hell is going on? The glittery fairy-girl suddenly transforms into a midnight secret operative? This is insane. She literally vanished. I'm even more shocked than when she went all trapeze artist-acrobat ten years ago and jumped into the Fox Inn dumpster next to me.

I slip back into the restaurant and reread the note.

Caroline, Celeste, Claudette. Just like that—Celeste Vaughn doesn't exist anymore, if she ever did. I knew she was too good to be true.

The reality washes over me, thick and overwhelming.

Celeste's gone. She's *GONE*.

I prayed for this day and here it is. The proof sits in the notecard pinched between my fingers.

She's gone.

Carlo steps behind me. He squirts the Windex bottle all over the emergency exit door. Blue liquid drips from the push bar. He definitely lacks Vincent's precision and artistry.

"The Madaleo guy, that's his daughter," I say.

"You two in a fight?"

"No." Not a fight, a battle. And I won. "They arrested her father tonight at Town Hall."

Carlo nods like it's no big deal but I catch the way his Windex-spraying slows.

"His daughter's running away, I guess."

This town's going to be overrun with missing person posters. At least now I know my hunch is right. Sometimes you leave because you want to. It's not always a bad thing.

Carlo's eyes run over the notecard in my hand. "Keep that note safe."

He heads back into the kitchen, but his words linger. I don't want to think about how Matty will lose his shit when he reads this note. I don't want him to know about it at all.

Keep the note safe.

I'll do one better. I'll keep it to myself. I owe Celeste absolutely nothing. Only a few more weeks remain before Matty leaves for Northwestern, and the last thing I need is for him to spend the rest of his time in Santa Barbara when he could be enjoying his final moments in Vista Buscato with us. With me. He drifted a little thanks to her, but I'm not letting Celeste Madaleo or Claudette Vaughn or Caroline Vega or whoever the hell she is take him away from me permanently.

I have a second chance. I won't blow this opportunity.

Matty never needs to know. This girl's sketchiness is a brand of happy he doesn't need.

I will always do what's best for Matty. I am his rock, his anchor.

The note is the only thing left to deal with.

I bite my lip and think.

Kill it, suffocate it.

I rush into the kitchen and slip into the walk-in freezer before my father and Vincent see me. Deep, deep in the back, on a shelf high enough to need a stepstool to reach, just behind a bunch of bags of mixed vegetables, I pull out an old box of frozen mozzarella sticks, decaying from freezer burn since the day my mother declared that Fox Inn would bend with the times and try the upscale approach with its menu. Inside, underneath the last few cheese sticks, sits my wad of emergency money, my escape plan. Blue rubber bands wrap around stacks of bills—everything from singles to fives, tens, and higher. I've taken a page out of Phil Fox's playbook and stowed it all here, where no one would bother looking. Last time I counted, I had nearly enough to leave. I tuck the note under it all, close the box, shove it back on the shelf.

I slip out of the freezer and shut the door. Snap, click. Done.

Celeste might know a thing or two about getting past a locked door.

But about love, she's positively clueless.

Chapter Eighteen

It's a slow lunch crowd at Fox Inn for a late July day. Some family festival sucked all our business to Ventura. Seems every person in Vista Buscato headed there to fly kites, get the kids' faces painted, watch street performers, all that fun stuff. Frankly, I'd love some street fair cotton candy too, but here I am. Apron on. Order pad ready. Hating every minute of it, but loving the growing bubble of cash stuffed into my apron pocket.

Outside, the sharp grind of skateboards against the sidewalk hits my ears. I know who it is before I see them. The door swings open, and my people burst through like a sunrise.

Sam's first. Lucky boy has a day off. He tosses his skateboard behind the host's podium immediately, perfect rule-follower that he is.

Joe follows. He doesn't let go of his board.

Matty staggers in last. Puffy eyelids, swelled cheeks. This is the new habit accompanying his incessant musing over Celeste's whereabouts—alcohol poisoning and the resulting hang-over bloat. I think drinking to oblivion dulls his ache for her. Wish I had the nerve to tell him it only messes with your balance and personality. Just look at my mother. But I don't bother lecturing him. Celeste is gone. Capitalizing on her absence is my best shot at love. Her disappearance means I've slid back into the open slot at Matty's side. There's no place better.

The guys hop onto bar stools. I pour mimosas for a table of women sporting diamonds as large as gumdrops.

Matty slaps his palms against the bar. He jerks his head to Joe and Sam. "These jackasses won't help me." Joe rolls his eyes.

"With what?" I ask.

"I need someone to get inside Celeste's house and leave a message from me."

I stay quiet and busy myself lining the mimosas up on a tray. On the inside I'm screeching, screaming, tearing my hair out with, *She isn't there! I erased her! She doesn't exist anymore! Forget her!*

Sam jerks a thumb at Matty. "He's talking about breaking and entering now. Climbing fences is one thing. Burglarizing homes is straight up crazy."

Matty waves him off. "I'm not stealing anything. I just need someone to make it inside. I tried doing it legit. Getting past the security guard is impossible. The guy looked like he wanted to throw me off a bridge. My only route is the fence out back. I keep leaving notes for her, but they're still there the next day. I need to get into her house, directly into her bedroom."

"Why don't you go over the fence yourself?" Sam asks, always the logical one.

"I can't get caught."

Like any of us can.

Defying all logic, Matty clings to the belief that there's a reasonable explanation for Celeste's abrupt disappearance two weeks ago. Maybe she went on a trip and forgot to tell him. Or maybe her dad's got her on lockdown. Worst-case scenario: an epic misunderstanding drove Celeste away. He thinks it's possible the two of them hit a blip without him realizing it, and if he could just smooth it over, they'd shift back on track. The idea that she permanently left Vista Buscato hasn't occurred to him. Even after two solid weeks without contact. His faith in their love—the sheer strength of their bond—kills me.

Life would be so much easier if I could tell him the truth: *She's gone. Gone.*

I've won.

But I don't dare open my mouth.

I got what I wanted. Their romance is over. That's what matters.

Knowing I'm the direct cause of Matty's disappointment burns a hole in my heart. It wasn't a courageous move; it was cowardly. But with love comes sacrifice. I can carry a little guilt. Just a few more days and the old Matty will be back.

I finish arranging the mimosas on the tray. "I didn't think you'd need help anymore," I tell Matty carefully. "I mean, she hasn't been in touch for two weeks. Seems like she moved on, right?" I throw a hand into the air weakly and laugh. It's funny, isn't it? He chases after a girl who vanished into the California beaches or beyond, maybe even off the continent for all we know, and I'm supposed to trudge through land and sea to find her, all when he could easily have me, the girl who loves him and never leaves his side. Inches away. Close enough to kiss. It's absurd.

"You think I should just give up?" he says, incredulous.

"No. I-I didn't say that."

I swallow and swallow until the ache of tears rising in the back of my throat subsides.

On the contrary, I did think he'd give up.

I did think he'd realize he loves me back.

I did think we'd be together by now.

Crazy fucking thoughts.

No one speaks. Matty turns pleading eyes on us all.

Joe watches me, running a thumb along his jawline.

Someone drops silverware at a nearby table and I take the opportunity to look away from them all. If I make eye contact with Matty, he'll take it as an invitation, a sign I want to help. And I do, I always do. But not with this.

"Forget it," Matty says finally with phony nonchalance. "I'll try schmoozing the security guard again. One day he's bound to crack, right?"

Sam laughs. "Either that or he'll crack you over the head."

"Yeah." Matty smiles, but only slightly, and it fades in an instant.

My skin gets all twitchy. A surge rises in my throat. I hate seeing him like this.

"I'll go." The words burst out before I can stop myself with smart things like reasons not to.

Sam shakes his head. Joe rolls his eyes and lets out a long, "Psssshhh."

Matty leaps halfway over the bar and throws an arm across my shoulder for a hug. "I fucking love this girl," he says.

For a split second, I don't know if he's talking about me or Celeste, until he follows with, "She never lets me down," and I realize it's me. Thank God.

Joe's eyes drill through to my core. *Always the sucker*, I bet he's thinking. He wouldn't be wrong.

I suddenly feel dumb and self-conscious. I pull away from Matty and say, "How do you suggest I accomplish this task without an arrest?"

"You'll have to climb the fence again."

Disappointment rips me open. I try to toss it aside, but it's in my eyes, my open mouth.

One of the ladies at table six makes eye contact. I hurry over with their mimosas.

The restaurant door opens wide. Gerard pops up like lightning, a bunch of menus in hand. In walks Detective Brimley with a younger officer in plain clothes, a shiny badge hanging from a chain around his neck. Another detective. Brimley holds up a hand, pushing off Gerard's greetings and menus. Gerard flips him off behind his back. I silently cheer for my asshole big brother who, at a bare minimum, seems to understand the fundamentals of good character.

Brimley approaches the bar. I make my way back with an empty tray.

Out of nowhere, my father pulls up alongside me.

"Game on," he whispers.

"Good morning, Detective," I say, hoping my eyes deliver all the nasty comments my mouth cannot. "Can I get you a drink? Bloody Mary? Mimosa?"

Maybe cyanide? Something stronger?

"No, thank you. I'm here on business." Like that's ever stopped him from a freebie.

Joe flicks a bored chin-nod at the detective as a greeting, like he doesn't have time for Brimley's bullshit. I wish I could do the same.

Brimley slides a picture from his pocket. "You kids know this young lady?" The detective passes it around.

The picture's rubbed raw around the edges and creased across the middle, no doubt from spending countless hours wedged between Brimley's ass and the police cruiser's seats. But the person in it shines bright, as always. Nothing dulls her sparkle. It's Celeste. She isn't the focus of the shot, though. Two little kids fill the center of the image, with orange wedges tucked into their mouths, the peels covering their teeth as they ham it up for the camera. Celeste stands in the far right background, smiling at something outside the frame. It's some kind of party, like a barbecue or get-together. Not the fancy, downtown Vista Buscato type, but the ones in the parts of town where normal people live. In the way, way, left corner of the photo, I spot the edge of a black lamppost with a house number dangling from it. The number's too far and too blurred.

But I know what it means. This was taken at Las Palmas Altas. Rumildo Walk.

Sam and Joe shrug. They never met Celeste. The girl in the photo is a nobody.

Matty's not paying attention. In the usual routine, my father slides him a bowl of Lucky Charms across the bar. Matty hovers over the bowl, as if he can bury himself in sugar-coated whole grains and marshmallows and pretend the detective isn't there. I can almost hear his theme song playing in the background—a sad whine of country music telling a tale of lost love, hangovers, and broken dreams. He shovels cereal into his mouth.

Brimley shoves the picture at Matty. He finally lifts his head to take a look. His entire face bursts open at the sight of Celeste. He snatches the picture. "Yes! I know her!"

"Can you tell me her name?"

"Celeste Vaughn."

The two detectives exchange a look I can't interpret. I don't dare acknowledge that I know her too. Or that her name is no longer Celeste Vaughn.

"You know her well?"

Matty glances quickly at me. "She's my girlfriend."

Her promotion to girlfriend blows my fucking mind. From the smirk on Joe's face, I see he wasn't notified of the official title change either. I want to sweep my arms across the top shelf of liquor bottles behind me and send everything crashing to the ground. After all the fireworks and declarations of love and pause buttons, it shouldn't come as a surprise. Still, I figured I could sidestep the actual words. Especially now with her gone.

Detective Brimley holds out a hand to take the picture back.

Matty pulls it closer to his chest.

The other detective slides a tiny notepad from his breast pocket, scribbles something. "Can you tell us where she is?" he asks, more urgent than Brimley. "This girlfriend of yours?"

Enough with that word.

Matty's eyes ping pong back and forth between the two detectives. "Is everything okay? Is she hurt?"

"That's what we'd like to find out."

"I haven't seen her in two weeks."

Brimley props a leg up onto a barstool's footrest. "No contact at all?"

"None."

"No calls? No texts?"

"No, no. Not at all."

A pulse of joy fills me when Matty affirms—again—that he hasn't seen Celeste in two weeks. I hope the daily count grows higher and higher, weeks turning into decades, until she's not even a name, she's that girl he only vaguely recalls, the one with the platinum hair.

"Can you give us her phone number?"

"She doesn't have a phone of her own. She picks up those buy-and-toss cells and dumps them once she eats up the minutes."

"What about a landline at home?"

"She...uh...I—I don't know." Matty's eyes flicker. "She never gave me the number."

Brimley's eyebrows creep together. I don't know if Matty is telling the truth or not. But I bet if there were a phone, Celeste's dad would not have shared the number. "How did the two of you get in touch if you have no way of reaching her?"

Matty breaks eye contact with the detective. It's monumentally embarrassing to announce that someone is your girlfriend and then admit your interaction with her has been limited. He must know how stupid that sounds. I think I'm supposed to do something supportive, like pat his back or offer an apologetic smile, but I take Joe's cue and don't move a muscle. "We had a routine," Matty answers. "Every morning we'd go to Bella Via Pharmacy. That's where we met."

"And one morning she didn't arrive as planned?"

"Exactly."

"And she hasn't been in touch since?"

"Right."

Brimley chuckles softly. "This is all very hard to believe, Matthew."

"It's true." Matty looks to me, then Joe, then Sam, like he can't understand Brimley's level of crazy, and can we? Sam rubs the top of his hair. Joe looks away.

"You sure about that?"

"Yeah. I've been looking all over for her."

"Really."

"Really!"

The other detective writes something in his notepad.

"Where have you looked?"

"Everywhere. All the spots we went together."

"Like?"

Matty shifts. "To a coffee place on Everdear Road—can't re-member the name of it. And to La Jolie Dame, Joselle's Sweet Shoppe, the ferry in Ventura, the movie theater in Oxnard." His eyes skim to me, then pop quickly back to the detective before he lets out the next spot. "To Huntington Beach, at a bed and breakfast that we stayed at when her dad left town overnight once. I thought maybe...I don't know...maybe she'd go back."

I clamp my teeth down on my tongue. If I don't do something to erase the vision of Matty and Celeste waking up in a romantic bed and breakfast, feeding each other forkfuls of waffles and whipped cream in the morning after a night of naked gymnastics in a fluffy rented bed with sheets as platinum white as her hair, I will lose my mind. I will lose my fucking mind.

Brimley breaks the silence. "Of course, you checked where she lives first, right?"

Matty stalls. His tone shifts lower. "I don't know where she lives, Detective. Her father doesn't allow visitors, so I never went to her house."

I sense the warning in Matty's voice: *Effie, keep your mouth shut.*

Brimley rolls his lips inward. "Hmmmm."

Something's off.

His nodding shifts from *Sure, sure, I believe you* to *You're talking shit, boy, and we both know it.*

Joe doesn't move a muscle. His eyes never leave Brimley's face.

Half packed with laughter and half choked with desperation, Matty blurts out, "You don't suspect I'm involved with her disappearance, do you?"

"Come on, Matty. Why would I suspect a good kid like you in the disappearance of two local women?" From his breast pocket, Brimley unfolds a yellow flyer with the face of the girl who went missing in May. "Are you familiar with this young lady?"

"Sure," Matty says. "That's Jessie Winters. She graduated a few years before me. We weren't friends, though. I only knew her in passing."

Prickles of doubt pass over my skin. That girl—Jessie. I thought for sure she was a runaway. She can't be a victim. She just can't.

Brimley slips the flyer back into his pocket. "How well do you know Celeste's father?"

"Never met him."

"Did she ever indicate what he was like? Was she afraid of him?"

"Not at all. He was strict. I know that. But she seemed cool with it." Matty's eyes dart to me. Again, another warning to keep my trap shut. Celeste didn't exactly seem like the type to tell her father off, but I wouldn't describe her as *cool* with his rules. "Detective, what's going on? Is her father in trouble or something?"

"Depends what you mean by 'in trouble,' son. He's disappeared too."

My father takes this tense moment to work the hell out of a silver cocktail shaker, one thumb clamped over the top, throwing it up and down like his life depends on it. Ice clatters inside. The sound fogs up Brimley's question and answer session.

Brimley tilts his head at my father and smiles.

No words, just a look. *I'm taking care of business here. Would you mind quieting down?*

My father sends back the same smile but keeps shaking.

Brimley's gaze lifts over my father's shoulder to the faces of Carlo and Vincent, their foreheads pressed against the kitchen door's panes of glass as they survey the situation like gossipy old women. Both heads simultaneously drop when caught by the detective.

My mother materializes out of nowhere, pushing plates of fruit salad at each detective. Vincent went nuts with artsy drizzles of caramel over the berries.

"Phil," the detective says, spearing a blueberry. "I'd like a word with your kitchen staff. Can you send them out?"

"No can do. My boys are on work time right now." The two men's smiles stay locked in place. It's like a physical anomaly. Who knew muscles could stay clenched that long? "An omelet can burn in less than a minute," my father explains. "Gotta keep my customers satisfied so they don't stray." He winks at the detective like it's some kind of filthy inside joke.

Brimley's smile frays at the edges. "That's a shame. I guess I'll have to order them down to the station for questioning then."

"Shut up, Phil," my mother growls. "I'll bring them out to you, detective."

My father's eyes bug. A frown pulls at his mouth.

Carlo and Vincent file out of the kitchen. My mother waves them on, practically dragging them by the sleeves of their white chef coats.

"Hey there, guys," Brimley says. "Fantastic job on these fruit salads. They're excellent."

Carlo and Vincent cast sideways glances at each other.

Brimley's smile is so fake I could gag. Matty throws me an eye roll. The detective rarely ever puts politeness or kindness above his arrest record or his desire for a promotion, which he is not shy about mentioning. He's up to something.

"So," he says, raising a finger. *Here it is,* I think. *The real reason.* "I'm looking for a man involved with the Dia de La Madonna Mission on Hibisco Street. Know anything about that place, gentlemen?"

Carlo's eyes flip from their usual sunny to a storm of clouds. A mumble leaves his lips.

The detective's eyes narrow. "Excuse me?"

Vincent smacks a hand against Carlo's pudgy arm.

"I know my rights," Carlo says. "You can't ask me stuff without a lawyer."

Joe smiles but pulls it off like he's chewing on the corner of his mouth.

"Correction, my friend." *Friend* comes out of the detective forcefully, deliberately. "I cannot question you in custody without a lawyer present. But you're not in custody. I'm free to ask anything I want."

"And I'm free to ignore you." Carlo shrugs.

My mother's mouth drops.

My father's head swings back and forth between them like he can't believe what he's hearing and he doesn't know how to stop the madness.

Detective Brimley directs his attention at Vincent next. "How about you, pal? Know anything about the people who work at Dia de La Madonna?"

Vincent shakes his head. A sheen of sweat glistens below his hooked nose.

"I'm looking for a guy who goes by the name John Vallone."

I've heard that last name before.

James Madaleo.

Kevin Vaughn.

John Vallone.

Celeste's father.

Chapter Nineteen

I am a stone. I don't move. I don't breathe.

I look at Matty for any sign of interest in the conversation. He's still busy staring at Brimley's picture of Celeste. Perhaps he's never met all the aliases. When it comes to Celeste Vaughn, he doesn't know the half of it.

Vincent's gaze stays fixed on the ground. He shakes his head some more.

"You don't know him?"

No response.

"Well." The Sherriff stabs a forkful of banana and bobs his head up and down in this condescending way, like he's negotiating with children. "Word around the precinct is he spends time at the shelter. If no one has any answers, I'll poke around there. Maybe I'll make a surprise visit. I hear drug dealers frequent that spot. We'll make some arrests while we're at it."

From the way Vincent gasps, I know it's not true.

My father tries to rope the conversation back a bit. "That's a pretty serious allegation. Carlo and Vincent only volunteer at the shelter every once in a while. We donate our leftover produce there. It's not a drug den. As far as I know, it's some sort of soup kitchen or…" He rolls his hand in the air, looking for the words. "I don't know. A homeless shelter or something. Folks there probably have enough heartache without being raided by the police."

"The Pope himself could work there and I wouldn't care. Between you and me, Phil, I'm banking on a high-profile arrest or two at that place. I could walk away with high numbers. The kind that makes people feel safer at night." The detective chews on a sliced strawberry.

"Right," my father says slowly. "Still aiming for that promotion, huh?"

They smile, but the air around them grows icy. The other detective shifts from foot to foot. He hasn't touched the fruit salad.

Carlo and Vincent hurry back to the kitchen. The conversation shifts, but the mood does not. Somewhere in between Detective Brimley concluding his interrogation of Carlo and Vincent and taking his last forkful of fruit, he shoots out about five veiled threats that Fox Inn might lose its liquor license when the new hotel opens up at the end of the street. This sounds like a steaming pile of crap to me. For one, how does he even know that? He doesn't issue liquor licenses. My mother frets over it. She hustles to the kitchen and returns with two Styrofoam take-out trays of apple pie for the detectives.

"Eh. Don't worry about it, Felicia," my father says. "We're in the clear." He shows his cards when he tugs the cigarette from over his ear and pops it into the corner of his mouth. Getting closer. Just a flick of a lighter and this week's smoke-free streak comes to an end.

"You sound pretty confident, Phil," the detective says.

"I've got an in with the Board. Peter LaRoche owes me."

"How?"

My father's eyes explode with possibilities. Like when he's rigged a new betting scheme to snake big bucks away from the top-shelf drinkers in town. I'm struck by how much his expression matches Joe's after being caught doing something utterly reckless and stupid, but perfectly amazing. He says, simply. "Favors go both ways in this town."

Brimley plucks the picture of Celeste from Matty's hand and tucks it back into his ass pocket. He and his lookalike file out the door, with Brimley carrying both apple pie bribes in his hands.

My father slams the cocktail shaker down on the bar. His smile is gone. A string of curses flies from his mouth, aimed at my mother. A few customers' heads turn. He's broken Fox Family Rule Number Two: don't air your dirty laundry in front of customers. My mother will tear his head off. They take their bickering to the kitchen, where my father swings the doors open wide enough that they bang back and forth.

An avalanche of fear rolls off Matty. "What the hell was that all about?"

Joe shrugs. "Celeste's dad probably owed people money. Maybe he stiffed the wrong person and now the cops are involved."

They discuss the whereabouts of the most impressive girl on earth. I try to stay a part of the conversation. I really do. But my brain can't help rewinding and freeze-framing at the moment I became a part in her disappearance. The information everyone wants is scrawled on a notecard and stuffed under some decaying mozzarella sticks a few feet away in the kitchen. The name—the name pings around my head. *Claudette Vega. Claudette Vega.*

Detective Brimley's looking for the wrong person. Or people.

The Vaughns don't exist anymore.

That girl was always too good to be true. My decision not to give Matty her message feels—finally—like the best bet. Whatever she's involved in, whoever her father is, whoever she is, Matty doesn't need to get tangled up in it too.

But he won't let it go. "What if something bad happened to her?"

"That doesn't explain why her dad's gone too," I say.

"What if he went psycho and hurt her?"

I shake my head. "Carlo and Vincent know him. He works at a shelter. He's good people."

"You don't know that, Effie. You don't know her like I did."

Sam spits out a laugh. "Bro, you don't get extra points because you got in her pants."

The image strikes me again, of the two of them in a romantic, quiet room in a Huntington Beach bed and breakfast, candles everywhere, a warm breeze blowing through the windows, his skin sliding against her skin, and all that comes after. *Oh God, no.* I don't know if it's true, but the thought—the mere idea of it—rips me apart.

I'm about to tell Sam to lay off, but the words stall in my throat. I'm sick, just sick.

Matty's not amused. He shoves his cereal bowl. Milk sloshes over the edges. He jumps off his barstool and grabs his board. No goodbyes. Fox Inn's doors slam behind him.

"Good going," I say and swat the side of Sam's head with my order pad.

Sam sighs and goes after Matty.

I turn on Joe. "Why can't you two be supportive?"

He pops a handful of salted peanuts into his mouth from a small bowl on the bar. Probably the only food he's eaten today aside from goldfish. "Listen," he says mid-chew. "I don't want her to be hurt or..." He looks like he might say something worse but thinks better of letting the words take shape on his tongue. "Or whatever. But..." Dark hair swings on either side of his face. He draws me closer with a curved finger. "I'm not sorry she's gone," he whispers. With an open mouth, I feign shock at his callousness. But I am the biggest faker alive. Because I totally agree. "Don't tell me you're not tired of hearing about that girl. The guy acts like he didn't have friends before he met her. Classic Matty."

Silently, I repeat his words until a hundred of them overflow in my mouth: *Classic Matty. Classic Matty.* That can't be true. It isn't.

He puts a hand on my arm. The warm feeling jars me out of my Matty stupor. "You still coming to check out the Wiley place tonight? Or are you getting sucked into Matty's problems now?"

Two battle plans have been drawn, and I'm some kind of general or lieutenant in each.

On the one side: Joe's Skate-ify The Town Movement.

On the other: Matty's Finding Celeste Crusade.

I love Matty, but I can't take much more talk of a girl I know isn't coming back.

"Sure. I'll meet you at Wiley after my shift ends," I say.

"Change of plans. Me and Sam will pick you up after work. I have to buy a mattress."

"What happened? Finally wet your bed to the point of disaster?"

He grins. "Nope. I'm moving out."

"What? How? Where are you going?" This is epic. It's the moment you live your whole life for. I have wads of money wrapped in blue rubber bands in the Fox Inn freezer for this exact reason.

"A place on Third Avenue. Bruiser's cousin needs a roommate." He shrugs, as if to say *might as well go for it*. "You'll come by when I move in, right? If you're still in town?"

I ignore that last statement. Who knows where I'll be anymore.

"Wow," I breathe. "That is so great."

"Figured it was time. My sister's growing like wildfire." His brown eyes always get sweet and sparkly he mentions her. It's adorable. "She'll need my room eventually. My mom and Tim think it's a good start, so..." His talking trails off.

Something tells me this move wasn't entirely Joe's idea.

Regardless, I'm happy for him. And more than a touch jealous. "I'm psyched for you," I say. I mean it.

His gaze drops downward. He doesn't look me in the eye when he says, "You'll come hang, right? Once I'm all moved in?"

My heartbeat pounds against my ribs, like it wants to fly the hell out of my chest. I'm suddenly warm all over. I suppose he caught the way I conveniently sidestepped the question a moment ago.

"Of course I will." I mean that, too.

He looks me in the eyes and smiles now. Something takes flight inside me again. He takes another scoop of peanuts, then slides off the barstool. A totally weird feeling of loss hits me square in the chest. I don't want him to go just yet.

"Guess I'm not the only one who likes your attention," he says.

I fumble for something to say.

A thread of weird tension hangs between us.

He motions to table four behind me. I spin around. The customers wave with the international signal for, "Get your ass over here with our check."

Joe drops his board to the floor and skates away. He pulls off an earsplitting, grunting powerslide just before he reaches the doors. It sounds like a zipper closing. Customers' heads snap up. Gerard whistles from the host podium. Joe's wheels leave a rubbery, opaque streak across the hardwood floors.

He tosses up a peace sign. "Catch you later." That grin is back—the one that acknowledges he's done something he shouldn't and you wouldn't dare counter with a ban on it.

Things flip over and under and back and forth inside my stomach. I try to shake the feeling—it's not normal, not the natural vibe between me and him. But it happens again, even after the door closes behind him.

CHAPTER TWENTY

Sam has a nosebleed.

He squeezes, he pinches, tips his face to the ceiling. Nothing helps.

We're in a mattress store on Condor Boulevard, and the bald guy pushing Joe to fork over a few thousand bucks for the Tesla of mattresses doesn't look like he has spare tissues in the pockets of his wrinkled, gray suit.

Joe presses each mattress until his fingers disappear into the memory foam. Sam and I hang back. Around us, everything is white, white, white. The mattresses, the pillows, the walls, even the catalogues propped in plastic stands beside each model. Everything with the exception of three small, round circles of blood on the tiled floor at Sam's feet.

"Shit," he mutters, backing away, horrified.

He jets outside, skateboard in tow. The bells above the store's door tinkle. I follow him.

I once watched Sam lean over a trash pail in English class until his nose dried out. Ben Dillon, your run-of-the-mill geek whose mother worked in our school's main office, kept shouting, "Out, damn spot, out!" at the trail of dotted blood Sam left between his seat and the trash. Later, Matty told me it was a line from Shakespeare. Figures. I never liked Ben Dillon.

Outside, the evening air envelops us. Blood drops to the sidewalk at Sam's feet. Desperation smothers his face. I want to help, but the last time I carried Kleenex in my pocket I was five. I'm useless.

He moans.

The store's doorbells chime again.

Joe marches out of the store behind us, eyebrows pressed together in concern. He yanks off his t-shirt and presses it to Sam's nose. Joe is more ripped now than I remember. Shadows and valleys of muscle ridges cover his chest and arms and stomach. This summer I've been working so much that I haven't seen him in a pool or at the beach or wherever. I've had no opportunity to see him shirtless. And maybe that's a good thing because I'm clearly embarrassing myself with the way I'm staring. I think he notices too. He presses his lips together like he's smothering a smirk. I struggle to focus on Sam instead.

Joe's cotton t-shirt is a dusty almond color, a shade or two lighter than Sam's skin, and the blood sinks into it, soaking through instantaneously. For a moment, I think the shirt's base color will mask the blood stain, make it appear more like spilled soda or a smear of chocolate, less embarrassing, less blood and gore. But no such luck. The stain balloons outward in a circle, bold and dark and bloody as ever.

"It won't stop." His words are throaty and deep. He throws his head back and piles the shirt on top of his nose and mouth.

"You'll be okay," I say, then quickly add, "Don't worry," though I know he will.

He mumbles something but it drowns in his throat.

Joe reaches past me and grabs Sam's shoulder. The brush of Joe's warm, bare chest against my arm ruins my focus. He's been shirtless around me one hundred thousand times over the years. But something about our skin skimming together now runs through me like a zap. Deeply, weirdly. I push the feeling away.

"Let's call your Dad," Joe suggests. "Maybe he can pick you up."

"No way." It's an epic, throat-clogging nosebleed, but still the words come out crystal clear. General Wills does not tolerate weakness. And there's nothing weaker than a future soldier sweating a run-of-the-mill nosebleed.

No one mentions Matty as an option. It's no secret he's role-playing Sherlock Holmes, hunting for clues at Las Palmas Altas to find a sweetheart who doesn't want to be found.

Two girls in yoga outfits walk by carrying takeout pizza boxes from the newest pizzeria on the corner, the one with the expensive, artisanal, organic crust, and brick oven-fired nonsense. God forbid we offer people plain dough, sauce, and cheese in Vista Buscato. No wonder everyone here is so damn spoiled. The girls' gazes linger on Joe's bare chest. As I watch them slide into a black leather-bedecked BMW, I want to shout, "You're not his type!" but they wouldn't hear me through the closed windows. Both of them missed Sam's predicament. Which is very much a good thing.

"I'm going home to change my shirt." Sam gestures to the line of blood down his front.

"Wait. We'll find you a ride." Joe whips out his phone. "I'll call Edgar."

"It's okay. I got my board." He gestures limply to the deck beneath his right foot.

"Dude, wait. We'll all go. We can skitch."

"No thanks, bro. I'm in no shape to skitch. I don't wanna die." Sam misses the irony in the pint of blood he's already lost. "I'll catch up with you guys at the Wiley place later." He takes off, lifting his non-bloodied hand in a salute. He lands a picture-perfect ollie off the sidewalk, even with one hand still pressed to his nose. We don't give that kid enough credit.

"He'll need a blood transfusion by the time he makes it home," I say.

"He'll be okay. He's tougher than he thinks."

I love Sam, but I'm not sure I agree.

Back inside the store, we bounce-test every mattress until the bald salesman exhales in rapid succession so heavily that I think he'll hyperventilate. Joe finally chooses a cushiony one. Not the upscale model, but not the bargain basement, either. Perfect for a guy on a budget who's saved a few bucks collecting a paycheck from a skate shop.

"They'll deliver it in three weeks," Joe says as we skate away down Condor Boulevard. I nod. I'm trying hard not to look at his tanned skin and ripped pecs. "Sam and Matty will be gone by then." I know this. I'm trying not to dwell on it. "That leaves you in charge of my housewarming party."

The same small grin he wore when he signed the sales slip is glued to his face.

I'm so jealous. Everything aches. Even my bones.

I wish I could have that feeling, too. I want to smile so hard on the inside that it busts its way through until I can't hide it.

Joe has the whole world at his fingertips. He can start fresh, do anything he wants. I wish I had those endless possibilities, open roads leading to a future where I'm not scribbling on an order pad about how some cranky old lady doesn't want onions in her arugula salad.

I want to be happy. I want something or someone real to care about. I want someone who cares about me. I know Matty does. But I want him to care *only* about me. Is that too much to ask?

"Come on," he says. "I want us to be the first ones there."

Joe cruises across the double yellow lines in the middle of Condor Boulevard on his brand new longboard with the pintail. His trucks are loosey-goosey, so he carves all over the place, and it's a wonder his wheels don't bite the deck on the turns. We roll together to the end of Condor Boulevard, where storefronts give way to the sloping lawns of Vista Buscato's Board members and other elites. My fingers itch to throw rocks at all the pretty things around me.

Joe waves me onto the turn at Halberd Court. The Wiley estate spreads before us.

The mansion itself is the kind of place you see aerial shots of in celebrity magazines. Except that since it's been abandoned, it's a wreck of out-of-control vines climbing the bricks, overgrown dead grass, and windows coated with grime. But beneath the layers of dust, I can easily imagine how beautiful it once was, when people gave a shit about it. It's the kind of impressive place you wouldn't see on the outskirts of town where us normal people live.

The lawn spreads and rolls in a speckled tan and brown cover of scorched landscaping that's been left to burn in the sun. It's been a few years since the owners left, when Fox Inn customers started whispering about bank foreclosures and liens and shit I know nothing about. A maintenance company came to drain the pool not long after the Wiley family left and the moving trucks disappeared. An empty pool with sloped sides is a supremely lucky thing for a bunch of skate rats. You know what they say about one man's trash being another man's treasure, right?

I follow Joe up the long driveway loop around the back of the property to the patio. We're first to arrive. To my surprise, Joe doesn't drop into the pool immediately. He leaves his board on the burnt grass and sits on the edge of the deep end. He scoots closer, then lowers himself a drop. His elbows bend, supporting all his weight. Locked muscles tighten across his chest and shoulders as he hovers there, legs dangling. I hang back, trying desperately not to stare at his bare skin, and brace myself for what this guy with the notoriously unpredictable streak will do next. He pauses—counts out loud, "*One, two, three*"—and lets go. In one swoop, he slides on his ass down the sloped wall of the pool to the deep end's bottom.

Somehow he manages it without ripping all the skin off his bare back. He lies flat at the bottom, hair splayed out around his head. The drain's a few feet away.

He waves at me. "Dive in, the water's perfect."

Black block letters on the stones around the pool's deep end spell out 15 feet. I would have guessed thirty. Looking down at Joe, it seems at least that much of a drop.

"Come in," he presses. "Check out the sky."

I follow his gaze upward. Stars pepper the night's ceiling. A few palm tree fronds float in and out of view, swaying, framing the picture.

I swing my legs over the edge of the pool, same as Joe did.

"There's a ladder down at the shallow end."

I glare at him. When have I ever taken the easy way out? I lower myself till my elbows bend as far as they can without snapping. The muscles in my arms quiver.

"Careful," Joe murmurs.

"Buzzkill." I wish he'd shut up with the human warning sign thing.

Matty's absence echoes off the sides of the pool. He wouldn't say something like that. He'd be my hero, he'd cheer me on. But he's not here, because chasing Celeste is all he ever wants to do. My arms quake at the truth I can't seem to win against. An image floats into my head space. It's Matty, freckles on fire. He races up and down the aisles at Bella Via Pharmacy, searching for Celeste, doing double takes at every blond he sees. He doesn't know he won't find her standing between the toothpaste and mouthwash in Aisle 3. He won't find her at all, ever. Because Celeste Vaughn put her trust in me, and I used all the courage in my soul to make sure she doesn't get her happy ending if it means she'll take away mine.

I lose focus on dropping into the pool. My brain doesn't fully sync up with my body and my elbows can't take the weight. I can't think clearly with Matty and Celeste filling all the available space in my head. I let go. I wind up at the bottom, curled like a newborn, elbows on fire. I gasp.

Joe winces. "I told you to be careful."

I jump to standing. Walk it off. "It doesn't hurt."

Explanations start spewing from my mouth, of why I dropped down like I have some form of palsy, because I feel the need to clarify why I'd screw up what should've been an easy motion. I wasn't afraid; I was distracted. It happens. Obviously I don't tell Joe that thoughts of Matty's vanishing act tonight tore my brain from my skull at a critical moment. I don't explain that the notecard I stashed in Fox Inn's freezer rents more space in my brain these days than the important things—like movement and whatnot.

"Here." Joe pats the space next to him.

I give in and plop down.

The cement's sort of cold, but it's refreshing. I kick my shoes off. My sweaty feet—gluey and wet inside my Vans—are grateful for the relief. After the initial shock subsides, I barely feel the ripped skin on my elbows. A kind of fiery numbness settles in. I'm fine. I've had worse.

Joe exhales with a little moan. "This is heaven."

"No. It's just Vista Buscato."

"It's still perfect."

Joe launches into a nonstop, ten-minute rundown of the plans he and Edgar devised to turn this pitiful, forgotten property into the skate park we've always dreamed of. Wedges and pyramids, steps, railings, a giant half-pipe. He reminds me about the shitload of people he invited to the Wiley estate later tonight, to test out the pool, check out the land in general, take a look at the patio steps to see whether they should stay or go. It sounds great. The only problem is the location. Dead end Vista Buscato.

"Joe, do you ever feel weird that you're not leaving? At the end of the summer, I mean. Don't you feel...I don't know. Stuck, maybe?"

"I can leave. I don't want to."

"Just so we're clear, I think you might be lying to yourself. Don't you want to see other places? I know I do."

"Who says we won't? We can travel any time we want. What does that have to do with the place we call home?"

"Being stuck here certainly makes going places hard."

"No." He shakes his head. His hair shimmies on the pool's cement floor. "I can have a future here, same as anywhere else, and I can leave any time I want. It's not about being stuck. It's a choice. Some people choose to go. I choose to stay."

"But why? Why would you choose that?" It's crazy.

He smacks his lips like he's given it great thought and his only answer is this: "Everyone I care about is here. Why wouldn't I stay?"

But that's exactly my problem, isn't it? No one here cares about me except Matty. And he's halfway out the door.

I sigh. "You're trying to give me the It-Isn't-Where-You-Go-It's-Who-You're-With lecture, aren't you? It sounds like a cop out. Especially because we're not the kind of people who are going places anyway."

"What's all this shit about 'going places'? Like you only live half a life if you don't work in a high-rise office building wearing a suit all day. Or if you only settle for one spot on the map. Look at this." He sweeps an arm around the pool and all that's above. "If this isn't the best place in the world, then I don't know what is."

I think about the palm trees tickling the sun, the never-ending way the cliffs at Buscato Point seem to climb into the sky and bring you with them. It's beautiful, no argument there. But just because Vista Buscato has palm trees doesn't mean it's paradise.

"Life keeps moving no matter what, Effie," Joe chimes in again. "What difference does your dot on the map make? Don't buy into that bullshit. You can search the whole planet, get yourself a camel ride in the desert, eat dim sum in Korea, ride a gondola in Venice, see the Mona Lisa, whatever. Travel around until you're broke. But when you're done, you'll want to come home and sit on a couch and bullshit with people you care about. For me, that's where my family is. I'm setting my camp up here." He slaps the cement.

Except he misses one crucial point: I don't have a family who cares about me. I have bosses and a screw-up for a brother with shared DNA. That's all. I will have no problem leaving this place behind. It left me a long, long time ago.

He taps the cement with his heel. "Takes more guts to stay than to leave."

I'm so over this discussion. He doesn't understand. "Whatever, Dalai Lama," I say. "You're in an awfully spiritual mood."

"I'm being serious."

"Obviously. Too. Way too."

He flips sideways onto an elbow. "Be honest. Do you really want to get out of here or are you just following him?"

My eyes fly to his face.

Him. The *him* that means everything.

I go for the nonreactive reaction. The one where I play off my immediate shock at his words as the need to cough. When I'm done pretending, I say, "I'm not following Matty. I'm just...ready to go. And since he's ready, too, it seems...natural." My bumbling words probably indicate that Joe hit a nerve or, more accurately, attacked the nerve with a sledgehammer.

He groans. "You're setting up your whole life and future based on Matty Pomerantz. Don't you realize he doesn't have a plan? He doesn't even have to. He's not leaving Vista Buscato for some courageous adventure. He's going to college. Good for him. I'm not knocking school, but when it comes to Matty, everything's all bought and paid for and it isn't even his money. He'll sleep in a cozy dorm room and eat three square meals approved by the dieticians in the dorm cafeteria. That's not reality, man."

I look away. He's wrong. But being defensive takes up too much energy right now.

"Where is he, anyway?" Joe asks.

"Where else? Looking for Celeste."

"I thought he'd be done by now. I told him to meet us here."

"He'll show up eventually."

"Whatever."

This new line of questioning bothers the hell out of me. "Why do you care what he's doing?" I say.

"Don't you?"

I shrug. But I do care. God, I totally, totally do. "I don't see why it matters."

"I thought for sure you'd be jumping fences with him. Like usual. Not here with me."

"Sometimes another friend needs moral support buying a mattress. I'm flexible like that."

"Speaking of support," he begins before a pause, "you're in on the Founder's Day protest, right? I can count on you?"

This is the part where I try not to outwardly cringe. Joe's bright idea to crash next month's Founder's Day Parade with a public protest will almost certainly result in my ass hitting a bench in a jail cell again. Aside from my parents' pain in the ass lectures about my future and responsibility and the fate of Fox Inn, I have no interest in sweating out all the moisture in my body while I roast in one of those tiny, cement hot boxes at the police station. God only knows why it doesn't bother him either. I heard his mom and stepdad forced him to stay in that holding cell overnight after the Town Hall meeting to teach him a lesson. I obviously don't need to point out how ineffective their method was.

Hope spills over in Joe's dark eyes. Above all else, I believe in him, and I think his push to fight for his place in Vista Buscato is a good thing. If Vista Buscato is where he wants to be, who am I to tell him he's wrong? Friends back each other's dreams, no matter what.

"Sure. I'm in," I say. "Whatever you need."

"Think we can get Matty there too?"

"Of course," I say, sounding a little too cheery.

"I'm not convinced. These days he's...I don't know. He's pretty much gone already."

"Not with me he's not."

I catch Joe biting his lower lip. "Sure about that?"

The question crushes me, squeezes me inside. "What do you mean?"

"I just want you to be careful, that's all."

The warning sounds suspiciously like the red flag you'd give a friend who's about to kiss the really hot, really delinquent guy everyone knows is bad news. Which, ironically, is the same speech I've heard countless girls recite to each other over the years in the bathrooms at Vista Buscato High School about Joe himself.

"What's the use of that?" I say. "Sam's careful. Look where it gets him."

"Some injuries you can't bounce back from."

His warning replays in my head. *Be careful*. We aren't talking about physical injuries. I think he means heartbreak.

"Shut up," I say, because I need a topic change, fast. "Are you stoned?"

"No. Gave that shit up."

"Really? When?"

"A long time ago."

"No," I say. "I would've noticed."

"When do you notice anything besides Matty?"

I ignore him because I don't have a good answer. "You're too serious tonight. What happened to badass Joe?"

He flips onto his back again. Throws an arm over his eyes. "Being crazy and flying on impulse doesn't always work. Not when you give a shit about someone. I'm still trying to figure out how to peel those two halves of myself apart."

I wish I knew what he meant by that.

Chapter Twenty-One

The dead grass around the Wiley estate is so parched and dry that I'm truly fearful flames will kick up if the cheap fireworks Bruiser and my brother are setting off throw out sparks. Because when people like us party, we go all out. 911 calls from terrified neighbors are the norm.

Joe eyeballs me from the crowd now gathered around the pool. Edgar's here too.

They both wave. I lift a hand, but my torn-up elbow barely bends.

They expect me to hang with them, talk sponsorships and comps and whatever. And I want to. But Matty's also here. It's been just a few hours since I saw him at Fox Inn, and he's now drunker than ever. He wags a blue glow stick in circles like it's his job. One critical element I've learned from having a mother who enjoys a cocktail or seven is that when you're this bombed, at some point everything will go one thousand percent wrong. I can't leave him. Bravery, or desperation, depending how you look at it, moved him to try (again) sweet-talking his way past the security guard at the entrance to Las Palmas Altas. Sam and I cringe as Matty reenacts how the guard shoved him so hard he fell onto a potted cactus at the front gate. A vivid pink welt swells above his right hip. For once, being the town's Golden Boy didn't work. I hope Matty doesn't take it personally. Unless I'm horribly mistaken, the security guard knows nothing. He doesn't realize the Vaughns are gone at all. True secrecy means not telling a soul. Celeste knows the rules, and so do I.

Evidently, hammering back an obscene amount of cheap whiskey helps heal Matty's cactus welt. I hope it heals broken hearts too.

Joe and Edgar hang with a group of people from Fillmore taking turns dropping into the pool. When it's Joe's turn, he grinds tail-slides along the lip like it's the most natural thing in the world—to be in someone else's backyard, sliding around their drained pool, playing in the remains of their misfortune.

Sam and I ollie down the patio steps near the monster mansion that sits atop a low hill a few dozen yards from the pool. I count seven steps, so it's the perfect height. Each jump lets out a sharp crack as wheels smack the ground again. It's heaven. I nail a perfect 360 down the steps. I can't help but check to see if Edgar and Joe saw it. They both smile, so I think they did. Some part of me wants to tell Edgar it wasn't a lucky try. I mastered that move years ago, back when he was probably still in Brazil.

Sam doubles back to the top of the walkway. He gestures to a concrete bench. "I'm about to attack this shit right here." His wheels sound off like an airplane engine. Some people gathered around the pool turn to watch.

My father would call two possible outcomes, each with equal odds.

One: Sam will ollie onto the first bench. His skating's improved recently. It's entirely possible he'll pull it off.

Two: he won't, and will soon wear pavement on his elbows again, which is a total shame because his scabs have finally healed.

I hold my breath, cross my fingers.

Hesitation hits him. You can see it in the weary lift of his front leg. His pop is low. He doesn't make it all the way up, and his board clatters down, followed by his limbs. Body meets concrete in a burst of bones and joints. He unfurls and blossoms open a few feet from the bottom of the benches.

Matty's all, "Ohhhhh. You need a medic, Sarge?" He finds himself hilarious.

A few people laugh with him.

Sam balls himself into a giant walnut. His old elbow scab is gone, replaced by an even deeper, brighter shade of red. There's an exact match on his right knee, too, peeking out from beneath the hem of his shorts. "Shit, that hurt." A rough exhale blasts through his lips.

Joe flies over to help.

Sam babbles excuses: I ollied too soon, my front foot snagged, my knee twitched, my trucks are too loose. The usual. He inspects his latest injuries. Joe pulls a skate tool from the side pocket of his torn-up Dickies, the camel-colored ones with strings trailing from the ripped hems. Sam takes the tool and spends the next five minutes tightening the bolts holding his trucks to the deck.

Edgar walks over. An entourage of lookalikes follow, all wearing exact replicas of Edgar's outfit or sporting less cool versions of his goatee. He squats beside Sam, who chucks Joe's tool onto the grass and says, "Shit. Busted a kingpin. Now I gotta buy a new truck."

"Nah, man," Edgar says, peering at Sam's board. "Stop by Skate Real tomorrow. I'll replace your kingpin."

"You can do that?"

Edgar pops his eyes open wide in amusement because *of course you can replace a kingpin.* But Sam's relatively new to this. He wouldn't know. "Yeah, I can do that," Edgar replies with a laugh. Behind him, one of his look-alike disciples snorts.

Sam's all happy now. He smothers Edgar with gratitude, slaps him on the shoulder. Edgar waves the compliments away with a flick of the hand, like he gets this all the time.

Edgar glances my way and I know it's not long before he—

"Hey, Effie," he calls, his voice cool with Brazilian swagger.

He holds out his hand like we've done this rehearsed hand-shake-slap-dance a thousand times before. I play along, and he laughs, elated. Apparently, he's already inducted me into his cast of disciples.

"What's up, kid?"

"Not much," I say, noncommittally.

He tips his chin at Matty. "How's it goin'?"

Matty fakes a grand smile, then burps. Charming as ever. I don't embarrass easily, but right now I want to die. "I need a beer. Nice seeing you, Eddie." He leaves, stumbling over a tree stump.

Edgar can't stop laughing. "Eddie," he says, shaking his head.

I'm inclined to follow Matty, just to keep an eye on him, but Edgar's blocking my way. Earlier, Sam and I left Matty to his own devices, and it turned out to be the worst decision ever. Matty thought it was funny to try shoving glowsticks up people's nostrils, and almost succeeded in getting jumped by one of Gerard's friends from Venice. I think the guy's name is Jason. He's short and thick, built like a solid tree trunk. And he definitely didn't give Matty a pass for being drunk. Joe and Gerard broke it up, but Jason still keeps an eye on Matty. He looks like he could mow down an army of General Wills types if he tried.

Edgar faces me. "Give any thought to the sponsorship?"

"Sure." And then I squashed those thoughts because they lead to places where Matty will not be.

"And?"

"I'm super flattered."

"Cool. Some dude who writes for *Transworld Skateboarding* is doing a story on me and the shop. Got the whole Skate Real team coming for a pic. They promised me the front cover. It'd be cool if—"

"Effie!" Sam's voice shrieks so loud I feel it in my bones.

Across the lawn, I spot him standing over Matty, who looks like he's fallen. He struggles to get up, but flops back on the grass all fish-out-of-water-style.

Sam waves at me, eyes wide, like, *What do we do about him?*

I don't know. I'm too busy pleading with God to let the whiskey erase Celeste from Matty's memory altogether. "Catch ya' later, Edgar," I say before I jet.

On my way to Sam and Matty, I pass Joe and the Fillmore kids. They forego glow sticks for sparklers and bottle rockets dug out of the box of leftover fireworks Bruiser and my brother hauled to the party. I recognize one guy from a skate park we hit there sometimes, this super tall surfer kid named Eric with shaggy blond hair who always wears the same trucker hat. Eric passes around a Zippo lighter. The flame peaks at the highest setting, casting a glow across his face and hat as he holds it out to light up everyone's stuff. The sparklers pop and ignite as they catch fire. Little explosive balls of wonder. Dogma is here too. She's with a friend. The two of them stand next to Eric, squeaking and squealing as they draw their names on the sky. Yellow streaks of light from the sparklers burn. The names eventually fade into nothing. Dogma waves and calls me over, and for a split second an urge to join her and forget about my screwed-up love life overcomes me. But I don't want to see fireworks again for as long as I live. The Fourth of July was enough.

When I reach Sam and Matty, they're arguing over two bunches of neon blue glow sticks. Sam tries to get Matty to drop them, to better his balance, but Matty's holding on. I have no idea why. He fumbles for a minute, but somehow manages to connect the ends of his glow sticks into a chain. He loops them around his neck and clutches a whole bunch more in his fist.

We help Matty up. The alcohol pulls him back down.

Joe comes over. He flicks his chin in the direction of the Wiley mansion. "Bring him inside in case he gets sick. Gerard figured out a way in."

"How? Isn't it all locked up?"

"Amazing what a baseball bat can do against a pane of glass."

"Are you kidding me?" Fucking Gerard. He's such a menace.

"Wish I was."

Gerard slinks over. "Get pretty boy inside," he says, jerking a thumb over his shoulder at that kid Jason. "He's pissing off Beats."

"Beats?" I can't help but laugh. "Isn't his name Jason?"

"He goes by Beats now."

"That's dumb."

"Don't say I didn't warn you, Effie."

Much as it pains me to admit, my brother is right. Jason/Beats can't keep his eyes off Matty. He and a crew of about five other guys swarm around each other. Their eyes pop in our direction. The last thing I need is Matty getting his ass kicked by a bunch of Venice guys, one of whom has enough self-confidence to reinvent himself as Beats.

Sam reads my mind. "Up you get," he tells Matty, and swings him over the shoulder, firefighter-rescue style. Sam doesn't even grunt. All those pushups his dad forces on him obviously work.

When we reach the mansion, I send a silent prayer into the universe for my brother's good timing. Gerard's busted a gaping hole in a window large enough to climb through. But from the looks of it, someone used their brain and unlocked the door from the inside afterwards, because it's wide open now. A thick cloud of mustiness seeps out. We sidestep shards of glass on the ground and enter a wide sunroom overlooking the pool. The scent of stale mold swallows me up, like when you step into an enclosed poolroom and hot steam's trapped inside. No electricity means no central air. It's dark but not completely black in here. It helps that the Wileys apparently spent a small fortune installing ginormous windows. Skylights let in a little glow from the moon. The place is completely bare down to the walls. Only the ghostly footprint of a large table and chairs remains in scuffs and scratches in the center of the room.

Dirty shoeprints trail off down a hallway to my right. Looks like the rumors of break-ins are true. I'm sure people like my dear brother have already worked this place over. What a waste of energy. What did they think they would find? Cash? If the Wileys had any, they probably would have needed it to pay their debts. Or better yet, put some gas in a boat and sail out of here.

Sam's itching to drop Matty on the floor. He sets him down in the middle of the room where the moonlight shines brightest. Matty slumps to his side. His arms are noodles. Sam slips back out the door and braces it open behind himself for a second, assuming I'll follow. It hovers for a moment, then closes.

I should really go with Sam. Let Matty sleep it off on his own.

But look at him. How can I leave him? Alone, especially. The last time I left his side he was at the candy display in Bella Via Pharmacy and by the time I found him at the cash register five minutes later he was running his mouth about the girl he just met in line. My life hasn't been the same since. His hasn't either.

Matty flips onto his back.

He mumbles a string of words. I swear I hear Celeste's name in the garble.

No, no, no. Not her. Not now.

She's here. She's gone but she's here and I'm sick over it.

I drop to my knees at his side. Up close, his skin burns a bright red, like he's run a marathon. I can't make out his freckles. Blue glow sticks still hang around his neck, and he has a bunch more in his fist. I realize that I, like an idiot, still clutch my own red one. I toss it aside. He reaches for it. With fumbling hands, he wraps my red one around his clump of blue to tie them all together.

He whispers the same words again.

"What?" I ask, tentative, weary.

"You're the best."

He presses the glow stick bouquet at my chest.

Oh. It's me this time. It's about me. Not her.

"Thank you," I whisper back.

His eyes close. His nostrils flare just the tiniest bit as he inhales. A furry line of reddish-orange eyelashes skims the tops of his cheeks. His mouth—where he binge-stuffed Lucky Charms this morning—opens slightly. When he sleeps, the edges of his lips curl upwards.

My fingers twitch like they have an energy all their own, like I can't stop them from reaching out. They buzz at the edges. The force of wanting to climb on top of him and press myself against him and mold my lips to his is so intense. One touch, that's all.

One finger. I'll just drag one fingertip across his lips. It won't be a big deal. Satisfy the urge, that's all.

I rock back onto my heels. Resist the impulse.

Reasons speed through my head as to why touching him in any fashion would be a bad, bad idea. Like, ruin your life bad. I tell myself it's easy, really, to do what sensible people do—keep it together, don't kid yourself, do not act on impulse. Back away. Back away.

Reminder: This is Matty. If he wanted to kiss you, he'd have done so already. Stay back.

The glow sticks clump together in my hand. I wonder what color Celeste would have chosen—blue or red or something different? Or if she would have needed to take one at all. Matty probably would have gifted her his whole bunch, including the one he took from me.

A wave of something gross and thick completely covers me until I'm suffocating. I feel sick. Pressing a palm to my chest does nothing to help me breathe. I think I'm dying.

I need to hold on to him. Just for this minute.

His chest lifts and sinks, pauses at the deepest bottom, then lifts and sinks again.

He's beautiful. He's perfect. He's everything.

Taking the craziest chance, I reach out and place one hand over his.

He smiles a little in his sleep. That smile means something, I think. It does. It does.

The impulse takes over. I give in to it.

I press my lips to the top of his head. Kiss his hair, his forehead, his flushed cheek. I steal more kisses than I bargained for, but I don't care. Finally, my lips float just an inch above his. Only centimeters fill the space between us. My breath and his breath mix.

Shaking off the urge is not easy.

He's right here. And if I don't make a move soon, joining him in Chicago won't matter. Here or there, I'll be just another friend, like always. The odds are clear—I might never have a chance like this again. We only have a few weeks left, really only a countdown of days. If I can't get out of Vista Buscato, this parting might be the beginning of the end for us. He'll be gone forever, and he'll return with a wife and kids and the only time I'll see him is when he's passing through Vista Buscato for a visit, maybe during the holidays or on his kids' summer break or for his tenth wedding anniversary. The same old stains will blotch up my Fox Inn apron, and he'll order chicken francese, and his wife will get grilled salmon, and I'll make sure there's enough tiny shards of crushed ice in her glass of mineral water that she chokes on it.

Fuck it. I don't second-guess anymore. I go for it.

He stirs. I freeze. Maybe my tangled hair tickled him awake. I'm not sure. A frightfest of images flash in my mind—of him shoving me away. But he doesn't.

His eyes flutter open, closed, open, and then they see me, for real, I think.

Lights finally switch on inside his eyes. His lips part.

Trusting, bursting, I press my mouth against his.

It's crazy and reckless but I don't care. I love him.

In my dreams, his kisses are sweet, like caramel or chocolate. The reality is this: his breath is half beer, half hot dog, and under normal circumstances I might go tell him to mainline a value-sized bottle of Listerine. But in this moment, the taste of him means we're together. I'm not just fantasizing about this. It's real. And he's kissing me back.

This is amazing.

His mouth stops moving. I open my eyes to look at him. His eyelids lift, but not all the way. Just about one-third, to the point where you can take things in, but the overload of information doesn't spring your brain into all-out alcohol throb.

I pull away. This is the moment when the realization will hit him, when the booze-fog will fade. *What the hell are you doing?* he'll say. And I'll need an explanation.

I was checking your pulse.

I was making sure you were still breathing.

I thought I saw a bug in your hair.

Every explanation is heinously inadequate. And I'm not sure it matters. He kissed me back and not because he was on autopilot. That kiss was loaded with feeling. My mouth burns.

I wait for his reaction, fully expecting him to jump up and declare an end to whatever it is we're doing, for his eyes to blast fully open and take in the absurdity of seeing me. On my knees. Like a beggar.

I am on my fucking knees.

Oh my God, what did I do?

The whole room reeks of desperation. Rewind, backspace, delete. Get me out of here. Take back every word I said about the kiss being perfect. This is horribly wrong.

I pull back.

"Effie," he groans, grabbing my arm. His voice comes out all froggy.

"Yes?"

"Effie," he says again.

My heart blossoms open. "I'm here, Matty."

He repeats my name again, but downshifts into a whisper.

There's a moan somewhere in the words. He won't let loose on my arm.

"Stay with me."

"Okay."

Of course. No hesitation. That's what you do when you love someone. You don't leave. You stay. So I lie down. His arms slide tight around me from behind and liquor breath puffs against my ear. It's heaven. I never, ever, ever want this to end. Ever. The only thing that could ruin this moment is if he says her name.

Please. I will do anything. Just don't say her name. Never again.

CHAPTER TWENTY-TWO

Sam's time is up, no matter how much we long to drag out the August days. He leaves tomorrow morning.

Seven of us pile into Matty's Jeep for a celebration of Sam's final night. Joe and I battle our way to the front passenger seat. He wins and snags shotgun first. My instinct is to argue with him, but he makes a peace offering by gesturing for me to climb aboard his lap. A warm flush heats my whole face. My cheeks tingle. The others take their seats as I stand there like an idiot, sizing up Joe's offer. Dogma slides next to me and jumps onto Joe's lap. He flashes me an apologetic grin. You snooze, you lose. I punch his arm. I'm demoted to sitting in the back with Gerard, Bruiser, and Sam.

Matty is no help on my behalf. But I'm not surprised. Neither of us has mentioned the fact that our lips and tongues were melded together one week ago. It's like our kiss never happened. I'm not sure he was conscious enough to remember it. Maybe this is my punishment for daring to make out with someone who'd already slipped into the REM stage of sleep. I can't decide if I'm happy or sad or relieved or pissed.

The Jeep races up the mountain road. The air feels thicker up here, less light and salty than the ocean-spiked stuff we breathe at Vista Buscato. The midnight blue views of the ocean slowly twist into the dark greens and browns of mountain shrubbery left to choke and die in the dry California heat.

I'm on Sam's lap. He's the only one wearing a seat belt. You can always count on Samuel Wills to worry about life expectancies and such, even right down to the final hours before the guillotine strikes. Tomorrow his parents will drop him at the Marine Corps Recruit Depot in San Diego where higher-ups will shave his head, hand him freshly washed and pressed fatigues, a toothbrush and a comb, and off he'll go in pursuit of courage. He'll enter a wimp and emerge a hero. A miracle in thirteen weeks. I give him credit, too—he spent the last few days waking at the butt crack of dawn to force himself to get used to the early bird program. He was the first employee to arrive at Fox Inn this morning for his final shift. I'll bet he popped one hundred curb ollies in front of the restaurant before we opened. It'd be nice if that were a useful skill as a Marine, but I doubt it is.

Sam's arms clamp around me from behind. I turn to check him out. His eyes are closed, his face tilted toward the open air of the ocean to our left. I squeeze his arms tighter around me. He pushes his face into my back. Fear rises in me, grips my throat. I've busted his ass for being a wimp for so long he'll never admit what's really on his mind tonight. But I know. He doesn't have to say it. I want to tell him it's okay to be scared. This enlisting thing—it's a big deal. And I don't want him to leave. Not for a career, not for courage, not for anything.

About a mile past Celeste's condo complex, on the outskirts of Vista Buscato, we pull into the parking lot of an old, deserted campground with a cheery wooden sign. *Welcome to Monteraro State Park!* Within five minutes of arrival, Gerard and Bruiser devise four different ways they can violate the sign and leave their mark on it. Sam talks them out of it.

Dogma forgets I lost the coin toss for designated driver on the return trip, and passes me the first beer from the case we scored with Bruiser's fake ID. I could like her if she quits pretending she knows anything about skateboards.

Matty sits on the ground next to the beer and motions for me to do the same.

Joe's head's been spinning in our direction ever since I walked out of the Wiley mansion last week with my bouquet of glow sticks, their lights dulled to a faint glow. Tonight's no different. He has no idea what happened between me and Matty. There's no conceivable way he would. But there's a knowing in the way he looks at me. He's putting something together, brick by brick, glow stick by glow stick. He coaches Dogma through the mechanics of a shove-it. I have to give her credit—she doesn't whine when the trick goes bad and her board cracks into her shins again and again and again. When she finally gets it right, her board spins underneath her feet in a perfect 180. She nails it and we all go crazy.

Matty's the only one not celebrating. He struggles flicking the cap off his beer bottle against the cement curb, like he's lost the muscle tone to handle the task. He sighs after the first sip. The sound is thick and broken. Forget about pause buttons. He's pressed stop on his life altogether.

"You okay?" I ask.

He shrugs. There's no bounce in him.

Guilt floods through me. He rings an arm around my neck. "Thank you. I don't say that enough, you know. Thank you." He smiles. "For everything."

Warmth returns to his eyes but it doesn't last. By the time I say, "Of course" it's fading.

He checks his phone for the fifty-seventh time. The phone never rang, never beeped, never vibrated. Why would it? We're all here, and we're the only people he should care about.

A little heartache in Celeste's absence was a risk, but I never expected this—cold, lethargic gloom that never ends. The sun could explode and asteroids could pummel the earth and our beautiful blue planet could spin out of orbit and the one and only thing on his mind would still be: *Has anyone seen Celeste? Where do you think she went? What happened to her?* He's taken to ripping down posters of Jessie Winters, the dark-haired girl missing since May, because he thinks if *that* missing girl takes center stage, then no one will remember to look for *his* missing girl. In the meantime, I don't think either of them want to be found, but that's another story entirely. And it's not like I can explain how I know. Some secrets are dead and buried and will stay that way forever and ever. The end.

Matty's gloom messes with my head. I pull my skateboard out of the back of the Jeep to let off steam, jump a few curb markers. Sam practices crooked nosegrinds along the ledge of a concrete fire pit. At a picnic table, Joe focuses his attention entirely on Dogma, who runs her mouth about economics and society and the class war in Vista Buscato. Again, I think I could like this girl. Intellectual junk spills from her mouth faster than I can process it. Joe's in complete rapture. This is the longest I've seen him hold a skateboard without riding it. Eventually, their chat turns to the big protest he's planning for the Founder's Day Parade. He throws out ideas—banners, picket signs, bullhorns—and Dogma offers up her artistry to help. "Yeah, man, whatever you need," she says over and over.

A nasty, biting energy crawls up my neck. I think I'm burning from the inside out with jealousy. Which is absurd. I churn out three kick flips, but the feeling won't go away.

Gerard and Bruiser concoct plans to rip the welcome sign off the post without tools. Joe shoots me a look—one that says I should control my brother, lock him back in his cage.

I shout the only truth I can think of to put a flame under his and Bruiser's asses: "We're out of beer."

I'm surprised when Matty's grunt of discontent is loudest.

Gerard calls out, "Buscato Beach!" Everyone agrees. Bruiser tries to load the campground welcome sign into the Jeep. He's such an asshole. The thing takes up the entire back seat. It's not happening.

I skate toward the Jeep. Joe pumps hard beside me, and we break into a race. Our hands slap the car one on top of another, with his hitting first. He smiles, triumphant. This earns him a punch to the chest. He locks my arms down at my sides. We're laughing as we wrestle. His eyes have that warm sparkle to them again. The play-fighting slows down, and it looks like Joe's about to say something to me, but out of nowhere, Dogma pushes between us. One of her dreadlocks skims my arm. It feels like grip tape. Joe blinks a few times, as if he momentarily forgot about her presence. I wonder if he cares that her dreads are going to scrape the skin off the side of his face on the ride home. I do.

Designated Driver falls on me, so I take the front. Matty tries for shotgun but it's too late. Joe shakes his head, and gestures to Dogma on his lap. "Beat it, bro. I don't care if it's your car. Rules are rules." It's about the only time I've ever heard Joe sing the benefit of a rule, regulation, or ordinance. And it's hilarious. Laughing, Matty grabs one of the side roll bars and hops into the backseat. Gerard and Bruiser join him, along with Sam. They're all squished hip to hip.

Even with my stupid brother present, we're all together. It feels good. Sam is here, whole and well, and not off in desert heat wearing camouflage and carrying a canteen and praying he'll make it home at the end of his deployment. Joe's here, too. He isn't rotting in jail over something he could have avoided if he'd kept his temper in check. Gerard and Bruiser—well, I can't get rid of them, so I guess they'll always be in the background somewhere. Dogma's put her econ lecture on pause for the moment. Her presence is easy to swallow when her mouth is shut.

I don't want any of this to end.

With Gerard and Bruiser's shouts—*faster, faster*—egging me on, I run us back to Vista Buscato with more speed than a sober driver should on a winding mountain road. The Jeep tilts around the turns, like we're kicking up onto two wheels. Dogma screeches, clutching the handle above the glove box. Joe screams out "Chicken bar! Chicken bar!" Everyone laughs. Gerard and Bruiser grab the roll bar over our heads and pull themselves to standing. Wind rips at their shirts, fanning them out like giant flags. Together, they bellow, "Wooooooo!"

Adrenaline floods through my fingertips. I accelerate. Hot air licks at my hair, my eyes, my mouth. Wind tunnels inside my ears. I rip my hair out of its ponytail. I take a glimpse at the sky, the stars, satellites. Anything, everything.

Bruiser takes his t-shirt off and throws it at the sky. It sails out for a moment, filling with air balloon-style, then flips and folds onto itself until it's nothing more than a white rope, rolling on the highway behind us. Gerard does the same.

I glance at Matty in the rearview mirror. He's grinning, swimming in booze.

Sam laughs. He's caught in the moment, free for once.

Joe tugs on my arm. He says something I can't make out over the screaming wind.

"What?"

He points at Gerard and Bruiser. "If we hit a bump, those guys will lose their skin!"

"If we hit a bump, we're all dead," Gerard cries out, laughing.

Joe flinches. He says something. It's hard to hear him over Gerard and Bruiser's shouts, over the noise, the wind, my own adrenaline. The backlit speed dial behind the steering wheel glows. We're doing seventy.

Joe tugs at my arm again. "Slow down!"

Matty yells into the air. I have no idea what he's saying. Wind strips his words away.

The speedometer hits eighty miles per hour.

Sirens wail in the distance. The sound shocks me back into reality.

I slide my foot off the gas. Gerard and Bruiser lurch forward over the roll bar.

"Down! Down!" Bruiser shouts, dropping to his ass. Joe throws both hands onto his head and groans. Dogma peers behind our car and says something about living in a police state. Bruiser warns her to shut her fucking mouth.

I check the speed gauge.

Back down to sixty. Okay. Better. Now fifty.

We slow and slow and slow.

The cops race behind us like we're armed bank robbers. Lights swirl, blinking, flashing. The sudden drop in speed and absence of wind in my ear canals jars me. I'm dizzy. Joe and Sam echo each other with a soundtrack of fucks.

Knowing the drill, I steer the Jeep onto the highway shoulder. We roll to a stop.

Miraculously, the cops speed past us, their lights continuing to whirl down Pacific Coast Highway, casting spotlights on the green and white signs marking highway exits. We watch, bewildered, so used to being the reason for the sirens. We can't calm ourselves.

Sam throws prayers up to the heavens. "Thank you, God. Thank you thank you thank you."

Matty shouts, "Quick! Follow them!"

"Are you crazy?" Sam cries. "We dodged a bullet!"

"Didn't you see? They took the exit to Las Palmas Altas. That's where Celeste lives!"

"She doesn't live there anymore," Joe shouts.

The three of them launch into an argument about the benefits and risks of following a cop car to its likely destination. The whole thing makes me want to die.

Sam pushes his motto again and again and again: "I'm leaving tomorrow! I don't have time for this shit!"

But Matty barrels forward. "I have a feeling about this, guys!"

"Sam and Joe are right," I reason. I force my volume up high, purposely. He needs a shock to his system. "Let's cut our losses. We don't know if that's where the cops were going."

His eyes narrow. All traces of the alcohol swimming in his eyes are replaced with clear, crisp anger. "Since when are you a fucking dud?"

I don't know what to say to that; I don't answer.

He busts out a nasty, choked laugh. "You never liked Celeste anyway."

Shock waves spasm through me. Joe puts a hand on my thigh, consoling me or trying to stop me from losing it. I'm not sure which. I alternate between wanting to throw a fist at Matty's mouth and wanting to deny his suggestion. He's wrong; he's right. My head still swims from hearing her name. That name. Always that name.

Joe saves me. "Check yourself. It's got nothing to do with Celeste," he says. "The cops are gone. Why push our luck?"

Matty turns on him. "Right. Like you've ever cared about getting pulled over."

"I care about *us*! You should too!"

"Man, fuck you, Joe."

Bruiser whistles, deep and low.

Joe's expression ices over. The shift isn't pretty. I fear for Matty's life.

A staring match begins between them. Two pissed-off cats, daring the other to blink.

Dogma squirms in Joe's lap. Bruiser coughs. Gerard sighs.

This is the most uncomfortable spread of silence ever.

Matty loses the game first. He runs a hand through his hair, and says, "Whatever. Bunch of fucking losers."

Joe shakes his head.

Bruiser mutters, "Sucker."

I wonder if the word is reserved for Matty or Joe. If it even matters.

My shirtless brother and Bruiser jump out of the Jeep onto the pavement.

Joe asks the thing all of us are thinking. "What are you doing?"

Bruiser grabs his board from the back. "This shit is beat. We're out."

"Yo, I'm not in the habit of following cops," my brother says.

I don't blame them in the slightest. But they're drunk and it's impossibly dark out here. We might as well be on the other side of the moon. They take this fact for granted, I think, because the Jeep's headlights are on. Joe chews on the end of a piece of hair and watches them skate in the direction of Vista Buscato. Dogma keeps saying, "Oh my God, oh my God," fingers pressed to her mouth. Sam babbles about the dangers of riding on a highway at night, like it isn't obvious.

In the glow of the headlights, my brother's bare back shines with sweat, same as when we were kids and our mom would punish him with an order to lift crates of empty beer and wine bottles to the recycle dumpster out back. I felt so bad for him. All those empties, all those heavy crates. The entire haul probably weighed more than his skinny ass. But Felicia didn't care. She wanted to teach him a lesson: no scuff marks at Fox Inn's entrance.

He grows smaller in the distance, skating away.

"Stay on the shoulder," I shout.

He gives me the finger.

Joe and Sam, and even Dogma, offer me apologetic looks.

Matty taps my shoulder. He's got to be kidding me. My brother and Bruiser could wind up flattened and bloodied because Matty can't shake Celeste out of his head. She's not even here and she's still fucking everything up. I turn the key in the ignition. We'll follow the cops in the direction of Las Palmas Altas. I'll give Matty what he wants, even when I know it's not the smart thing to do.

Inside, I'm one part angry, seven parts sad, and twelve parts sick. Matty sits up straighter, suddenly alive.

Chapter Twenty-Three

Three police cruisers block the entrance at Las Palmas Altas' security booth.

Matty was right. That fact almost makes him hyperventilate. His intuition felt something, and he followed it—*we* followed it. The idea that there's some kind of metaphysical connection between him and Celeste sickens me.

We park behind the cop cars, then weave on foot along the cactus-lined walkway into the center courtyard of the complex. A police officer stops us a few feet past the guard's booth.

"You kids live here?"

"No," we say in unison.

"I don't have to answer your questions," Dogma says, and leans forward to peer at the officer's badge. She finishes with, "Officer Pembrook, badge number 14276."

Matty stares at her like she's just lit herself on fire. Joe and I say nothing.

There's brave and there's stupid, and I'm not sure either of us has figured out the fine line between the two. The cop sets his mouth open like he's about to say something but stops when two other cops emerge from the darkness up ahead along the walkway. Between them is a man with his arms behind his back.

"Vincent!" Sam cries out.

Then Matty. "Vincent?"

What. No.

As they grow closer, the man's features come to life under the center courtyard lights. It is Vincent. Handcuffs clamp his wrists together.

I bolt forward without thinking.

"Whoa, whoa." Officer Pembrook grabs my shoulder.

Sam points at Vincent blocked by a bunch of police. "But we know him."

"Oh yeah? He just broke into one of the cottages here. Still sure you know him?"

Sam swallows. His Adam's apple slides up, then down. "We work with him at Fox Inn."

"Looks like his day job doesn't pay enough." Pembrook laughs at the crack.

He couldn't care less about us or Vincent or anything. If you want answers, talk to the people in charge.

I push forward again.

Joe calls out, "Effie, no!"

Pembrook fumbles, but he's not fast enough to catch me this time.

I hear Matty's voice. "Let her go."

Let her go.

Because he knows he can count on me. And I'll bet anything he wants me to come back with answers about precious Celeste and what business Vincent has being anywhere near her condo. I want answers too, but not for the reasons Matty does. We're not on the same page. I don't think we ever were when it comes to her. I press the thought out of my head before I lose focus.

One of the officers eyes me approaching and signals the rest of them.

It's me against a line of cops. I remind myself I am a Fox. Losing is not in our genes.

"Who's in charge here?" I say, sounding exactly like a woman named Felicia.

One officer steps forward. "Something we can help you with, miss?"

He smiles but it's that vague tug of the mouth where you can't tell if he's being kind or he's amused by your naiveté. I decide I don't care.

"That guy." I point to Vincent. His head whips back and forth in a violent shake. Lips say nothing, but his eyes scream at me to shut the hell up. "I know him. He's not a criminal."

The cop chuckles. "I think the term you're looking for is burglar."

Vincent's eyes can't grow any bigger.

Soft lighting illuminates the rows of neat little cottages along Rumildo Walk up ahead. Matching palm trees, matching lampposts, each with a stubby cactus beside the front door. Somewhere in the middle of the row, I spot Celeste's house—lights blazing, front door swung wide open, police milling about inside.

The air in my lungs suddenly thickens. Vincent was in Celeste's house. Fear licks at my skin. I'm hot, I'm cold. My gaze meets Vincent's. His eyes scream NO. His fear matches mine.

A cop trots down the walkway toward us. "Perimeter's all clear. There's no sign of him."

A voice that is unmistakably Detective Brimley's roars through the darkness. "Damn!"

I think I know who they're looking for. But the Vaughns aren't there anymore. Neither is the Vallone family. Or the Madaleos. Pick a name, you still won't find them.

Brimley ambles to the courtyard, flanked by two other detectives.

Vincent glances at me. He shakes his head again, like I didn't get the message earlier.

When Brimley spots me, he rotates through three expressions: shock, confusion, and complete, utter, face-reddening irritation. I'm reminded of the Detective Brimley legend—he always carries two sets of cuffs. One for hands, one for feet. Like shackles. To be used together in the case of super unruly, pain in the ass perps. And with the way he glares at me, hands resting on hips, eyes narrowed, I think he considers me a colossal pain in the ass. "Did your father send you?" he barks.

"No?" The puzzle piece bearing my father's name does not fit into this scenario.

Brimley spits on the ground. "Damn it, Phil."

"Detective, I don't know what's going on here, but you know Vincent." I wave a hand at my co-worker. "He's a good guy. This has to be a misunderstanding. He would never rob anybody's house."

The spotlight's on Vincent, who looks like he'll shit his pants.

"Come with me," Brimley says, snagging my elbow.

I follow him halfway down the road in the direction of where Matty, Joe, Sam, and Dogma still wait. When we're at the perfect length of distance between the two groups of people—my friends and the cops—he tugs a photograph out of his pocket. With a penlight, he throws a glow on the picture. It's a perfect match for the one he showed Matty a few weeks ago with Celeste in the background. But in this one, an unmistakable image of Celeste's father blots the very furthest left corner of the photograph. He stands beside a barbecue grill holding what looks like a hamburger, smiling at someone off camera. I bet it's Celeste, and that's why she's smiling in the other picture we saw of her.

The detective whisper-hisses, "Do you know this man's name?"

It's a simple question. Just two words—a first name and a last. But given the mile-long list these Vaughn people answer to, I'm not sure I know how to answer. Plus, if Vincent didn't tell, why should I?

"I'm not sure." I squint at the picture.

"The hell you're not."

"I'm really not sure." It's not a lie.

"I'll tell you then. It's John Vallone." The name is spoken—first and last—with a flattening emphasis, each part carrying its own dead weight. "He's the person Vincent came to see. Do you know him?"

"How would I know him?"

"You're ballsy. Like your dad." He nods. "That's good, that's good."

The way he's manic-nodding makes me think it isn't good at all. No one ever describes my father in a positive light. "Tell me where John Vallone is or your buddy's behind bars tonight." He jabs a thumb at Vincent standing in the center of the group of cops. His head hangs. It's pitiful. "Don't play games with me. I've seen you with Vallone's daughter."

Something inside my body starts to squeeze and contract. I fight the urge to run.

In the courtyard, Joe calls out, "Effie, you okay?"

Dogma shouts, "Ask for a lawyer."

It occurs to me that the two of them are the bravest people I know.

With one thick, stiff finger, the detective pokes me hard in the chest. "Don't be foolish, Stefanie. John Vallone's a criminal. He did a terrible thing."

"Did he kill someone or something?" I brace myself for the response. Holy shit, I don't want to know if he did.

"He's a kidnapper, and who knows what else. The FBI's been looking for him for years. I'm going to make sure he doesn't do it to anyone else. I care about this town. And it's my job to keep everyone in it safe. Now please, tell me what you know."

That's the first time I've ever heard him say please. Even when he orders coffee from me, I don't get the pleasantries. But he can't sugarcoat his way into my head.

I shoot a glance at my friends in the courtyard. Dogma and Sam sit on the lip around a giant rock garden. Joe and Matty stare back at me. Matty looks like he wants to leap at us, Spider Man-style. One massive scream into the air from me, "SHE ISN'T HERE!" would burst his bubble. Because come on—that's all he cares about. I wish it weren't so, but the truth hit me hard tonight.

I bang my toes against the pavement. Let time pass while I think. It doesn't get easier.

Brimley folds his arms and waits for my answer.

I don't owe Detective Brimley. And I certainly don't owe Celeste and her kidnapper father either. But Matty. Betraying the Vaughns-Madaleos-Vallones would kill him. If he ever found out how dirty my hands already are, his feelings for me, for all of us, for Vista Buscato, would die.

Assuming, of course, he ever finds out. What are the odds he will?

I glance at Vincent again. The poor guy's neck must ache from the shame pulling his head down. Just a few words—a name, a notecard, an address—and my life will go back to normal. Vincent's cuffs will come off and Detective Brimley will chase John Vallone out of this town forever. He might even chase him out of the state, out of the country. Satellites won't be able to find him.

Matty will never hear from Celeste again. Ever. Life on our side of the globe will spin and spin and spin, just as it did before Celeste and her angel white hair swept away my dreams.

Matty never needs to discover my part in it, and life will go back to normal.

The detective leans forward. My answer's teasing at him. "Give me information on John Vallone, and I'll let Vincent go. It's that easy."

"Okay," I say, finally. "Vega. He goes by the last name Vega."

Brimley's entire face ignites. He rips a notepad out of his breast pocket. "Anything else?"

"They're in Santa Barbara," I offer.

"Santa Barbara?" he says incredulously, like he can't imagine how the man skirted capture for so long and is only one county away. Every quick-thinking officer here with a gun and a badge can't catch one guy with a kid. It's pathetic.

John Vallone is the most clever dude in this whole game.

And even still, I suddenly feel like I'm the one winning.

CHAPTER TWENTY-FOUR

My father slams his office door shut behind us.

"What the hell were you thinking?" He looks like he wants to choke me. An unlit cigarette bounces in the corner of his mouth. "You ratted them out?"

"I got Vincent off the hook!"

"You also implicated him!"

I'm struck dumb by this. How?

Sam and I stare at my father.

He rubs his temples. Invoices and fresh produce packing lists litter his desk. Three stacks of cash, thrown together roughly, pile up in towers at the center. No less than twelve takeout coffee cups teeter around the room on shelves, papers, chairs, wherever. Surprisingly, this is neat for my father. Usually it's worse. Especially during tax season. He presses a few buttons on the security camera. The screen lights up. Two detectives pull away from the curb in front of Fox Inn. He casts a glance at Vincent and Carlo.

In all the years I've watched Vincent in the kitchen, I've never seen him sit until tonight. He slumps behind the desk in my dad's chair, like the entire mass of the earth presses down on him. Carlo stands to his side, one fat hand patting Vincent's shoulder. Every now and then Vincent dabs at his wrinkled forehead with a linen napkin. There's no sweat as far as I can see. Maybe he just expects sweat to be there. Or, possibly, he's gotten so used to standing in front of Fox Inn's million-degree grill all day all week that it's a habit.

Detective Brimley's never seen this side of Fox Inn. And he certainly wasn't invited into this meeting after he escorted me and Sam to the restaurant. Matty couldn't pass Officer Pembrook's sobriety test, so they ushered him into the back of a police car with a promise to bring him home. Judge Pomerantz won't be happy at the sight of Matty, but if I know anything about how this town works, the cops have probably already finished tucking Matty into bed without bothering to wake the judge with silly things like drunk grandsons and police escorts. Dogma and Joe skated off down the road. Pretty much every law enforcement official present at the scene decided that getting rid of Dogma was a good thing. When it came time to deal with me and Sam, Sam pleaded not to be taken home. "My dad—my dad—please! You don't understand!" Brimley finally called off his officers. He offered to bring me and Sam to Fox Inn himself. "Your pal Vincent needs a lift back to work. And I need a word with your father, Effie."

He thinks I care about all this nonsense. I really don't. I got Vincent off the hook. I did my good deed for the millennium.

But apparently no one is grateful for my selflessness, and it occurs to me that they might see the extent of how not-so-selfless it really was. Sam's confused as hell, but even he knows something's up. He hasn't asked one question.

My father pauses, eyes jumping to Sam, sizing up his trustworthiness. "Vincent is artistic. He's very skilled at what he does," he says slowly, eyes scouring mine for realization.

"At what? Cooking?"

He rolls his eyes. "At creating documents where there are no official documents. For people who need them. Catch my drift?"

"He makes...documents?"

My father nods slowly.

"What does that mean?"

Sam pipes in. "I know what it means. I saw it on a show once. He makes fake papers."

"Exactly." My father nods. "Papers. Identification. Passports, birth certificates. You name it."

Vincent grimaces at the list of transgressions.

"Keep this between us, Bubble Boy." My father points at Sam, who offers up a dozen assurances.

My glare tightens. "Why do I sense you're involved somehow, Dad?"

He shrugs, surprisingly sheepish for him. "Times are tough. I partner myself in any and every lucrative business deal I can find."

Vincent moans out a prayer in Italian.

Questions break into a boil inside my head.

My father must spot the confusion on my face. He sighs. "Vincent did not burglarize John Vallone's home. Believe it or not, Vincent has a key. He was there *with permission*," he emphasizes, "to retrieve something John left for him."

"What kind of something?"

"Money."

"Why would John Vallone owe...?" No sooner do the words leave my lips that I hear their stupidity. Of course. Vincent created fake documents for someone who needed a new identity, who seemingly takes on new names for the fun of it. But that somebody, according to Detective Brimley, is a kidnapper. And possibly worse.

"Dad, you guys don't want to be involved with this man. John Vallone is wanted by the FBI. It's serious. They're saying he's a kidnapper."

Carlo blows out a lungful of air in disgust. I'm not used to seeing him without a big grin, and that total absence of gleaming teeth and round, happy cheeks—throws me off balance.

Vincent presses the napkin to his forehead again. It droops over one eye. He doesn't lift it. "He's not a kidnapper."

"Why else would they be looking for him?"

Words rocket out of Carlo's mouth. "John Vallone came to California a long time ago with...with..." He glances at Vincent, who rubs his face. "I don't know. What's her name now?" Vincent mutters something. Carlo nods vigorously. "Right, right. With Camille."

"Who's Camille?"

"The girl. That's not her name?" He glances at my father, who shrugs.

"You mean Celeste?"

"The girl with the pretty hair?"

I resist the urge to groan. "Yeah, that's her. His daughter."

Carlo purses his lips together. "That's the problem, kid. She's not his daughter."

Sam gasps.

"What?" I say.

Carlo heaves a giant sigh. "It's complicated."

"Try me. I'm pretty sharp."

My father lights up a cigarette. I get the feeling this will be a long story.

Carlo begins. "The little girl—Camille, Celeste, whatever, I can never remember—her mother died young. She had problems with drugs. John Vallone—he worked at a shelter in New York City. He did everything for the people there. He counseled them, fed them, prayed with them. That's where he met the mother. She was just a little older than you. Pregnant, too. She hung around the shelter a lot and she cried to John that she couldn't get off the drugs." He nods to see if I follow. I nod back. This is a shitload of information to take in, but I pay attention when it matters, when I care. And for some reason, I do. "John Vallone did everything to help. He even stayed with her at the hospital when she gave birth to the baby. She told John all the time—*all the time*," he repeats the words, eyes blasting open to twice their size, "that she wished for a good life. She wished for a good daddy for her baby girl. Someone like John."

He frowns and shakes his head. "The real father—what a lowlife. The people at the shelter didn't like him. He was feeding the poor girl the drugs."

My father grunts with the cigarette in his mouth. "That's only one-tenth of what he did to her, from what I heard."

Sam exhales sharply beside me.

Following this story makes my brain ache. Information overload pings around my head. But I need to understand Celeste, the little girl who hopped into a dumpster thick with garbage to make a friend. With every ounce of focus I can scrounge up, I coax the puzzle pieces together.

Carlo goes on. "In the end the drugs killed her. She got all high and crazy one night and died like this." He mimics a seizure or something. "The shelter people and the ambulance guys tried to save her." He pushes chest compressions on himself, enjoying the visual effect. "The whole time John Vallone held the baby and watched. But the mother died anyway. The baby was very small then. Tiny. And the father—he didn't care. When she was pregnant, he told everyone the baby wasn't his." Carlo looks like he could spit. "But after the mother died, John had trouble with the cops."

"Why?"

"The mother's family wouldn't mix with her after she got into the drugs, you know? They were proud people, so they disowned her. The big rumor was that she had a trust fund she couldn't touch until she turned twenty-five or something like that. That's why that asshole drug dealer hung around. He saw dollar signs. So when she died, all that money passed to the baby now, see? The minute the father heard the mommy died, it was like he hit lotto. He was all, 'I'm the daddy, I'm the daddy!'" Carlo waves his arms in the air in a fake embrace, then launches back into his story. "So, John Vallone did what he had to do. He kept the baby. He ran."

"You mean he kidnapped the baby?" I say softly.

Beside me, Sam mutters, "Shit."

Carlo squeezes his eyes shut and shakes his head. "He did not kidnap her! He saved her. I don't care what anybody says about it. That's his baby, his little girl! God wanted it that way. And the mother wanted it that way too. He lives for that kid."

Vincent murmurs from beneath the white napkin. "John Vallone is a good man."

"Where do you fit in?" I ask Vincent.

My father answers. "John bounced around with the baby for a while. Big cities, places he could mesh into a crowd. He obviously couldn't touch the girl's trust fund or they could trace where he was. Besides, John had savings to tide them over. He pulled off odd jobs and carpentry. Mostly cash-paying gigs, nothing traceable. But the money ran out. Over the years he kept in touch with his buddies at the New York shelter. They kept his secret. When he told them he had nowhere left to go and not a whole lot of money, they referred him to Dia de la Madonna."

"That's the place Brimley was asking about a few weeks ago?"

"Yep. That's where John met these two." He tips his head at Carlo and Vincent. "They volunteer in the soup kitchen. He opened up to Vincent during a prayer session. So, we put our heads together to help him out. The rest, as they say, is history." He sweeps his cigarette hand through the air. "John Vallone had a fresh start, a new identity, and a set of perfect documents, thanks to Vincent. John felt good about settling here. Vista Buscato was a better life for his daughter than being on the run. He started working at Dia De La Madonna as a counselor. It was a big risk. But the reward was happiness. It took a lot of courage to plant roots here. He took the chance and stayed." Relief skips off my father's words. He takes a drag and blows out a long stream of smoke.

Happy is not how I would describe that life. A constant threat hanging over your head. Your home as your very own prison. Locked up tight. No friends, no family. No one to care whether the two of you survive through the night. Even with all my bitching about Fox Inn, I know at some point someone will notice if I'm gone. I can't imagine how it must feel for people like Celeste and her father. To never fit in anywhere, with no one noticing if you slip off the map. Dread and fear are one thing—a fugitive can outrun them. But the loneliness follows you everywhere. It's no wonder Celeste and her dad cling to each other. They're all they have in the world.

"Things were good for a long time. But then he got himself caught up in that stupid Town Hall nonsense. A neighbor said she saw Celeste at the protest and John got worried. When he called me from the police station, I thought for sure we were all found out. But Brimley didn't make the connection between John Vallone and Kevin Vaughn. He didn't even recognize him, the idiot. He's not as quick as he thinks he is."

"You're the one who bailed him out?" I say.

He nods. "I said he was an old friend. John split later that night. Got a little gun-shy after spending a few hours in a jail cell."

Detective Brimley knows who John Vallone is now. And with two girls gone missing in Vista Buscato in a few weeks' span, John Vallone's arrest is Brimley's ticket to the promotion he's been telling my father about for years. It also didn't help to find Vincent in John Vallone's home, claiming to have permission to enter and yet also claiming not to know where the man is. If Brimley didn't suspect Vincent and Carlo's involvement before, he certainly does now.

"Brimley thinks he's doing the right thing," my father mutters. He drowns his cigarette in the bottom of his gin glass.

Carlo pulls a sour face. "Pffft."

"That's why he's poking around. He knows Carlo and Vincent volunteer at the shelter."

"And now he knows John Vallone's new name and where he's staying. Because of me," I say.

"Shit," Sam repeats.

Vincent moans. Carlo pats his shoulder and soothes him in Italian.

My father rubs the back of his neck.

The room drops into quiet.

"I—I'm sorry. I didn't know. I—I—" I cover my mouth. I did so much harm I can't breathe. To Celeste, her father. To Matty, myself. I single-handedly wrecked more lives than I can count—each domino collapsing against the next in line.

There's one critical driving force behind every toxic couple—Bonnie and Clyde, Sid and Nancy. They share one common thread: they'd do anything for each other. And when you're reckless and stupid and you'd do virtually anything in the name of love, bad decisions float to the surface faster than any other choice. It's sick and completely psychotic. *Depraved*, Detective Brimley would say. But I understand it. I've always given Matty what he wants. My love for him created a shitstorm of problems for everyone around me.

My father's voice softens. "I contacted John. We'll get him new papers. He and his daughter made a move already. They're not in Santa Barbara anymore. I hooked him up with a new place after pulling in a few favors."

"That quick? How did they pick up their whole life that fast?"

"You learn to live lean when you're on the run." My father's gaze sharpens. Here comes the lighter. A new cigarette sizzles, red beneath the flame. "But listen up, Effie. No messing up this time. Keep the detective happy. One call to the FBI and we're all screwed." I nod. Anything. I'll do whatever it takes. "And don't tell your mother. She's always thought helping John is too risky. She's the reason I asked him to move out in the first place."

That's right. Celeste, the friendless girl in the window, lived in a tiny, rented room above Fox Inn once and drew a castle in chalk on the sidewalk there. John Vallone and his stolen daughter came and went in the blink of an eye. Once, a long time ago.

I wonder what their names were then.

Claudette Vega.

It's a stupid name. A made-up name.

She's a nothing girl; she doesn't exist.

But even as nothing as she is, Matty wants her more than anything. I split her love story with him apart and stuffed it beneath a bunch of cheese sticks, and still my life isn't the dream I imagined it would be. Still I'm not better off. Nobody is.

And the fault lies with me.

Sam and I shiver our asses off in Fox Inn's walk-in freezer. I need him with me for a boost of courage. After what we learned in my father's office, I knew I'd lose my shit at some point. I didn't want to be alone when it happened. My own side of the story—the role I played and how it affected Matty—itches to burst forward. Standing here in the freezer, I finally let it all out to Sam. He doesn't judge. He knows how very much I adore Matty, even if I've spent the last year pretending he doesn't. He also knows how brave I can be, and the lengths I will go to.

But bravery doesn't count for shit when you know what you're doing is wrong. I didn't force Matty and Celeste apart, not exactly, but I didn't give him the tools he needed to find her. And how can you claim you love someone more than anything else, more than your own life, when you'd willingly hide the key that unlocks that person's happiness? That wall between the two of them wasn't built by me, but I did nothing to help tear it down when I had the chance. An opportunity to watch Matty and Celeste reach the dead end of their relationship presented itself, and I took it. I reveled in it, rolled around in it, rejoiced over it. I'm absolutely disgusted with myself. A stupid, ridiculous, feverish jealousy of Celeste twisted me into a girl I don't very much like. I want the old Effie back. The strong Effie. I don't care the cost.

I hold the envelope filled with new, clean, folded white pages—two IDs, two faux-faded birth certificates, and two new passports, just in case. I close my eyes and make tons and tons of wishes. I wish that I never screwed up, that I never betrayed Matty or Celeste or her father, that I was smarter, less selfish, less impulsive, that Sam wasn't leaving in a few hours time, that I could leave too. But I don't see any genies popping out of magic lamps to grant wishes. Unless you count Vincent and his magic document-making.

The responsibility of getting these new documents to Celeste rests on me. It's fitting, really, considering I'm the reason she needs them at all. Obviously, her father can't show his face in public. And with Vincent sparking suspicions, the police will watch him like a hawk. Carlo too. They're always together. My father offered to make the exchange, but I insisted it be me. For Matty's sake, I need to make sure Celeste and her father get out of here safely. Together.

I hate playing a role in her disappearing again. I never should have played a part in it in the first place.

Love makes you do crazy, insane, cowardly, *cowardly* things.

Sam's teeth clatter. It's subzero in here.

He whispers, "Eff? Why are we in the freezer?"

"There's something I've been saving...you know, for when I leave."

"Where are you going?"

"I don't know."

My determination and hard work, my pipedreams, and my ticket to freedom are all stowed inside this walk-in freezer. Blue rubber bands wrapped around wads of cash, worn green bills with food stains, some still stuck together. Someone else needs that money way more than me. One thing I learned from John Vallone's story: love and sacrifice go hand in hand.

"Give me a boost," I tell Sam.

He laces his fingers into a basket. I place my foot inside and haul myself up. I reach behind the bags of frozen vegetables on the top shelf and slide out the box of mozzarella sticks. I dig around. Finally, my fingers run against a crisp, folded notecard, exactly where I shoved it deep under the cheese sticks weeks ago, when fireworks lit up the sky and spelled out a love story that wasn't mine.

Claudette Vega.

I tuck the notecard in my pocket.

My heartbeat's pumping crazy fast and strong. I can feel it in my throat, my fingertips.

I grab the folded stack of cash that I counted and recounted for the last several months in hopes of leaving Vista Buscato. Each dollar earned and stowed with dreams of my big, fat exit in mind, the biggest trick I ever hoped to pull off. I've suddenly never been more certain that this is the right thing to do. Celeste's dream of college hit a roadblock, thanks to a quick and necessary name change. She almost got away, too, but not after I stuck the nail in the coffin and ratted her out to the police. After the way I helped screw up her life, I'll do whatever I can to give Celeste and her father a happy ending. I'm not sure what will become of me tomorrow or next week or next year, but at least I'll know my future wasn't built on the destruction of somebody's else.

I drop to my feet.

Sam watches as I take the money, my dreams, and shove them deep inside the envelope for Celeste and John Vallone.

Sam's mouth is open. "Damn. All that money's yours?" he asks.

"Not anymore."

He inclines his head like he wants to ask me something, but the words get lost between his heart and his mouth. Like a whip, he reaches out and yanks me toward him, hugs me tight. My sweet, sweet Sam. We stand there clamped together until my fingers ache from the cold and I can't feel my nose. But I know tears run alongside it. They drop from my chin as I lay all my fears out for Sam—I'm going nowhere, I'm stuck, my future's washing away, all I see are pause buttons.

Sam shushes me, says everything will turn out fine, I'm the strongest person he knows.

But I don't know if he's right. Strong people aren't supposed to get hurt.

CHAPTER TWENTY-FIVE

The Founder's Day parade rolls down Buscato Drive. Horn blasts and drumbeats grow louder as marching bands draw near. Kids watching from the sidewalks lick matching lollipops from Joselle's Sweet Shop. The little pieces of red candy on sticks spell out "VB." The whole town turns out for the parade, lining the streets from end to end of Buscato Drive, stopping at Halberd Court. Peter LaRoche leads it all with a grand marshal sash. He waves at the crowds like a beauty pageant contestant.

I pop out onto Fox Inn's front steps to join Joe and Matty—the captain and his lieutenants surveying the field before battle. A crew of skateboarders collects in the parking lot across the street. This is it. We're prepped and at attention. We have our orders. Keep things under control at the Wiley estate, chaos-free. Spread our message. Our voices will not go unheard. There's a place for skaters in this town, and if others won't make room for us, we'll do it ourselves.

Joe stole his lucky, white, Bones Brigade cap back from me under protest. He wears it now, and underneath its lid, his eyebrows squeeze together. I'm about to ask him what's wrong when he taps Matty's arm. "Detective's here. Keeping an eye on things."

Matty's eyes run over the crowd swelling in the street.

He and Joe slap out a bro handshake that pauses at the end. Hands still joined, they stare into each other's eyes. Something indescribable passes between them. Matty nods.

Behind us, my parents step out of Fox Inn. My mother's cheeks are red. Her blood's boiling beneath her skin, I bet. She stares at the skateboarders gathered across the street like she wants to hurl a stick of dynamite at them.

Suddenly, their raised voices chant, "We want a park! We want a park!"

I cringe. *Not yet. Wait.*

Some of them bang skateboard decks against utility poles. The clatter is outrageous. It drowns out the cheery sunshine of drums and trumpets marching by. Joe chews on his bottom lip. This wasn't the plan. They're supposed to wait until the parade moves to the Wiley estate. Every nerve in my body fires up with worry.

A man and woman stroll up to Fox Inn. Oblivious, they chat about the parade in an exchange of "Oh! Did you see those adorable children waving flags from the sidewalk?" and "Nothing beats a good tuba blast, I tell ya'!"

I roll my eyes and step aside to let them pass.

My mother flits into a dance routine of the usual tricks, smoothing down her skirt, fixing her necklace. Showtime!

"Are you open?" the woman asks.

Felicia Fox flashes a smile reserved for paying customers only. "Seven days a week! Come on in!" She shoos Joe away with a shove to the shoulder.

From somewhere in the crowd of skateboarders, a bottle sails high into the air and cracks against the pavement in the middle of the street. Glass scatters in a billion directions. Mothers on sidewalks gasp. Fathers square their shoulders, protecting their young.

On Fox Inn's steps, we all stiffen.

"Let's take care of that," Joe mutters. "Can't have people in cuffs before we get the message out."

I certainly cannot end this day in handcuffs.

The Vallones are counting on me. My father made contact with John. It's unspeakably dangerous for John to meet me himself to pick up the new IDs, so he'll send Celeste. Our meeting place? Las Palmas Altas, as positively insane as it sounds. The feds are so preoccupied with finding John Vallone elsewhere that they've stopped surveillance on his old house, a place they've checked and rechecked and come up empty every time. Celeste will wait for me there, hidden brilliantly in plain sight, as she collects the last of her belongings, which I'm sure aren't many. As my father recited the plan to me, it all sounded like choices in a chess game, and I totally understood why this Vallone dude has evaded capture for as long as he has. Anyone who takes a million hours to deliberate a move will probably make the right one.

Matty steps into the street.

Joe follows, then looks back at me. He stretches out a hand. Hope forms a question in his dark eyes. He waits for my move.

My mother calls out, "Effie, get in here. You have customers."

I glance at my father. He lights up a cigarette, flicks his chin at me in acknowledgement.

He knows what I have to do.

I grab Joe's hand and take off.

We beat the parade to the Wiley estate. It isn't hard. We're all on wheels, after all.

But we didn't beat the cops. Enormous wooden barricades already ring the perimeter of the estate, blocking us from access to our paradise inside. They're painted blue, with white letters spelling out "Vista Buscato Police Department."

Brimley underestimated us. We won't be silenced or pushed away. Dogma made banners. She and a few others pull folded red and black swaths of fabric from their backpacks and stretch them out. Soon, flags fly from lampposts like pirate sails. They're tacked and stretched across the barricades, displaying "Skate Free or Die" in Dogma's freeform art.

As the parade moves closer, Vista Buscato residents pile up along the sidewalks to watch the show. They take one look at our banners, our boards, our clothes, and gravitate to the opposite side of the street. There's no real fence erected in the middle of our two communities, no true walls dividing the haves from the have nots, and yet here we are, them on one side and us on the other. The narrow street spreading between us might as well be galaxies wide.

Keeping myself focused on the protest is a monumental challenge. I'm set to meet Celeste once the sun goes down. Snippets of blond hair appear everywhere. She's all I see. This must be how Matty felt when he first fell in love with her. And to think all I saw was glitter and fairy dust. She's so much more than that.

I get to work passing out American flags attached to sticks from two giant cardboard boxes that Edgar shows up with. Soon, everyone's got one. From every angle, every left-to-right switch of your eyes, they fly overhead. Joe smiles at me. "Genius," he says. I can't take credit for the idea. Sam came up with it. Before he left, he managed to convince his father we needed as many flags as we could get our hands on for a summer street fair later in the month. Of course, General Wills supported Sam's show of national pride and had the boxes shipped to Skate Real. The General would have a stroke if he knew the real story. Three men across the street with matching Vista Buscato Golf Club polo shirts glare at us, at our flags held high, and snicker. How absurd that the same flag could mean two different things depending on who's holding it.

Joe climbs on top of a barricade and hooks an arm around a nearby palm tree trunk. Like his guru Edgar on the ground next to him, he's wearing a Skate Real t-shirt with a skull and crossbones design on the front. The bones are actually skateboards.

Dogma passes Joe a bullhorn. Edgar clutches the handle of one in his fist, too.

"We are here! We are here!"

First Joe starts the chant, each word slow and deliberate. Then Edgar joins in.

The crowd—*our* crowd—cheers. On the other side of the street, parade-goers pass each other looks that are either frightened or disgusted. I wonder what would happen if Joe dressed the part, like he did at the Town Hall meeting. Maybe the rest of the town would take him seriously then. Who am I kidding? If they didn't respect him that night, they never will.

Dogma hands me and Matty each a bullhorn.

I don't waste time. I wave my board over my head with one hand, raise the bullhorn with the other, and explode with "We are here!" The words rip my throat open. Who knows how much longer I'll be stuck in this town, but whether it's days or weeks or years, I won't let anyone push Joe or my friends out. Thanks to Celeste and her dad's predicament, I've spent some time imagining what being bounced from your home feels like. Nothing comes close to matching the despair. Joe deserves to live in a place that is his. He deserves friends who come through for him. He needs people who care. He certainly cares enough about us.

Matty pulls his own bullhorn to his lips and joins our chorus.

People follow my lead and lift their boards high. Decks and wheels and American flags wave overhead, like how people hold up lighters and cell phones at concerts. I think our boards shine even brighter than those lights and flames.

I'm overwhelmed by it all—the flags, the chanting, the unity. I never knew all of us could care so much about a town that doesn't even want us here. To be honest, I never knew I cared about this town at all. I thought for sure I didn't. Today, I don't know.

Everyone goes wild. I can't hear the marching bands anymore.

Some mutant tosses a soda can at a palm tree. It explodes and fizzes brown liquid in all directions. Screams and laughter bubble up from the crowd. At the exact same time, Dogma and I yell at the guy. She grins at me, and I return the sentiment. It feels oddly good being on the same page as her. For the first time in my life, I feel like the place where I belong might be a little bigger than I ever thought it was. Maybe I'm even bigger.

Edgar waves to an older guy with a huge black backpack and a camera the size of a boulder swinging from a strap on his shoulder. The guy drops to one knee and starts snapping pics, but not of the parade, of *us*—Joe and Edgar and Matty and me. He scoots closer. His focus shifts. He zeroes in on me.

Some messages don't need words. I drop my bullhorn to the ground.

With both arms I lift my board up.

I turn my face up to it. From end to end, the deck blots out the sky. It's over my head, as high as I can reach, scraping the clouds, breaking into the heavens. Dogma waves one of her red banners. It swishes against my shoulder.

The photographer shoots and shoots. My arms shake from holding the pose.

Behind me, others catch on and do it too.

Our boards are aloft, blocking the sun. We eclipse everything.

Over time, with all the energy coursing through us, the barricades shift onto the Wiley estate. Cops push the barricades forward, locking us out of the Wiley land, pressing us back to the sidewalk. The only direction left is into the street, and unless death by a marching band stampede is the way to go, we're all screwed.

Joe's still perched on the corner of a barricade. A cop shoves the other end, not realizing his move shifts the balance. Joe freefalls in slow motion and hits the ground to a collection of gasps and "Oh! Shit!" from the crowd. In the fray, his hat tumbles off. The photographer snaps away. Joe's hair sticks to his cheeks in spots. Fury builds in his eyes, dark and raw, and I'm reminded of the Joe I've seen other times. The crazy, super reckless Joe. He pops to his feet, but with so many people and arms and legs and skateboards pressed around him, his balance is sketchy. I reach an arm out to steady him. Before I can help, he stumbles backward toward the street, taking down an entire row of cymbal-clashers in the parade.

Two cops bolt at Joe.

I scream, "It was an accident!"

The crowd stirs.

They tackle him.

Joe shouts, "We want our voices heard!"

The horde of protesters rumbles and moves in a wave. Edgar raises hands, trying to calm the masses. The photographer keeps clicking. A cop approaches him. Like lightning he pulls a lanyard from around his neck to reveal a laminated square attached to the end. Funny—he has a right to be here even when we don't.

A scraping sounds stirs up. A barricade crashes onto its side. More cops rush to fix it, but the damage is done. People pour into the Wiley estate, commemorating their win with declarations: *Skate Free or Die!*

I spot Joe on the ground, face down, arms beating the ground, fighting still. With a *click-click*, handcuffs pin his wrists together. The photographer snaps and snaps and twists his lens. The marching band walks on. Baton twirlers dance all around them.

I snatch Joe's hat off the ground. Precious things need protecting. I shove it on my own head.

"Shit!" Matty shouts. He sees Joe too.

"We have to help him," I say.

Anxiety sets my muscles tingling, popping.

I can't risk getting swept up in this if it turns south. The love of Matty's life needs to make it out of Vista Buscato safely, with John Vallone by her side, not orphaned by law enforcement. Celeste handed me a notecard and in return I will hand her a ticket to a new life. This is the only way I can unscrew all the things I screwed up so royally for Matty this summer. Back at Fox Inn, a folded manila envelope sits in my brother's hands, stuffed with identification and cash wrapped in blue rubber bands for a man and his daughter. When Gerard brings me those documents after his shift ends, everything will backslide back to normal. I will make things right.

Tugging me, Matty bounces toward the other side of the street—the safe side—where his grandfather and other families and happy parade-goers watch in confusion. Judge Pomerantz sees us and approaches very, very slowly. His eyes run a full body scan over me, from the Vans I wrote on yesterday while my tables were slow to the t-shirt I stole from my brother, and Joe's hat, underneath which my long, brown hair needs more than just a simple comb-through. I'm acutely, painfully aware of what a mess I am.

To my surprise, he smiles. "Stefanie. It's nice to see you." He presses a hand to my shoulder.

I want to correct him and say, "Effie," but my name feels stupid in my mouth. Not classy, not pretty. My life could have been so different had my name been beautiful. Like Celeste. Or Caroline. Anything but my own.

Matty's cheeks are pink and bright. He speaks in a rush. "Pops, they arrested Joe. But he wasn't doing anything wrong. He lost his balance and stepped into the parade route when they shoved the barricades at us."

The old man's eyes widen. "He'll be charged with disorderly conduct again."

"You have to help him."

"The friction is this town is reaching an unmanageable level. One side will have to sacrifice something or things will break down entirely."

My intention isn't to argue with the judge, I'm certain I'd lose the debate, but I can't help jumping in. "Judge Pomerantz, the protesters..." I correct myself, "I mean to say *we*...have nothing left to sacrifice."

"Yeah, " Matty agrees. "Their voices are all they have." I'm struck by the way he says *they* instead of *our*. But I can't dwell on it. This isn't the time.

"Perhaps you're not the side who needs to sacrifice then," the judge says. He looks at me with a little nod, a trace of a sympathetic smile. "In the legal world, righteous evidence is the answer to everything, you know." The judge's voice is soft, always soft. Like he spent years shouting over lawyers and prosecutors and defendants and now he's spent, rung out. But for all that, he's still the kind of person you do not interrupt. You wait for him to finish speaking, even when you have no idea what he's talking about—like right now. I think that's the kind of person Joe wants to be. Someone people listen to.

Three men and women I recognize as Board members move beside the judge. Outrage sharpens their features; it threads through their chit-chat. They aren't quiet about it.

Brimley has his hands full with that Monroe kid.

I heard his mother has no control over him. Stepfather couldn't care less.

It's a shame. What a waste.

We'll see how brave he is in prison someday.

I run my fingers along the top of Joe's hat. The photographer snapped a pic of me grabbing it off the ground.

"Judge Pomerantz? I think the photographer caught pictures of the sequence of events. Maybe we could ask him for copies to show the police that Joe wasn't at fault."

The judge smiles. "Now you're thinking like a lawyer," he says. "Come with me to the police station. Sounds like our dear friend Joseph needs advocates." His eyes flick to the commotion near the upended barricades at the Wiley entrance. This is not how tonight was supposed to go down. We were supposed to speak our minds, make progress, not chaos. And I was supposed to fix the terrible things I've done in the name of love.

My cell phone buzzes in my pocket. It's Gerard. His shift ended ten minutes ago.

My heartbeat pounds and pounds and pounds.

Time ticks away. I need to split. Gerard's on his way. He'll be looking for me so he can pass that manila envelope over, and I cannot screw this up.

First one step, then two tiny steps backward.

Matty looks at me. His hair's bright, and his eyes are even brighter. I think he senses that I'm halfway gone.

"Effie…" he says slowly, like a warning.

I back away some more. "I can't."

"What are you talking about?"

His eyes are full of questions.

The realization doesn't strike him that Celeste is the answer to them all.

I break into a run. Matty calls out my name.

I try not to dwell on how shitty it feels to leave him and how that feeling will smother me again when he's gone for good. For now, I focus on the good parts of all this—Judge Pomerantz will protect Joe, I'll protect Celeste, and Matty will never know. Everyone's taken care of. Except me. My eyes burn. But I don't cry. Because it's time to be strong.

I find Gerard waiting in Bruiser's pickup at a street corner three blocks away.

My brother's eyes are glassy. Who knows what he's inhaled to clear away the stink of Fox Inn on him. In the driver seat, a wool beanie sits low on Bruiser's forehead, but I spot a fresh line of blood slashed across the top of his right eyebrow. He sported the exact same cut last year when he was baked out of his mind and wiped out in the rain off Fox Inn's front steps. Being fun and reckless is one thing when you're on wheels, but it's a different ballgame when your future is on the line. I'm not sure if Bruiser or Gerard care.

I jump into the pickup. Gerard passes me the manila envelope. For the first time in my life, he's come through on a promise. I fold the envelope, then stuff it down the front of my jean shorts and tug my t-shirt over it. Within minutes, we're cruising up the mountain to Las Palmas Altas. Gerard laughs and laughs over how the sun drops low and round in the sky, like a giant orange Skittle, which makes him think of candy, which makes them stop at a gas station for snacks.

Minutes pass by on the dashboard clock. I shake my foot one thousand times a minute. Gerard returns with a Red Bull and hands it to me. I realize I don't know my brother's favorite drink or movie or pro skateboarder or anything. I'm too busy counting the hours until I can get away from him and my parents and Fox Inn. He rips open his pack of Skittles and declares them the greatest food on earth. I vow to remember that one stupid detail about my brother, even as it drowns in all the other details in my head tonight.

They drop me at the back of Las Palmas Altas, where Matty coaxed me over a black painted fence at the beginning of summer. I harass them as best I can. *Go straight back to Vista Buscato! Put away the weed! Get off the road!* They yes me to death. My brother's already baked himself into oblivion. Bruiser says goodbye and Gerard lifts one hand in a lazy wave. No questions, no answers. They don't care what I'm doing, but then, I've never given them a reason to.

Chapter Twenty-Six

I am so over climbing fences.

This sucks.

With my toes dug into one of the diamond cutouts in the fence, I grab the top crossbar. It's still California-warm, of course. The sun set not too long ago. A grayish-orange haze still clings to the sky. With a heave, I pull myself up. Grab some leverage. Okay. I'm good. I can do it. I've conquered this climb on more than one occasion. My fingers wrap around the spokes.

I swing one leg over.

Below me, a voice whispers, "Effie?"

It's Matty. My muscles light up with fire.

He cannot be here.

His voice changes everything. He's on the right side of the fence, the inside. Or the wrong side, depending how you look at it. My mind shifts focus from getting through the task at hand to his presence and what it means for my meeting with Celeste.

"What the hell are you doing? Go away," I hiss.

He stares up at me like I've gone off the deep end. "What's going on? Why are you—"

"I'm doing something for Gerard."

"What are you talking about? I just saw him on the road. He has no clue what you're doing here. Care to fill me in?"

"Never mind me. What are *you* doing here?"

"Joe and I were looking for you."

"I thought you were bailing him out?"

"Pops took care of it in less than three minutes."

"Cool. Tell Joe I took his hat."

He ignores the comment. "Get down."

"I can't. I have to—" *What? What?* "I...I have to—I need to—"

A rustle shimmies the bushes behind Matty.

"Matthew?"

I know that voice.

A figure shifts forward, pulls down the hoodie. Celeste. Even with her hair pulled back and her face wiped of the usual joy, she's still the most beautiful person I've ever seen.

Matty doesn't move. Several seconds slide by.

"Ce-Celeste?"

They throw themselves together. An excited blend of words and phrases and affirmations rises around their entwined arms and hands and fingers and lips:

You're here!

Where did you go?

I missed you so much!

I love you!

I love you too!

I'm sorry!

I hover on the fence. My hands slip on the warm metal. I'm sweating. My muscles ache, arms tremble. I don't think I can hold on much longer and I can't fucking concentrate with their delirious voices in my head. My body feels off, like I suddenly have too many moving parts. My legs dangle on either side of the fence, dragging me down, willing me to drop. I'm not ready. I'm too busy watching them kiss and I can't center my brain. My torso pitches too far to the right.

I fumble. *Shit.*

The drop to the ground is fast. I hit bottom. Hard.

The thing about getting cut is you don't feel it at first. You almost sort of hope that you imagined the injury, that you didn't get sliced up, even though you know it's just a pipedream, because you totally did. It isn't till you move that the sting runs through you. The pain waits until then. That's when your hope runs out.

Of all the falls I've had in my lifetime, not one has hurt like this. This one, this kills.

The pain bursts open and multiplies inside me.

I feel the thick bump of Joe's lucky hat pinned under my shoulder, which means my head probably met with the earth first, I think. I don't know. I'm face down. Everything's dark and out of focus. Dirt sticks to my cheek. I'm here on the ground but I'm not grounded, which makes zero sense. Efforts to lift my head result in tipping and swirling—not of me, but of the planet. So I stay down, hands and cheek pressed against the earth. Skaters are led to believe we're strong, toughened up, because cement is the hardest place to fall. I'm not so sure. Any fall is a fall, and if the landing isn't soft, it's all awful.

Celeste and Matty's voices ping around my ears but I can't process their words. The pain running through my nerves burns like acid.

I bite back the urge to lift myself up and look at my chest. Judging from the burn I feel there, it isn't going to be pretty. The fence's spokes of doom got me. I wince. My hand is on fire too.

From somewhere above, I hear Celeste say, "Effie? Effie?"

Matty grabs my bad hand and tries to yank me up. I scream.

"You're good, you're good. It's just a little blood." His voice shakes.

A sound blares in the distance. Cops? An ambulance? I don't know. Lights pass on the road behind us. Red and white and they're spinning.

That singsong voice with the hidden question marks says, stiffly, rocked with sudden fear, "Cops! I have to go."

"No! No!" Matty shouts. "Don't leave again!"

He drops my hand.

I watch Celeste's feet backpedal. Her sneakers scrape against tree bark. It makes me think, *Yes, smart. A tree would have been easier to climb than the fence. Should've thought of that. Next time.* But I don't see myself taking chances like this anymore. Not for Matty, not for anyone else.

Something shoots sharp inside me, low, on my right. I gasp, struck by some internal pain I can't identify.

"Matty," I say. Everything comes out choked, like I'm gasping for air.

But Matty's looking at Celeste, not me.

The sirens keep going.

Celeste slips over a tree branch and drops to the other side of the fence.

"NO!" Matty screams, scrambling up the tree, craning his neck at a spot in the distance, in the hopes his angel won't disappear.

What's the use? We were all fools for misjudging her. She's an expert at vanishing. One minute she's here, and the next she's gone, and it all would have gone perfectly to plan if I'd given her the documents still tucked into my waistband. All would have been fine if Matty didn't show up. Now, it's a disaster.

"Matty, Matty." Over and over I call him. I'm afraid to move.

He drops down from the tree, sways from foot to foot, eyes jumping from me to the tree to the fence, and to Celeste's imaginary path in the distance, probably calculating how far she's run and whether he can reach her if he leaves me here and chases her on wheels.

"Did you know she'd be here?"

I ignore him.

"Do you think she got far? Can I catch her?" He nearly hyperventilates. I'm reminded of the crooked, flipped version of him I saw in the mirror that night at Fox Inn—the one Joe seems to know so well and I denied existed.

Fighting against the pain, I push myself up on my forearms. Lightning shoots through my wrist. I bite back another scream. Looking down, I catch a glimpse of my chest. No amount of gauze will slow what's flushing out of me. It's more than just a little blood. A deep slice rips open my t-shirt. But it's not even my shirt, I remember. It's Gerard's. He's going to freak. It's his favorite. Covering my wound seems like the sort of thing Sam would tell me to do if he were here, so I put pressure against it with one dirt-caked hand. Red blooms beneath my fingers.

Matty's head keeps swinging back and forth, from me to invisible Celeste in the distance.

Beneath the gash on my chest, a river of something else starts to flow, something other than blood. Rage. The longer I look up at him, hoping for a different reaction, for care and concern, the more I want to burn this whole fucking town to the ground.

"I'm bleeding, Matty," I say, more calmly than I feel.

"I—I might have something in the Jeep. Band-Aids, maybe?"

"Does it look like a Band-Aid will cover this?"

He eyeballs my wound. "You'll need more than one."

"Sure." White-hot pain rips through my chest. I gasp. "Head to Walgreen's. I'll wait here. But make sure you spring for the biggest box they sell. I'll need the whole thing. Go for the Superhero ones if you can find them, too. I'm always saving your ass, aren't I?"

"Effie," he says, and the pain in his voice pisses me off even more.

"I'm hurt!" Shouting makes that low, down-deep pain inside me throb even more. I try to get to my feet again, but my forearms can't handle the pressure.

"I know. But it'll be okay."

"Are you really trying to convince me this isn't a big deal?" I look up at him, trying to make sense of what—who—I'm seeing.

His head swings around again to look at the fence. "Do you know where she went? Do you think she'll come back?"

I have no response. Only angry, angry thoughts: *Shut up. Just shut your fucking mouth.*

The shakes set in. I shiver. My forearms give out. I drop to the ground and press one cheek into the dirt again.

Oh my God, I lied to myself.

Hope got the better of me. He never, ever felt the same way. The sheer impossibility of this one final truth weighs my heart down. He only kissed me back because he was drunk. He was only pretending I was her. I'm sickened.

Arteries leading to my heart close off as he continues the bombardment of questions. I can't process his words. My head floats on the inside. I feel like I'm falling again, except I'm already down here in the dirt in a spot where the grass on this side of town doesn't grow green but alternates in checkerboard patches of dusty brown and gray. The sky's turned dark overhead, inky blue and purple. Only a scrape of light glows on the horizon. The whole of Vista Buscato stretches for miles around me, the land spreading down the hills to where the ocean meets the land, the waves rolling into endless possibilities, limitless dreams, and for me, Matty Pomerantz is no longer in any of them.

He is everything to me.

No.

He *was* everything to me.

Nothing anyone said could pull me from him. Not another guy, not my gut feeling, not Joe's hints, even when I wondered if he was right. Nothing could break that loyalty to Matty. That is love. That is caring, devotion.

And now, his lack of concern rocks my fucking world.

The person standing beside me, not tending to my wound, not fussing over me like Joe would, or holding my hand like Sam would, is not the same guy I continually risk everything for. Whatever concern he once had for me is gone. I pushed those concerns away; I told him not to worry, I am tough, I can handle it. I let him think nothing was off limits or out of bounds or undoable. His love for Celeste will always come first. I lay here bleeding, maybe dying, and he can't focus on anything other than her.

He tips his head, pleading. "Do you care if I go after her? I mean, you're okay, right? I can't let her get away. You don't mind, right?"

Someone thunders over to us. The ground pulses beneath me with hurried footsteps.

"What happened to her?" a voice shouts.

Joe. *Joe.*

Gentle hands flip me onto my back. Joe kneels beside me. I ache so badly for him to wrap his arms around me and tell me I should have been more careful. Next time I'll listen. He tries to pull my hands from my chest, but I don't let him. There's so much blood. The palm of my hand covers my heart, but blood leaks around the edges anyway, an outline in red.

Matty finally gets the idea that should have occurred to him eons ago and kneels, too.

"Let me see, Effie," Joe says softly. "How bad is it?"

"Bad, I think." My voice doesn't sound like my own.

A flash of my white bra peeks through the sliced fabric of Gerard's bloodstained t-shirt. I'm split open, everything inside me pouring out. I spread my hands across my chest.

"It's just a cut, it's just a cut," Matty says over and over. "Cover it up."

Joe turns on Matty.

"What happened to her?" His volume cracks the sound barrier in half.

"I don't know. She fell, I think."

"What do you mean, '*you think*'? Weren't you with her?"

"I was—I was..." I can see his thoughts and they're miles away, on the other side of the fence, down the road, chasing after a mystery girl.

"You selfish fucking prick," Joe growls, his brown eyes full of adrenaline and fury.

Matty's eyes shift, stunned.

"Haven't you looked at her?" Joe rages on. "Haven't you seen the blood?"

Joe pulls my hands away, revealing my wound.

"I don't want to see it!" Matty roars. "I know she's hurt!"

Carefully, slowly, with endless tenderness, Joe pulls at the torn pieces of the t-shirt, where the Vans logo splits apart into VA- and –NS, where the fabric opens up and my heart spills out. He pulls it together, closed and whole, as it should be. He insists on helping me to my feet, even though I'd rather plunge a stake right through the hole in my chest to finish the job than take aid from anyone. I sway. Joe lifts me straight off the ground and into his arms.

I feel like a ragdoll. Small and stupid and reckless and ridiculous. There's no fight in me anymore. I burrow my face in the crook of Joe's neck. His skin's soft and smells like sweat and lavender.

"She needs a hospital," Joe says.

Matty looks at me, then back at Joe.

The struggle is painfully obvious. Taking care of Effie means throwing away his chance to find Celeste before she gets too far away. But ignoring Effie means being an irrefutable asshole. I'm so angry and hot with rage that I second-guess who he is underneath it all. I think he might actually go the asshole route. But after a pause, he nods. "I know."

Matty leads us through the complex. We pass through the center courtyard where I spilled Celeste's secret to Detective Brimley. My stomach lurches at the memory. The security guard steps out of his booth. He asks if we need help. An ambulance? A first-aid kit? As if he cares.

Joe shifts and grunts as we reach the Jeep.

I moan. Breathing is hard, sharp.

"It hurts, Joe," I whisper. "It really hurts."

"It'll be okay. I got you."

Tears spill down my cheeks. I don't bother hiding them. Something tells me Joe doesn't mind. He never did.

In Matty's hands, the keys to the Jeep jingle. Joe loads me into the backseat. It's hell getting in. The pain burns, inside and outside my chest. Matty tosses the keys to Joe and jumps in next to me. Sitting up properly against the backseat is nearly impossible as we bounce down the hill, on our way, Joe insists, to Vista Buscato Medical Center's emergency room. My lips are shut, but somehow the grunts of pain still leak through.

Matty tugs my head and shoulders down to rest across his lap. It burns to twist my torso this way. He runs a hand over my hair. The top is down, the wind blows us skyward.

I rub my eyes. The ache in my head intensifies. I wince.

He pets my hair again. "You'll be okay."

No, I won't. I'm never going to be okay after this night. It's over.

He whispers, "What was Celeste doing there?"

Her name is a blow to my already throbbing head.

She's here, even when she's not here. Always, always, always.

I will never be more than a visitor with luggage waiting for a ride at the airport, a friend passing through town who wants to say hi, a girl he once used to hop around on skateboards within the streets of his hometown.

It's over. This is the end.

I dig into the front of my jeans, pull out the blood-stained manila envelope. This package was meant for Celeste. And so is Matty.

He takes the envelope, slides the contents out. Papers and wads of money fall into his hands. "What is this?" he asks.

"Celeste's new name and address."

His face goes frozen. Beneath my head, his legs stiffen, muscles clench.

"I don't understand." He shakes his head. Wind tugs his orangey hair skyward. His freckles vanish. "Why do you have this?"

Do it. Just say it already. He deserves to know.

"I've known where she was since she disappeared."

He stops poking through the documents. "What?"

"She asked me to tell you, but I didn't."

Matty does something weird with his lips—a licking, biting, pressing movement. He's considering my explanation, trying it on for size. I don't think it works for him. He pulls the paper in his hands taut. I wonder how long he'll stare at it, if he already has the new name and address memorized.

The silence sucks. I try my best to explain but it doesn't make sense, even to me.

"You wanted her gone," he says slowly, sorting through a catalog of thoughts.

"Not like that. Not in a way that hurt you."

"You kept me from her." Blame sharpens each word.

Can Joe hear us? If he can, he doesn't say anything. He doesn't save me. I deserve this.

The Jeep flies down the road. I watch the sky shift above us.

My heart's pounding so hard. It thrums in my ears.

"Why would you do that to me?"

"I—I—" The stars whizz by overhead in a circle. I feel so far away. Matty shoots out more angry words, but I can't grasp them. A buzzer goes off inside my head. I keep watching the stars, but it only makes me more dizzy. I hear Matty, I know he says my name, and the sound flips from pissed to urgent all in the space of a second. But I don't have the brainpower to formulate an answer to each question. His voice grows softer, a little frantic at the edges. The words run in and out of my head just as fast as he says them.

"Effie? Effie!"

"I'm sorry," I mumble. Too much ringing in my ears. I can't hear myself. I hope he can. "I think I loved you a little too much."

I close my eyes.

He holds me, shakes me, frantically shouting in the hopes I'll hear, wherever I am.

Stars surround his head.

I let him fade away. I let go.

Chapter Twenty-Seven

They say the more you love someone, the harder it is to see them clearly. Something blinds you, hides all their imperfections. I didn't want to see anything in Matty other than spontaneous, hilarious, boundless energy. But that Matty, the one I always loved, split at the seams. The other parts of him bled through to the surface.

My eyelids flutter open.

Matty stands beside me, a hand on my arm. And it's like I'm seeing him for the first time.

Every part of him is exposed, highlighted and in bold. He's beautiful. But other, not-so-beautiful things come to mind too. A thin thread of selfishness sews him together. He followed his heart and forgot about me. He kissed his dream girl under a sky where fireworks flashed so hard and bright that they overpowered everything, even his love for me.

I see him now. No filter.

Every one of us has flaws. Even the greatest among us is human in the end, after all.

"She's awake!" Matty shouts.

He fades away, and Joe steps into his place.

"What's up, Foxy?" His smile slingshots me into the present. "You're all banged up."

I blink.

Daylight blazes above us. Too bright.

I throw an arm over my eyes, but only succeed in clunking something thick against my forehead. A soft cast extends from my forearm to fingers. And it's wrapped up in a cheesy sling, too.

It isn't daylight at all, but lights shining overhead in a giant, open room of beds and beeping machines. People shuffle around in green scrubs, stethoscopes ringing their necks. Someone coughs behind a curtained-off area.

You are here: Vista Buscato's emergency room.

Déjà vu spins me back to eighth grade when I broke my ankle. In this very place, the orthopedist told my parents I'd be off my skateboard for at least four weeks, maybe even as much as six. "Come back for follow-up x-rays in four weeks. Maybe then we'll talk about cast removal." We didn't go back. After two and a half weeks, I took utility scissors to that cast myself and threw the thing in the dumpster behind Fox Inn.

The déjà vu moment clears.

A soft wrapping is on my wrist this time, with a plastic board tied up with it, holding my wrist firm and straight within the sling. A sure sign that a hard plaster cast is in my future. Also, my chest aches. I'm wearing a hospital gown. Under it, Gerard's ripped, bloodied t-shirt is now completely severed down the middle, like someone took scissors to it. A giant gauze pad's taped in a six-inch long line between my boobs and halfway under my blood-soaked bra.

The night's events rush back, filling my head with a million thoughts and feelings I wish I could push away. I failed at everything. Joe was arrested. Matty knows what I did. He sees me for the selfish, cruel person I really am. And I didn't transfer the papers to Celeste. I could have cracked every bone in my body, slashed every major artery, and it wouldn't hurt as bad as my reality.

More people rush at me: my mother and father, Judge Pomerantz, Carlo and Vincent. Joe's still by my side. Matty hangs back behind his grandfather. A nurse pushes through them all and adjusts the blood pressure cuff on my arm. She pauses, waits for a number on a computer screen to the left of my bed, and seems satisfied with the answer.

My mother shoves her aside. "We're here, Effie. The whole family's here for you." Her eyes are watery, bloodshot. Faded lipstick bleeds into the fine lines along her upper lip.

Joe takes my good hand. He's soft, careful, like his touch might crack me in half. If I weren't so damn exhausted, I might be annoyed by his kid glove treatment. I'm not a delicate flower. The proof is in the fall I managed to survive. But I kind of appreciate that he's thinking of me and my pain. It's comforting.

The nurse presses them all backward. "Give it a few more minutes, guys. Then I'll move her upstairs." Matty and the judge back away. The rest of them won't budge. The nurse sighs.

"No smoking in the building, sir," she says to my father.

"Oh, it's not lit." He smiles. "I don't smoke."

Her second sigh is a millimeter away from an outright groan. She hates us already. She pads away toward a station in the center of the room where other nurses scurry, carrying folders or holding tiny cups of multicolored pills.

"What's she talking about? Upstairs?" I ask.

"To a room," my father explains, talking around the cigarette between his lips. "You hit your head pretty hard. You're staying overnight for observation."

"No, I'm not."

Carlo and Vincent don't even bother hiding smiles. Joe lets out a soft chuckle.

"She's exactly like you, Phil," my mother complains, and spins off toward the nurse's station.

"We tried telling them you're a combative patient," my father says, shrugging. "But I think they remember her as the problem." He pokes a thumb in the direction of my mother now arguing with a nurse. Loudly.

"Get her out of here," I mutter.

My father puts up his hands in surrender. "I'm on it, I'm on it." He trots away to throw cold water on my mother's steaming attitude. At the nurse's station, she shouts a string of tirades about wait times and lazy staff and incompetence. My father tugs on her arm, attempting to wedge himself between her and her prey, a team which has grown to two doctors and three nurses, from what I can tell by their differing scrubs and lab coats. That's small potatoes for Felicia Fox. She won't cave, not ever.

A thought pops into my head as I watch my family behaving badly. Again.

"Carlo, if all of you are here, who's at the restaurant?"

"You really care, kid?"

I shrug. Doing so pulls on the muscles in my chest. It hurts. "Not really."

He smiles. "Nobody here cares either."

Turns out I broke myself. Literally.

I fractured two bones in my right hand, one in my wrist, and a rib on my right side. A Frankenstein seam containing twenty-six stitches runs down my chest and a giant ace bandage wraps around my middle. And according to the neurologist, a mild concussion knocked my brain around.

I have a good mind to tell her that my head thumped against concrete harder, and repeatedly, when I taught myself to pull a 360 ollie down the steps at Town Hall. But why point that out? My mother would freak. Carlo and Vincent finally calmed her down. We don't need Felicia Fox breathing fire again. As it is, her hair frizzes out all over the place. She tugs ferociously at the clip holding it all together. When she bent to kiss me earlier, after her verbal sparring match with the baby-faced attending orthopedist, the one who was eager to put pins in my wrist, I didn't detect any traces of alcohol in her breath. Just coffee. It smelled weird on her, but I could get used to it.

I decide not to pitch a fit when the pissy nurse orders me into a wheelchair for my ride upstairs. Her biceps are the size of my thigh. She looks like she can throw a stiff punch. Behind my wheelchair, the Fox crew marches single file down the hall. They cram into the elevator, shoulder to shoulder. Carlo and Vincent purposely slide between my mother and the nurse. Those guys always know the right thing to do.

My hospital room is small. And vomit green. I absolutely will not survive an entire night in this prison cell.

As if to further declare my night a success, I have a roommate. She's about four hundred years old. When the nurse flicks on the light behind my bed, the old lady sighs with more force than I expect from a woman whose collarbones poke hard and sharp underneath her skin. I should tell her to run. With the Foxes around, mayhem can only worsen.

The nurse hooks me up to the blood pressure machine and slips the heart rate monitor clamp over my finger. Leashes and chains and shackles hold me down from all angles. I'm about ready to lose it.

The nurse leaves.

I immediately fly into a rant about the absurdity of it all. I'm okay. Slightly dizzy, yeah. And I have a rip-roaring headache. But I'm not dying. I want out of here.

My father rubs the back of his neck. "Just...do your best," he says.

"What does that mean?"

My mother's face is dead serious. "Your bones are broken."

"So what? I've had broken bones before."

"Yes, but you also have a concussion. You need rest." She helps adjust my pillow. "For once in your life, will you listen to us?"

The nurse pops her head back in the doorway. "Room 304. The floor above this one."

"Thank you," my father mutters.

My mother readjusts her hair clip.

"What? What's in 304?" I ask.

Silence blankets the room. Vincent and Carlo won't make eye contact. My mother covers her mouth. I am appalled—no, *terrified*—as she chokes back a sob.

"It's Gerard," my father says.

A storm kicks up inside me, somewhere deep. No, no. "What happened? He left the protest with me and Bruiser."

"After, Gerard and Bruiser were driving around with...some people." He looks to my mother to fill in the blanks. But she can't help him. Neither of them knows Gerard's friends very well. I'm surprised they remember Gerard himself when he isn't holding a stack of menus. "We got the call about him as we were on our way here for you."

"Oh no, oh no, oh no," I say. I should never have let him drive off with Bruiser. My brother. My stupid brother. The guy with no rules and no direction and no parents. Someone should've been looking out for him. "What happened? Did they get into an accident?"

Please don't let it be awful.

The blood pressure cuff squeezes my arm. The machine beeps.

"No, no. Nothing like that." Again, his gaze darts to my mother for help. Both hands cover her mouth now, like she can hold the sobs in if she tries hard enough, keep it all from pouring out. I know the feeling. It never works in the end. "He overdosed on something. They're not sure what yet. They gave him medication to reverse the effects, and he regained consciousness. Thank God."

"Dad..." Words can't cover this. I don't know what to say.

I should have done more. But knowing Gerard—knowing *myself*—it wouldn't have worked. You have to hit bottom on your own.

"It's okay." My father nods.

"No, it's not," I say.

My mother shakes her head. I think she'll disagree. Tell me to shut my ungrateful mouth, go put on some lip gloss. "She's right," she says. I don't recognize her voice. "It's not okay."

My father rubs a hand over his face. "No. It's not."

For the first time in my entire life, all of us find common ground.

My mother grabs a tissue. She doesn't bother turning her back to blow her nose. Carlo pulls her into a hug.

Two children. Two hospital rooms. Same night.

What kind of odds would my father have given this game?

My mother steps over to kiss me on the forehead. "I'm going upstairs, okay?"

"Sure. Go, go."

She doles out rules. "Get some sleep. Don't leave this bed."

Carlo and Vincent each kiss me goodnight too, whispering Italian words and phrases I sort of remember. A little bit of cooing, a little bit of "baby girl." They leave with my mother to check on Gerard. Down the hall, elevator doors go ding ding, swooshing open for them.

My father must recognize the futility in my mother's rules because on his way out he adds, "Just don't wander the hospital. Stay in your room, at least."

The old lady roommate shrinks under her covers.

I should tell her not to worry. I'm not an animal. *We* are not animals.

We're Foxes. Just a family, like any other. We screw up, we make mistakes, we suffer for it. Our priorities are out of whack. Sometimes it takes a monumental effort—near death—for us to see what's plain to everyone else. But we do care about each other in our own messed up way. At the end of the day, that's what matters.

"Wait," I say as my father reaches the door.

He turns, readjusts the cigarette now perched in the fold above his ear.

"Is Matty still here? In the waiting room?"

"Where else would he be?" He snickers as he leaves the room. I'm sure he thinks it's obvious that the boy will never leave my side.

But he doesn't know about our ride to the hospital with Joe behind the wheel. When everything changed. Sometimes wishes and prayers don't work, and sometimes taking chances and going after the things you want don't either. Because the things you want aren't things you're supposed to have. End of story.

I have one final task tonight. I need to untwist the knots holding me and Matty together.

Chapter Twenty-Eight

Matty steps through the doorway of my room. His skin glows pale and white. Freckles burn orange patterns across his cheeks and nose. A silver can of Red Bull's clutched in his right hand. He holds it out. A peace offering.

He looks like his old self. Adorable, sweet, silly.

I could love him now more than ever if it weren't for the mountain of impossibilities wedged between us. It will never go away.

This summer, each time Celeste's name passed through Matty's lips, he slipped further away from me. No amount of hoping and praying pulled him back. I was scared. So scared that I let myself sink low to keep him. I didn't just risk life and limb for him, I risked the lives of others. Celeste and her father have me to blame, not Matty, if their lives flip into chaos. I can point the finger at him all I want but at the end of the day it was my choice to make stupid, stupid decisions, with every outcome colored by Matty's name. And he was never mine to have anyway.

It's like Joe said. You can't always be reckless when you care about someone. You need to be smart, careful, controlled. There are two sides to life: the fun, reckless side, and the side that gives a shit. The trick is learning how to split them apart when you care about someone.

Matty sets the Red Bull on the tray-on-wheels beside my bed and sits. "How are you feeling?"

"I'm good."

"That's a lie."

"I've had worse."

He glances at my chest, the wound covered with gauze under the ugly blue hospital gown. The cranky nurse told me, "We'll need to change the dressing again in the morning, you know."

Except I don't plan on being here in the morning.

Matty lifts a hand weakly in the direction of my chest, then thinks better of it, and scratches his ear instead. "Does it hurt?"

There are so many ways I could respond: a lie, a small warping of the truth, a half-truth, or the real deal. In the end, I choose not to hide it.

I nod. "Yeah. It hurts."

He nods too, then folds his lips inward and looks away, blinking, blinking, blinking. From this angle, it's clear—his nose really is a little off-center. I noticed it once in his reflection. But I chose not to acknowledge it. I liked my perfect version of him better.

On the other side of the room, my old bat of a roommate couldn't care less about my pain. She huffs to let me know, and turns over in her bed, gingerly.

Matty and I look at each other and smile.

The tension pops and fades away.

"The doctors said you were probably in shock when you went unconscious. I thought I lost you." He touches my hand, the one all wrapped up. My fingers wiggle out to reach him. "You said something before you passed out." He roots around, carefully. "Do you remember?"

I shrug. The movement pinches my chest. My heart's busting out ollies, higher than the ones Matty can pull off. Of course I remember.

"What you said—I sort of knew already."

I run a finger along the edge of my cast and wonder if he thinks I still love him.

"I remember that night at Wiley," he says, eyes fixed on my soft cast. "Not every detail, but the important stuff." He glances at the old lady and licks his lips. "I shouldn't have let it go on like that. I should have stopped you. No. I mean, I should have stopped *myself*." He keeps looking at broken wrist. "The next day, I knew we should talk about it, but you acted like it never happened. And that was such a relief. I knew if we got into it, things would change. And I didn't want that. Because I really do love you, Effie. I do. You're my best friend."

"I love you, too," I say. Just not that way anymore.

We're quiet. The kiss didn't change anything. Celeste did.

Finally, he looks at me. "I'm sorry."

"I'm sorry, too," I whisper.

A thousand apologies won't change what I did, but it feels better to acknowledge it.

"After what you said tonight, on the ride here, I think I understand."

"What I did was inexcusable."

"You had a reason. Maybe not a good one. But still."

"I don't care. I was wrong."

"I care."

Satisfaction floods through me. I'm glad he still cares because the kind of love we have can't be turned on and off with a flick of a switch. We're best friends. And even now, after everything, I still love him. I'll go to my grave loving my friend with the freckles and the insanely high ollie pop. But the intensity is gone somehow.

I try to smile but it comes out feeling sadder than I thought it would. "I don't think you care enough."

His gaze drops to his lap.

I squeeze his hand with just my thumb and the tips of my fingers. He squeezes back.

The pressure hurts. It hurts so fucking bad. I let go of his hand.

He pulls the manila envelope from the back pocket of his cargos. It's battered and warped and bloodied, but still intact.

"This..." Matty holds it out. "I don't know what to do with it. Why do you have it?"

John Vallone's life story is not mine to tell, so I give Matty the abbreviated version. I only explain my part in it—the part where I ratted Celeste and her father out and couldn't live with myself for it. I tell him about the exchange that was supposed to happen tonight. I like my new role in the story better. It's where I do the right thing.

"Have you found her yet?" I ask.

"I haven't looked. I've been here all night."

"What are you waiting for?"

The beeping machine behind me hiccups into a faster pace.

A part of me died tonight. She was the side of me that didn't give a crap. But the rest of me is still here, alive and kicking.

I formulate a quick and dirty plan and pass it by Matty.

"I—I don't know." There's a shift in his eyes, like a longing. But it disappears in an instant. The thing he doesn't say is clear: he wants to go but he, like me, is doing the right thing. And I'm so grateful he's here, and that he cares, and I know we'll be okay. But enough's enough. I won't let guilt hold him back from his dreams.

I rip at the blood pressure cuff, tear the clamp off my finger.

I'm on my feet again. It feels so good.

"Whoa." Matty stares at me like I've gone wild. Who the hell knows where my mind is after the night I've had. He throws hands up, as if that will stop me. "Sit down."

"I'm fine."

"You're not fine."

"I have a few broken bones. It's not a tragedy. I've had worse."

"I think the concussion's messing with your head."

The old lady roommate turns her head slightly to see the show. "Where are you going?" she says in a scratchy squeak.

"Busting out of here."

Joe Monroe never walks when there's an opportunity to ride.

Down the hall from my room, the elevator dings. Doors slide open. Something hits the ground with a whack, and a smooth hum rises up after that. There is nothing on earth as beautiful as the sound of wheels in motion.

Joe reaches the door of my hospital room in less than three seconds. Somehow the lucky Bones Brigade cap is back on his head, its white cotton marred with the same dirt that's under my fingernails. He's got two skateboards tucked under his right arm, and his own set of wheels underneath his feet.

Thank God for him.

He ticks his chin up at me, casual as ever. "Welcome back." A smile twitches on the side of his mouth. "That was some wipeout."

"Nothing I won't recover from." I take my skateboard from him with my good arm.

Matty takes his, too.

"You look good in anything, Effie, but hospital gowns don't suit your image." Joe wriggles out of his shirt and holds it out for me.

I'm a little spazz about how to get myself untangled from the gown and the sling holding my bum arm. Joe slowly loosens the strap of the sling, then slides the gown off my shoulders. I toss

Gerard's torn and bloody t-shirt on the hospital bed. I am suddenly acutely aware that, aside from my bra, Joe and I both stand facing each other shirtless. A soft smile breaks through the hard angles in his face. A spell grips me. I can't stop staring at his eyes and the way they sweep over my body.

Matty clears his throat.

Joe tosses out one of those breathy laughs he's so good at and gets to work pulling his t-shirt over my head. He helps fasten the sling back in place, then pulls the lucky hat off his head and stuffs it on mine. This hat's been through the ringer today, but it still smells amazing.

"Here," he says. "You need the luck more than I do."

No sense in arguing with logic. Besides, I really love the hat.

"How'd you find it? I thought for sure I lost it at Las Palmas Altas."

"I got lucky."

"Wouldn't be the first time, I bet."

"Won't be the last, either." He reaches for me. The way one arm slides around my waist and pulls me to him is more delicate and gentle than I thought he was capable of, and it feels good. I have no idea what's going on between us right now, but whatever it is would certainly make that blood pressure machine go haywire if I were still wearing the cuff. Matty fusses with the laces on his sneakers, but I know he's listening. He doesn't say anything.

The old lady across the room sits up on her elbows. She's coming out of her shell. Beeping from the machines behind her picks up pace.

"What are you doing?" she says to no one in particular.

"Making a scene," Joe says. "Want to join us?"

Her wrinkly pink lips curve upward for the first time. "If I didn't have a broken hip, I might take you up on that. This place is for the birds."

"Tell me about it," I say.

Her grin is huge. At least three teeth are missing on the left side.

Matty steps out into the hallway, board dangling from his right hand. Joe brings up the rear. "Think you can handle being on wheels while you're dragging around that monstrosity?" He motions to my cast.

I nod. I can do anything.

The elevator brings us down to a corridor with no obvious way out except through the emergency room where we came. Matty lets his board drop to the speckled white tiles on the hospital floor. Joe and I do the same. Together, we explode down the hall. People start diving to the left and right, running every which way, climbing the walls to get out of our path if they can. Joe kickflips over a stack of files some guy wearing scrubs dropped as he pitched himself away from us. The hospital staff doesn't care very much for my discharge strategy.

We pump toward the sliding doors where they wheel in stretchers and unload the ambulances parked outside. They're marked with red, cautionary words: NO EXIT, ENTRANCE ONLY. Joe reaches the doors first. He digs his fingers into the rubber groove between them to pry them apart.

An alarm rings off. Heads turn in our direction.

Even the cranky nurse lowers her clipboard to watch. A crew of security guards rush at us. There's a lot of shouting and commotion, but it's all behind us.

We're too fast, too smart. It's all about the wheels.

CHAPTER TWENTY-NINE

The documents I hold in a manila envelope feature a girl named Carly Victor.

Also known as Celeste Vaughn and a million other aliases.

She's not far from Vista Buscato. Maybe twenty miles away, in and out of hills and tucked into the side of a mountain, in Escondido, a town with a lot of charm and a heavy dose of pretty, Spanish architecture. She hides with her father one block from a bus station in a studio apartment above the Happy Healthy Heart vitamin and supplement shop. Given the condition of my heart in the weeks since Celeste arrived in my life, I find this name dreadfully ironic. A CLOSED sign dangles from a chain on the shop's door. A sandwich board perched on the sidewalk outside reads, *Wheatgrass Wednesday! Free shot with every $20 purchase!*

Joe and Matty are with me. The three of us look up at the tiny apartment above the shop. Shades cover the windows. Without Vincent's help, we never would have found Celeste and her dad here. This is certainly not the most luxurious of circumstances, but it's better than the adorable haven at Las Palmas Altas if that's where the feds think you are. I don't know John Vallone. But I'd like to think Escondido works for him. I hope he's happier here. If for just a moment until he needs to jet again.

Matty takes a few quick, sharp, in-and-out breaths, then presses the buzzer at the door beside the vitamin shop.

We wait.

A soft voice calls out, "Matthew?"

I see her. Celeste pokes out from a window with no screen, wearing all white, the only thing still shining because the sun set ages ago. She slips back inside. Footsteps pound down the stairs, locks click open. The door swings outward. Her hair swirls in white gossamer threads.

Celeste launches into Matty's open arms.

Joe steps back.

I hesitate because old habits die hard and I'm used to being the one by Matty's side. But I step back too. It's best for my sanity to keep a healthy spread between us all. Joe slides closer to me, presses his shoulder against mine.

"I found you," Matty says, the words muffled into her hair.

They kiss.

My heart breaks again, but not because of a loss. It's different this time. I'm struck by the realization that this is one of the last moments I'll ever know Matty. *My* Matty. He's shifting into Matthew, and maybe that's for the best. Joe loops an arm around my shoulders and squeezes, like he can sense that I'm tense all over.

John Vallone steps out after Celeste, darkness slipping off his shoulders. His eyes zip from street corner to street corner.

I pull the folded manila envelope from my back pocket and hand it to him. He takes it, pinches it between two fingers. I'm reminded of the man I once saw bent over a chess board as he held the pieces, freezing them in place before he worked out his next move. He looked different then. I suppose I did too. His eyes run over the blood stains dotting the envelope. He doesn't ask. Everybody has a story. His troubles are way more complicated than mine. I'm sure he's seen worse than a few drops of blood.

He tucks the envelope beneath his gray jacket and drags the zipper upward. All the plans for my great escape disappear when the zipper—metal into metal—locks closed. I did it; I sealed the deal. Everything I ever wanted is gone now. It's okay, though. It wasn't right for me. I have to let it go.

"Thank you," he says. His voice is gruff. It matches the gray of his clothing, the wrinkled pieces thrown together in a rush. "Tell your father and Vincent I'll try my best to get in touch. Soon," he adds, though it comes with no guarantee. His head swings around, taking in the street behind us. It's dark and well into the wee hours of the morning. But John Vallone doesn't strike me as someone who takes chances. He used up all his stores of courage when he stayed in Vista Buscato the last ten years, and now he's ready to run.

He glances at Celeste and Matty, then averts his eyes. I wish I could tell him it's okay, I understand. It used to be hard for me to see it too. You just have to get over it. Somehow.

They pull apart, finally.

Celeste turns to me and Joe. "Effie! I was so worried. Are you okay?"

"Broke a few bones," I say, all shrugs and smiles. I want to be good at this, I really do.

"You poor thing. It must hurt."

"Not really." Joe pinches me. "Okay, okay. Maybe a little."

Matty runs an arm around Celeste's waist. He bounces on the balls of his feet, and she matches his rhythm. They turn to face each other and bounce faster, purposely. Joe and I laugh. He's back—my Matty. Except that he's her Matthew now, too. Witnessing it doesn't tear me apart like it once did.

John Vallone clears his throat. "We're catching a six a.m. bus in the morning," he says. "The apartment's bare. But you're welcome to come up. It's better than being out on the street." You don't need to be a rocket scientist to read between those lines.

He opens the door to a tiny vestibule. A narrow staircase leads to their second-floor apartment. Celeste slips in first. Matty follows. Their voices fade as they bound up the stairs. John Vallone holds the door open for me and Joe. He gives me a small smile. After what I did to ruin his daughter's life, I don't expect it. He must not know that part. In all his maneuvers and artistry, Vincent conveniently forgot to mention why the need arose for John Vallone to pull a new identity over his head in the first place. I'm grateful.

I hesitate at the open door. "I think I'll say goodbye now."

I jump onto my board and skate away to the town square a few blocks down the avenue. Joe shouts my name. His wheels rip across the asphalt behind me, but I don't turn.

The square is a collection of benches, low stone walls around a water fountain, and sloped wheelchair walkways. The perfect playground for anyone on wheels. But I don't have the strength to pull off a trick. My head throbs my chest, too.

A poster sticks to a tree trunk. I stop to take a look at its yellow, frayed edges. And there she is, smiling at me again: Vista Buscato's dark-haired missing girl, Jessie Winters. Big, black letters spell out the word MISSING in an act of desperation. People care about her. They want her home. Jealousy runs through me, sharp and biting.

Joe pops up onto the bench next to me, then fakies back down.

I wrap a hand around my soft cast and squeeze.

"Everything okay?" he says.

Everything I've held back for weeks starts to crack and break. I fray at every edge. He's all over me then, arms looped around me in a hug, pulling me to him. We sway a little. Tears start falling before I can bite them back. They soak through the front of his t-shirt, the wetness turning the heather gray a shade closer to black.

"We always knew he'd leave one day," he says.

"I'm not crying for him. God!" I pull away and wipe my face. "I'm crying for us!"

Joe's eyes scrunch up, bewildered.

Matty's gone; Celeste's gone; Sam's gone; everyone's out the door.

But here I am. Still. I'm twisted inside.

"We're the only losers left. Even Gerard will probably get out of Vista Buscato one day."

Joe's head tips to the side. "We'll be okay, Effie."

Frustration boils within me. "How do you know that?"

"I just do."

"That's not good enough for me. I'm leaving." I throw an arm out, reaching, reaching, I don't know where. Anywhere but here.

"You can't run away. You *are* Vista Buscato. So am I. So is Matty, and Gerard, and your parents, and my mom. Even Sam will come back one day. It's ours, too."

I glance at the yellow poster on the tree. And what about Jessie Winters? I wonder if Vista Buscato belonged to her. If that's the case, why's she still gone?

"What about the Board?" I say. "Do they think Vista Buscato is *yours*?"

"I don't care what they think."

"People like us don't belong there."

"People like us *are* Vista Buscato. We are reality."

I shake my head. He's longing after something he can't have. Not in his wildest dreams.

"Listen." He bends his neck lower to look straight in my eyes. "It's late. Or early, depending how you look at it. Ever catch a Vista Buscato sunrise? It's the sickest thing you'll ever see."

Give me a break. Sunrises are the same all over the world. It's just one immense star, and we're all spinning around it, too dizzy not to notice that we've seen it before, day after boring day. It's all a big game of pretend.

"No. I can't. I...I have to go." I edge away from him. I step back onto my board.

"Effie," he says. "Don't leave."

"There's nothing here for me."

"Please don't say that."

I hesitate.

His face squeezes in on itself. Like someone just told him he'll have to make the biggest vert drop of his life, and he'll definitely eat it on the way down. He looks like he anticipates the pain.

I have one leg kicked out and ready to push off, to cruise the hell out of here. The urge to split is still in me, so strong, but I don't move. I can't. Not while he's looking at me like that. Warmth and concern and something even deeper, like a rolling wave of longing, rushes at me. It grips me, crushes me from the inside out, locking around my ribcage, pressing against my heart. When I open my mouth to tell him why I must leave, nothing comes out. I'm not sure I know why anymore.

He reaches out a hand, palm up, an offering.

"Stay with me?" The little uptick in his voice breaks me.

In the middle of freshman year, I made my first vert drop down a ramp. It wasn't good, and when my body hit bottom, people went, "Oooooohhh!!!" Joe rushed to pull me up. I smacked his hand away not once, but two times. He wouldn't leave. His hand stayed outstretched like it is now. He only lowered it after I scrambled to my feet and walked away. That was before I understood that there are two sides to Joe that snap together. One wild and reckless, and the other that cares enough about people to pick them up after a drop. Joe came all the way to Escondido in the middle of the night, after spending the day fighting for everything he believes in. Maybe all of that is just his wild side. Or it's his careful, measured way of ensuring I didn't disappear like Celeste. And it means he can split those two sides of himself apart.

A thought passes through my head: life could be better when Matty's gone. I can't imagine what it will feel like in his absence, what my future holds. But maybe things could be better then. Somewhere along the way I equated him with my future. I confused Matty with things that only I can accomplish down the road. I suppose I could leave for another spot on the map, but maps mean nothing when you're constantly in motion anyway. So long as the wheels underneath me keep moving, I think I'll be okay. So long as the people I care about move with me, wherever I go, even if it's in circles, I'll be perfect.

I put my hand in Joe's.

Several seconds pass. That longing in his dark eyes draws me nearer. My foot's still poised on my board. I take it off, inch closer to him on two feet. He steps off his own board. Now, for once, we're on solid ground. We lean toward each other, making the drop even though we both know we're going to fall. As his lips meet mine, a hot, explosive feeling detonates inside me, bursting outward and upward. I throw my good arm around his neck. He grips me so tight it hurts my broken rib.

He's so warm. He feels like home.

His kiss is fireworks. And I know a thing or two about fireworks.

His kiss is fireworks. And I know a thing or two about fireworks.

CHAPTER THIRTY

We take the hard plaster cast off my arm—against doctor's orders—with the same technique I used in eighth grade. Utility scissors and a lot of patience. Honestly, I amaze myself with how still I can sit when there's an end goal in mind and I want it that badly. My skin's super white and oddly wrinkled by the time the cast finally thumps to the ground. That's what solitary confinement does to you. Matty picks up what's left of it, all mangled and split open.

"I'm totally taking this with me to Northwestern," he says.

Joe sniffs. "It smells."

"I'll put it in the glove box."

"That's nasty," I say.

"It reminds me of you."

"Dude. You can just call me."

His blue eyes spark with an idea. "You know how people put stickers on park benches and bus stops and stuff? I'll do that with your cast. I'll leave it outdoors. It'll be like a piece of you in Chicago."

It's sweet, all this talk of Matty taking pieces of me to college. At one time I would have ached over it, but now it feels good. He's all set. The Jeep's crammed with everything he needs. Playlists are cued up with my favorite songs for a road trip I won't be on. And that's okay. Celeste waits for him in Chicago. She's a different girl now—a new name, new birth certificate, new social security number. The seat for Celeste Vaughn at the University of Michigan will stay empty because Celeste Vaughn doesn't exist anymore. But Chicago's full of possibilities. Vincent's already brainstorming. I'm sure he'll come up with a piece of artwork that will open every door for her.

"Better yet," says Joe, "Take a stack of mags and tape them up all over campus." He tosses a rolled-up copy of *Transworld Skateboarding* to Matty. "You can tell everyone your friend's famous."

I roll my eyes. "Hardly. It's Vista Buscato that's famous now, not me."

It never gets old, staring at the cover of that magazine, at what Judge Pomerantz continually refers to as Exhibit Number One, better known as *righteous evidence*. The photographer at the Founder's Day parade snapped hundreds of shots, capturing every misdeed on both sides of the debate in digital form. The best of all is on the cover. It's a shot of me at the perfect moment—arms raised high overheard, skateboard lifted to the sky, my face tipped upward, as if I'm sending up a prayer at the altar of skateboarding. An army of people behind me do the same. The featured magazine article inside pulls no punches. It tells the story of a town divided by culture, class, trends, and four wheels bolted to a piece of wood. It tells how we tried to change our little corner of the world for the better.

Judge Pomerantz is the first to say goodbye.

"I'll call you as soon as I hit the first rest stop, Pops."

"Good boy," the judge says.

Matty and Joe grab each other in a bro hug that lasts longer than any I've ever seen. Enough back-pats to last until the next school break.

"Take care," Joe says.

"Stay out of trouble."

"You know I won't."

Matty pulls one of those crinkled-eye laughs that makes all of us smile, even the judge.

"Come here, you," he says, pulling me in for a hug.

I close my eyes. Saying goodbye is never easy but letting go is much harder. I already figured that part out, though. He kisses the top of my head and whispers, "I fucking love you, Effie Fox."

"I love you, too." I pull away. There's no regret. Only strength.

When Matty finally turns the key in the ignition and waves one arm out the Jeep's window, kicking up the dry, dusty California earth beneath his tires, it no longer feels like a loss. I've grown accustomed to his absence a little more each day. I'm okay with it. He'll be back.

I wave with my newly freed and (hopefully) mostly mended wrist, thinking how incredible it is that bones inside me snapped in three different spots and now they're back together, supposedly, hopefully, even stronger than before.

Joe lands a crooked nosegrind along a low concrete divider that separates the lawn from Matty's grandmother's flower garden. Judge Pomerantz watches him. The first time Matty tried to ollie onto that divider, we were in sixth grade. It was the only time I ever heard his Grandma Helen yell. Matty never did it again, even after she'd passed away. Joe shears the nose of his board against the divider again with a loud scrape.

"I'll tell him to stop," I say. "He has a hard time controlling himself when he sees an opportunity to pull off a trick."

The judge smiles. It cuts through the tension. "Let him be. I'm not bothered by it."

"Most adults can't stand it. He's not allowed to do it in front of Fox Inn."

"My educated guess is that your parents' rule has nothing to do with Joseph's enthusiasm for skateboarding, but rather, his penchant for attracting the police."

"You could be right."

"I'm always right." His face breaks open with the same silly grin Matty wears when he's just one-upped you in conversation. I look back at Joe and wonder how he doesn't see us watching him. Is that how it feels to shut out the world?

"Joe told me you persuaded Peter LaRoche to vote in favor of a skate park at the Wiley property. I can't tell you how happy that's made him."

The judge nods. His white hair bounces on top of his head. I bet it used to be red like Matty's, once upon a time. "After the Founder's Day parade, it seemed like a genuine concern among our community's young people. Of course, news coverage shed light on the topic as well. I may be old, but I'm not blind." I hide a smile with a bite of my lip. "Crews are set to demolish the place shortly, in preparation for the retail shops that will be built there. I couldn't stop that process. But Joe and I did secure a sizable area on the property for a skate park."

"I doubt Detective Brimley is happy about it."

"We've swapped a few favors over the years. I'm sure he'll come knocking on my door to cash one or two in once the park opens. I intend not to be home when he rings the bell." He raises his eyebrows. A thread of mischief laces through his words.

"Good call." We both laugh. If anyone can win against the detective, it would be the judge.

"Besides," he continues. "You needn't worry. Detective Brimley will be covering the streets less these days. His promotion is a given at this point. Did you hear about the missing girl he located?"

I stiffen. Please don't let him be talking about Celeste.

"Jessie Winters?" I ask.

He nods. "Brimley found her in Las Vegas late last night, unharmed, though a little world-weary from being on her own since May. They say she was thrilled people were looking for her. She was desperate to come home. My guess is that shame kept her away."

"Wow. I hadn't heard."

"It hits the papers tomorrow. Finding her will boost his likability. The detective doesn't need to chase skateboarders any longer. Mark my words: he guaranteed himself a spot as Commander."

I nod, but I'm not thinking about the detective's long-awaited promotion. I'm thinking how Jessie Winters was never kidnapped, just like I thought. She ran away. She left of her own accord, and used the same technique as John Vallone, hiding in the midst of millions. It works for some, and others it doesn't. Depends how badly you want to stay gone.

Joe's board cracks out the loudest hit so far. He stumbles.

"Sorry," I say again.

"You know, I was a lot like Joseph when I was younger."

"What happened?"

"You assume I've changed," he says. There's no question mark at the end.

"But—"

"You think wearing judge's robes alters who you are on the inside."

Again. Not a question. He's very good at statements, pronouncements of truth.

I shake my head. "It's hard to believe someone like you was ever like Joe. I guess I picture you as more like Matty. Off to college and then on to bigger things."

"Like what?"

"Well, like important things. He'll be r—"

"Rich," he interjects.

"No. I was going to say *respected*."

The caramel brown of his eyes is sweet and soft. I never noticed it before. "People don't respect me because I held a judge's gavel for a living. They respect me because I care about them and treat them well. I suspect Joseph does the same."

"Maybe. But I'm not sure Matty's got a whole lot of respect for Joe."

"My grandson respects ambition and education. That's fine. But he's forgetting about integrity. Joseph could work on controlling his less productive impulses. But when it comes to integrity, he has it in spades." The judge watches Joe nosegrind against the concrete divider again. "And as for ambition, one day he'll discover that beneath the skateboard there's a passion that compels him to accomplish things. If he focuses on what he truly cares about, and keeps the rest of the noise at bay, he'll achieve everything he chooses to. Still with a skateboard under his feet." He chuckles a bit. "I hear you've experienced your own success. Isn't a sponsorship in the works?"

I toe the ground. My old, torn-up Vans hit the dumpster a few days ago. I'm wearing a fresh pair of white skate shoes that are in serious need of breaking in. A gift from Edgar. They're so cushioned inside, I can barely feel the ground. I'm floating. "Yeah. I signed with the Skate Real team a few days ago."

One thing Joe is good for: showing me what I truly love. And it isn't chasing rainbows to Chicago. It's what makes me feel best on the inside, no matter where I am. The thing that makes my heart bounce out of my chest is being on wheels. So, I signed with Edgar's team. I'm a part of the Skate Real family. A stack of red and white Skate real t-shirts sits on my dresser at home. My mother grimaced when she heard, but ultimately only asked that I not wear anything other than a Fox Inn t-shirt during my shifts. My father was more enthusiastic. Dollar signs glowed in his eyes. His first question: "So how much dough does a pro skateboarder make?"

The judge smiles. "See! Success found you! You followed your heart. It's that easy."

"Is it, though? Joe and I—we aren't like you and Matty. We weren't born lucky." I hate myself for saying it, but it's more truthful now than ever.

"Luck has nothing to do with it."

"It feels like it does sometimes."

"You say these things to a man who was once a boy with holes in his shoes and barely a penny in his pocket. I was as unlucky as any other kid playing stickball on city streets."

This is a piece of a story Matty never told about his grandfather. I've heard tons—how he sentenced a guy to life in prison for kidnapping and torturing some little girl, how he helped put a bunch of casino moguls away for racketeering, how he loved to sail on his off days, how he adored his wife, but hated her garden. But I don't know the Honorable Justice Bertram T. Pomerantz's life as a street kid.

He grabs my hand, covers my pale, wrinkled skin. "I have a great story. Did you know a bird pooped on me once?"

I laugh.

One day the scar on my chest might pale, too. I'm glad it's there, though. A memory from when my heart opened and spilled all over. I was stupid and reckless. But I made the drop in, wiped out, and walked away. Maybe with a few more scrapes than I'd have liked, but at least I'm on my own two feet now. There are a million ways to waste time in this tiny little town. I can think of so much worse than caring about something enough to throw my heart into it. If that's not bravery, then I don't know what is.

CHAPTER THIRTY-ONE

An envelope arrived for me at Fox Inn yesterday afternoon. The return address is MCRD San Diego. It took a second before I figured out what I was looking at. The mystery unlocked when I recognized Sam's handwriting. I didn't open the letter, but saved the moment for my pre-dawn meetup with Joe.

I miss Sam so much. I'm genuinely stoked to read all the tiny details in the letter, even if it would bore me to tears coming from someone else's mouth. He'll probably moan about jogging for miles, digging trenches, pounding out push-ups or sit-ups or whatever other orders his drill sergeants shout out. The Fox Inn staff all placed bets on the amount of weight he's dropped. My father said 10 pounds, Carlo said 20, I said 30. Vincent hedged all bets by saying Sam won't even mention weight loss in the letter. Vincent will probably come out the winner. He always does.

In the sleepy, five a.m. darkness along Buscato Drive, I fold the letter in half, then half again, and stuff it into my back pocket.

I skate past Fox Inn. Amazing how one minute you look at a place and loathe everything and everyone inside, and the next minute it's just a building. A dumpster out back, a business hours sign in the window, and a front door set to open in a few hours to welcome the hustle of a new day.

I won't be carrying an order pad today. My parents and I worked out a new schedule so I could fit in training time with the Skate Real team. Four regular shifts a week—no doubles. My father said, "We'll figure it out," to my demands. My mother just nodded. I didn't expect her to say anything. Between Sam and Gerard leaving, and me dropping shifts, she'll have to hire someone to cover. Not having a say in the matter kills her. But this was a long time coming. One of her kids is currently getting his act together in rehab, while the other—me—has a plan for herself that doesn't include working at a restaurant permanently. I have no idea where this sponsorship will take me, but that's okay. Starting at the bottom is still a start.

I roll up to the Wiley estate, kicking up pebbles under my wheels.

A construction fence rings the perimeter of the property. But this time, for once, it's not a wall keeping me out. The gates are open and I enter a world that's mine. I skate through the opening in the fence where the driveway unfolds onto Halberd Court. Eventually, gravel and other bits clog my ride, so I pick up my board and walk.

Joe waves at me. "Right on time. Sunrise is any minute."

He stands atop a dirt-packed mini-mountain—a by-product of the construction crew's leveling phase last week. Several dirt mounds run along the edges of the property, all spaced throughout. Much of the place looks different. The house was demolished to make room for a food court and skate shop. But I'm happy to see that the pool stayed. It's one place that makes Vista Buscato feel bigger than it really is. I'm counting on discovering more places like it in my free time. On wheels, of course.

I join Joe and survey the property in its state of in-between. Peter LaRoche and Judge Pomerantz met with Joe and some Board members earlier in the week to talk with the architects about their plans. Now Joe knows things about water tables, soil depth, cement and something called rebar. He points around the new foundation of the property—now skimmed to a perfect, even surface—and dives into details of where they'll place different aspects of the skate park. A quarter pipe here, wedges over there, an eight-foot-high concrete pyramid in the center, rail slides along the edges, rolling transitions all around. The park's official name, so far, remains unknown. Ultimately, the Board has the final vote, but Judge Pomerantz asked Joe to submit a list of possibilities to the Board, and they'll choose from his picks. Bruiser thought it was stupid. That we should be the ones with the power to label it. But it's compromise. I figure any input is better than no input. We've come a long way. It's a good start.

Joe wraps arms around me from behind. I press my head back into the warm nook between his neck and shoulder. We fit together better than I ever imagined.

A white and yellow haze bleeds over the horizon, turning the sky heather gray, brightening everything over Vista Buscato. It takes forever. I'm afraid to look away, though, because each second brings a new color to the spectrum. Beautiful things like this went unnoticed by me until recently. Like the fact that our futures aren't measured in achievements and awards, but moments with the people we care about. And everyone I care about has a place here. I'm not prepared to split. Not yet. Try as I might, I can't leave my parents when they need me, not just as an employee, but as their daughter. And Joe's here. Suddenly, all these people I thought I didn't care about care about *me*. Leaving them behind to do nothing in another town or city doesn't feel like progress. Maybe it is for a guy in Matty's position, where progress means something different, but not for me.

Joe whispers, "Here it comes."

My patience runs on empty, but this suspense is better than any freefall drop. I can't quit tapping my fingers against Joe's hands—my only outward sign of impatience. He turns me around and pulls me into a kiss that sends heat straight into my toes.

Joe pulls back and glances at the horizon. "There it goes," he says.

When the first pop of sun finally lifts above the hills, it's magic. It's a thrilling possibility, a new beginning.

"I bet Sam sees this every morning while they've got him pushing out crunches. Lucky bastard," Joe says.

"That reminds me!" We break apart. I reach in my pocket for the envelope from Sam. Joe knows the sender immediately after he spies the label. Sliding my finger under the envelope's flap, I rip it open and, of course, manage to slice a grisly paper cut through my skin. "Shit. Ow. That stings."

A pearl of blood grows along the edge of my index finger.

Joe slaps my hand away. "You're becoming a real whiner, you know that? I think Sam rubbed off on you."

"Shut up."

I pull out the letter.

Words written in Sam's usual stiff and twitchy way fill the page. I read them aloud:

Dear Fox (that's what you'd be called here—FOX—because they call everyone by their last name, and I would shit myself laughing if I heard it because I know you'd freak out),

Joe throws his head back and does, indeed, laugh his ass off at this.

I shove him with my non-bleeding hand and continue reading.

Things are good. I know this sounds crazy because I wasn't doing cartwheels at the idea of coming here, but it's fine. I'm <u>OKAY</u>.

He underlined the word and added little dashes all around it.

On my first day I fell and scraped the shit out of me knee. Dude, I swear the chunk missing from my kneecap was deep enough to see bone. You know me. I was losing my mind. But they didn't let me wallow in it. I had no choice but to keep going. A few drills later and I forgot about it. Not permanently though. I'm not crazy. Yo, my leg was on fire when I got into bed that night. But they gave me ointment and gauze, so it's all good.

Joe and I chuckle at the image of Sam sliding into his cot all mummified in white cotton gauze.

Turns out I'm the strongest guy in my unit. Can you believe that?

Joe says, "Yes," like it's the most obvious thing in the world.

I never would have guessed that about myself. But even more than that, I FEEL strong.

More underlines and dashes.

I never thought I'd be brave like you, Effie. Coming here's forced me to look at myself differently. I think I might have some courage now. Is that okay for me to say? I know you're laughing, don't deny it.

I'm not laughing anymore and neither is Joe. Tears slide down one side of my face. Joe slings an arm around my shoulder, kisses the side of my head. I sniff and let them flow, let them all out. Sam's words swim in my vision.

I can't wait to see you guys again. I hope you'll visit on Family Day. But if you can't, that's okay. I'll be back to skate at Wiley Park before I ship out. My dad's filled me in on the progress. By the time I get home I hope you and Joe figured things out. Say hi to Carlo and Vincent for me.

Peace,

Sam

Seeing *you* and *Joe* connected in the same sentence sends a rush through me. It's unexpected and surprising. But it feels good. I refold the letter and slide it back into the envelope. Sam's words grow into a symphony in my head. *I hope you and Joe figured things out.*

344

"Wiley Park," I say. "I like it. It's simple. Smart kid, that Sam."

Joe's eyes go stony, serious. "I'll need help, you know. Getting the park up and running."

"Okay. Of course." I doubt he'll need me. He's the kind of guy who gets things done, Joe. But I like the idea of helping him. Making this place a little better. Like Matty said, there are a thousand ways to break out of being stuck. This feels like one of them.

Joe keeps going. "Edgar introduced me to this guy in Santa Barbara who's on a park planning committee. He has a degree in engineering or some shit like that, which blew my mind because if you saw the aerials this guy can pull off..." He blows a stream of wonder out in a whistle. "Anyway, he said I could help sketch the rough layout of a new park they're planning in Ojai. It got me thinking—I could take some classes or something. Maybe learn more about drafting and planning."

His hopes and dreams come out in a rush, racing with excitement.

"That sounds awesome, Joe."

He smiles. "You know, Edgar told me about a girl who made a shitload of money shaping handmade decks for a bunch of pros, and now she's looking for a place to open a shop with a partner. Edgar thinks this place might be the perfect spot. You should talk to her."

Sounds great; sounds like a dream. But what do I know about opening a skate shop? My work experience is in hauling plates of food. "I'm not sure I have anything to offer."

"Fox Inn probably taught you more about running a business than you realize."

"Maybe."

I know a lot about Felicia and Phil's way of doing business. Finding my own groove will take time. But what a great groove that could be.

We stay a while longer, watching construction workers and cement trucks file into the site and start pouring.

Joe gets that wild, reckless look on his face, like when Town Hall's doors are wide open but he can't stop himself from sliding down the railings one more time. He tugs me down the dirt mound to a spot near the front of the property, where the first drops of liquid cement poured out a perfect entrance road.

A little time has passed, so a matte haze covers the concrete. It's not as liquidy; it's hardening before our eyes. Joe kicks around on the ground until he finds something good enough to pick up. It's just a twig. But when he bends down to the edge of the cement slab, the twig becomes more than a useless, little stick. It's a tool.

He pulls away. A small and careful *JLM* brands itself into the concrete.

This place is his; this place is mine.

My turn.

I press the twig into the cement. I carve out my initials next to Joe's.

I am here.

Also By Jeanmarie

In Between Them
a YA contemporary romance about
friendship, forgiveness, and the price of betrayal.

Acknowledgments

The cast of Rebels & Romantics has lived in a small corner of my brain since roughly 2014. I am so grateful for the encouragement of friends and family who loved the idea of a cranky skate rat named Effie, even when I wasn't so sure anyone would want to read about her.

To my dear writer friends, Alexis Bass, Shelley Batt, and Tanya Spencer, who encouraged my nutty idea of a spin on the old Les Miserables story: thank you, ladies. To Kat Ellis, whose positivity always makes me feel like I should keep pushing forward, I'm grateful for your friendship over the years.

Thank you to my dad, who taught me how to assemble a skateboard when I was in kindergarten. Who knew it would turn out to be an important life skill? And thank you to my mom, for always, always, always having my back in everything I do. I love you.

My three daughters, Josie, Jackie, and Roxy, are my motivation to keep chasing my dreams. I love you girls so very much.

My husband deserves an extra helping of gratitude just for being who he is. Thank you for listening to me whine about publishing this book—the ups and downs over the years have been a crazy journey. I wouldn't have had faith in this story without your constant encouragement. I'm so glad you let me ride on the badass Surfrats's skate ramp when I was a dorky twelve-year-old. I love you with all my heart.

About the Author

Jeanmarie Anaya writes contemporary romance novels. She loves food, wine, the beach, and preferably all three of those things at the same time. She lives in New York with her husband and three daughters.

For more about Jeanmarie's upcoming releases and sneak peeks at new projects, subscribe to her newsletter at www.jeanmariewrites.com. You can also chat with her on Instagram, Facebook, and TikTok.

Jeanmarie would love if you'd leave a brief review of Rebels & Romantics on Goodreads or your favorite book-selling platform!